SPECTER IN THE MIND

DOCTOR WISE BOOK 7

ARJAY LEWIS

MIND
BENDER
PRESS

Cover Design: Marianne Nowicki; PremadeEbookCoverShop.com
Editing: Brandi Aquino; www.editingdonewrite.com

SBN-13: 978-1732659339
ISBN-10: 1732659338

Published by:
Mindbender Press
474 South Main Street
Phillipsburg NJ 08865
www.mindbenderpress.com

DEDICATION

To my wife Debra,
who continues to surprise me
in new and delightful ways

"How does one kill fear, I wonder? How do you shoot a specter through the heart, slash off its spectral head, take it by its spectral throat?" — *Joseph Conrad*

"Ah, Death, the specter which sate at all feasts! How often, Monos, did we lose ourselves in speculations upon its nature! How mysteriously did it act as a check to human bliss-saying unto it: thus far and no farther!" — *Edgar Allan Poe*

PROLOGUE

The sun was a dying ember, bleeding its last light across the San Francisco Bay, when Joseph Thompson turned his back on the view.

He didn't care for the fiery horizon; he was looking at the monster behind him. The mansion sat atop the hill like a gargoyle of stone and soot-stained brick. Its twin turrets reached into the darkening sky, silhouetted like the horns of a buried titan.

Encircling the property, a wrought-iron fence stood like a line of spears. Jagged and threatening points marked the eight-foot metal posts, which rust had pitted. If not meant to keep people out, the fence kept something very specific trapped within.

Parked at the curb was a windowless white van, in stark contrast to the overgrown driveway. From its rear doors, thick black cables spilled out, snaking across the dead grass to the house.

Joseph reached into the back of the van and gripped the pull-cord of the gasoline generator. With a violent yank, the machine coughed, sputtered, and then roared into a rhythmic, grinding life.

Up the hill, the house reacted. In the hollow sockets of the windows, yellow light flickered on — wan and sickly. The glow didn't make the place more inviting; it only highlighted the neglected abode.

Joseph ignored the sudden prick of dread at the base of his neck. He marched up the carved stone steps, stepping over the thick power cables to walk through the front door, propping it open like an unblinking eye.

He told himself it didn't matter. There was nothing left to steal. The house had been a hollow shell for years, its true treasures — the artifacts and the "echoes" — stripped away two years ago.

By *him*. Leonard Wise.

Joseph's jaw tightened. Even here, in the silence, Leonard's shadow felt heavy. He could still hear Doctor Kohl's voice, thick with academic worship, droning on about his "most brilliant protégé."

He remembered the way Anna Chou's almond-shaped eyes would soften, lit from within by a flame Joseph could never kindle, whenever anyone mentioned Wise's name.

To Anna, he was just "Joey." A diminutive. A child's name. It sat in his gut like lead, especially knowing that even her roommate, Zabella, seemed to command more of her attention than he ever could.

Joseph had the gift — the tests proved he had psychic potential — but it was a flickering candle compared to Leonard's bonfire.

Tonight, Joseph thought, his fingers twitching, the candle becomes a sun.

As he stepped into the foyer, the cool air hit him. It was August in California, a sweltering evening, yet the interior of the mansion was tomb-cold. The scent of stale dust and damp masonry filled his nose, thick enough to taste. He pulled his jacket tight, his boots echoing hollowly on the scarred wood paneling of the great hall.

In the center of the room stood the Accelerator. It was a jury-rigged nightmare of wire coils and copper plates bolted to a cheap folding table. It looked small, almost pathetic, beneath the towering fireplace.

Joseph caught his reflection in the massive mirror above the mantel. The silvering was peeling away, making his face look fractured and ghostly. On the top of the mirror, in red spray paint, the words GET OUT stood. A gift from a squatter who hadn't lasted forty-eight hours in the house before fleeing into the night, screaming about "the sounds."

Joseph's thin lips twisted into a jagged smile as he looked at the machine. Leonard hadn't built this. He had. Taking Kohl's cryptic notes and the University of Maine's raw specs, he breathed life into them. He hadn't just replicated the machine; he'd optimized it. He'd rewritten the software to do what the others were too afraid to try.

The plan was a team effort. Safeguards. Peer reviews. Boring, cautious science. But Joseph knew the machine could be more than a sensor. It was an amplifier. If he ran it alone, the feedback loop would funnel directly into the only psychic receptor in the room: his own brain. This was his chance to one-up Leonard Wise in a single night. The Accelerator would allow him to see things Leonard couldn't imagine.

He would earn that adoring look from Anna.

His fingers danced over the laptop keys. The activation sequence hummed, a low-frequency vibration that he felt in his teeth. It would take ten seconds for the machine to warm up.

"Ten minutes," he whispered to the empty, freezing room as he set the sequence timer.

Even if the "bad things" the rumors whispered about were real, ten minutes wasn't enough time for a haunting to take root. It was a calculated risk.

He hit "Enter."

The countdown began: 10:10... 10:09...

Joseph stepped back, his heart hammering against his ribs like a trapped bird. Outside, the last sliver of the red sun dipped below the Pacific, plunging the world into a bruised purple twilight.

He closed his eyes, surrendering to the growling, electric roar of the Accelerator as it surged to full power. The air ionized, and the scent of ozone struck his nose. He felt a sudden, sharp pressure behind his eyes — a door unhinging in the back of his mind.

It was the last thing Joseph Thompson ever did in his right mind.

1. HAUNTED

I used my cane to push myself up to my feet. "My name is Leonard, and I am an alcoholic."

"Hi, Leonard," the group of men and one woman spoke back to me in singsong unison. We all sat in a circle of folding chairs that faced one another.

"It's tough, sometimes," I noted, my hand gripping my cane so hard my knuckles were white. "Because no matter how long it has been since I've had a drink, the desire is always there, just under the surface. And when... bad things happen... it's the first place I go."

I hastily sat down, and the group murmured, "Thank you."

I would've said more, but the emotions that bubbled inside me were too strong.

Not that I hadn't had a rough time with my emotions in the last month or so.

But here on this Monday morning in August, with a group led by my comrade-in-arms and sponsor, Lt. Bill McGee, I didn't want to start whining and moaning.

Another member of the group stood. "My name is Dave, and I am an alcoholic."

We all murmured, "Hi, Dave" in reply, and he began the litany of his personal experiences with drinking.

I only half-listened, too lost in my misery. I had to admit, my morose attitude was starting to bore me.

At the end of May, I had faced a monster. Literally, a demon in human form which almost killed me. Worse, it had almost killed my girlfriend, Assistant District Attorney Jyanette Emery.

We'd been dating for about eight months, but the experience had been so terrible that she decided it would be best if we no longer saw one another.

It had been a devastating blow to me.

I mean, we were serious. We confessed our mutual love and met each other's parents. I knew she was upset that I kept showing up bruised and battered from my work with Bill McGee and the Mountainview Police Department as an unpaid civilian consultant.

But I thought we would continue.

I had invested in the concept that it wasn't her and me anymore, but us — a couple, a pair who could face the world as an unstoppable duo.

I had been wrong.

I have had little luck with relationships. A car crash killed my fiancée the night my psychic abilities manifested, and I saw something in the road.

Nothing much — just a giant demon.

After that, I studied to be a psychiatrist in a psychiatric fellowship, where I attempted some relationships with several women, none of which lasted.

Then I discovered my mentor, Doctor Kohl, who trained me how to use my strange abilities. I didn't have any stable relationships and only became involved with a woman when I returned to New Jersey. She ended up murdered right before my eyes.

Like I said, not a lot of good experiences.

Even Jyanette had been the victim of a mad therapist who hypnotized her and turned her into a weapon. But we had gotten past that, as well as the holidays, family, and the inevitable disagreements all new couples must face.

But to see her lying in that hospital bed after the incident, telling me quietly and firmly that we couldn't see each other anymore, broke me.

It broke me more than fighting a demon and almost losing my life.

I woke out of my reverie as Bill McGee stood and thanked everyone for coming. He finished with, "Work the program, and the program works."

Everyone stood up and milled around. It was an early morning meeting, finishing at 9:00 a.m., so people were in a hurry to head for the door and get to work.

I put the chairs away as Bill came over to me.

"You okay?" he asked. "You seemed to be in your own world there at the end."

I grimaced. "Nothing you haven't heard before, Bill."

He nodded sympathetically. "It's been tough with everything so quiet."

I shrugged. "I got the novelization about the Mishan case done and submitted it to the agent who was interested."

"Well, that's good, isn't it?"

I nodded. "I never thought I'd want there to be a major crime wave, but I have to admit, my classes don't start for three more weeks, and I could use a distraction from my own thoughts."

Bill shook his head. "Well, you have my number. If you feel you need to drink, you call me."

"I know, Bill. It was only that one night…"

"But like you pointed out today, an alcoholic is always near the edge. I want you to know I'm here for you, Len."

I forced a smile. "Thanks, Bill." I glanced around the room. "Why don't you go? I can finish the clean-up."

He glanced at his watch. "If you don't mind. I can't have the lieutenant showing up late."

"I've got it, Bill."

"You'll be here Wednesday morning?"

No, I won't…

The thought passed through my mind so quickly, I almost didn't recognize it as a 'buzz.' That's a term I use for a quick flash of insight that often comes to me unbidden. I take those little buzzes seriously, as they have saved my life on more than one occasion.

I attempted to recover from the sudden mental burst. "Uh… sure… if nothing comes up."

I felt that was a safe enough reply. Bill smiled, nodded, and headed for the door. I continued to fold chairs and put away the coffeemaker and the condiments of creamers, sugar, as well as the plethora of other sweeteners.

It only took about ten minutes, and then I was alone in the church basement where the meeting had taken place. All at once, a memory of Jyanette hit me so hard I had to sit down.

It was January, and I had just returned from Maine, beaten up from an altercation during the solving of a murder in a haunted house.

We were naked in my bed, my light flesh against her dark African-American skin. We clung to each other, having just made love. Her amazing hair spread out like a pillow beneath her, and the dim light made her even more beautiful. I felt sated and happy — a happiness I hadn't experienced since leaving for Maine.

"Was that good make-up sex?" she asked, her breasts still heaving from our shared exertions.

"Best I've ever had," I panted.

"You look like hell, you know."

"Classes don't start yet. I'll heal," I said almost dismissively.

For a moment, I saw it clearly in my mind's eye. The look of worry and annoyance that passed over her face. I pulled her to me, and we kissed and soon fell asleep in each other's arms.

Slumped in the chair in the church basement, I stared at the cobra-headed cane that I carried. When you have a bad leg, it comes in handy.

I cleared my mind and rose, but the clarity of the memory had startled me. It was a waste of time and energy to keep dragging up recollections of what I'd lost.

But what else did I have?

I drove my specially equipped van back to the house I shared with my landlady, Mrs. Higgins. The van was a gift from a grateful client, equipped with controls on the steering column for accelerating and braking.

This is quite useful because I lost my knee in the same accident that killed my fiancée, and now my right leg is permanently stiff. I could never have afforded a new van designed this way, but the rich client could.

It was also during that case that I met Mrs. Higgins, and we hit it off. An older Irish woman, she had been a cook and her husband a chauffeur for several rich families. He had passed away back in the 90s, but she had continued to work and saved enough money to purchase the house we both resided in.

It was a wonderful opportunity when she invited me to live in the extension built onto the older building. I had my own bedroom and a sitting room that I used as an office, but I also shared the house with her: the kitchen, living room, and all the amenities, including her amazing cooking. I do what I can to keep the house in good repair and help as she needs, but the rent she charges me is much less than the market would bear.

At least I could be grateful for that.

I'd been helping a lot lately, in between finishing the novel I had been obsessed with. It was based on the first case I'd ever done with Bill, but fictionalized enough so that I would not get sued by any parties involved or cause an uproar if people found out the Mountainview Police were using a psychic to solve cases.

Besides, technically, my actual job is teaching at nearby Garden State University in the only parapsychology program on this coast.

With my classes done for the summer, I helped Mrs. Higgins with the house while I finished the book. The manuscript was in the hands of the literary agent I'd been lucky enough to find, who was shopping it out to publishers.

I also celebrated my 31st birthday in July. It was a sober affair with just Mrs. Higgins, Bill, my teaching assistant Teddy Santos, and Jon and Jenny Baines. Mrs. Higgins made a delightful meal for us, and we ate at our big dining room table with the china and the good silver. At the end, there was a birthday cake, and everyone did their best to lift my spirits.

Now I had a lot of free time to catch up on my brooding.

I pulled into the circular driveway and parked my van. It was only 9:30, and an entire day opened in front of me with no projects on the horizon. Maybe I could go to some sad movies and really get myself into a state of deep depression.

I opened the vehicle's door, turned my special bucket seat to face outward, and the lift lowered my seat down to the ground before automatically retracting back into the vehicle. I locked up and limped to the house, cane in hand.

The day was sunny and not yet as hot as it would become. It was August in New Jersey, and the dog days of summer made me want to hide in glorious air-conditioning. Perhaps I could review my class plans for the fall. I knew my personal computer geek and teaching assistant, Teddy Santos, had finished those. He had already posted them online, but I could review them.

I went up the steps to the front door and was soon inside, where the smell of baking filled the air. A combination of cinnamon and sugar wafted through the house, and I was suddenly hungry. I hadn't eaten when I'd gone off to the early morning AA meeting.

As I pushed the swinging door into the kitchen, I saw Mrs. Higgins. Matronly, with her hair up, a few wisps of auburn mixed in with the silver. She turned to me with her green eyes, an old-fashioned apron on her stout, all-of-five-feet frame. She gazed up at me with a smile.

"Ah, good mahrning, Doctor," she greeted in her lilting brogue.

"Good morning, Mrs. Higgins," I replied. "What smells so nice?"

"Makin' a few things for the church bake sale. It's this weekend, don't ye know?" she explained, a smile on her face.

"Isn't it a bit early in the week to start baking?"

"No, I have a lot to do. I think I want to do a couple of pies and some biscuits and all."

"Better label them 'cookies' here in the States, Mrs. Higgins."

"Aye, that'd be true," she said, and didn't meet my eyes. "How are ye feelin'?"

I smiled wanly. "You ask me that every day."

"And ye have yet to give me an answer I like," she chided. "I'm worried about ye. All of this with Jyanette—"

"Mrs. Higgins," I sighed. "I'll be fine."

"Well, ye haven't been foine, if I do say so meself."

I forced myself to be patient. I knew that Mrs. Higgins often thinks she's my protector, or even a substitute mother. But at times, it's a bit much.

"Mrs. Higgins, I've finished the book, assembled my fall lesson plan, and even done the repairs to the house—"

"Like a robot, ye have," she complained. "No joy in it a'tall."

I sat heavily on the chair at the kitchen table where we often shared a meal. "I'm still processing," I defended myself.

"It t'were a terrible thing she did to ye. Breakin' up with ye in the hospital and all, with ye all bruised from savin' her life."

I hung my head. "Please, Mrs. Higgins, not again."

The room was silent as she busied herself and I tried to just let it all go. As she passed me a second time, I heard the sound of a porcelain mug land next to me on the table. I brought the steaming coffee to my lips and took a sip. "Thank you."

"I think some breakfast would be in order," she insisted.

"I'm not hungry," I attempted, knowing it was a lost cause.

"T'weren't a suggestion, Doctor. Yer far too thin, and ye've all but stopped eatin' the last two months."

I considered it. Had it only been two months since Jyanette and I had broken up? It felt longer, each day dragged out. I reflected on the ten times a day I thought of calling her, texting her, not to pursue her, but just to be reassured that she was all right.

I had wisely not done it. The last thing I needed to do was become "Leonard Wise: Stalker."

She pulled out a frying pan and made some eggs. I sipped my coffee as silence again filled the room. This was not like us. Mrs. Higgins and I have always been able to talk. But I was just too frayed since the breakup, and one night she'd gone on a tirade about how insensitive Jyanette was, and I wouldn't hear of it.

Mrs. Higgins had liked Jyanette a great deal, and our breakup had been hard on her as well.

In a few short minutes, scrambled eggs mixed with a sharp cheddar cheese appeared before me with rye toast. I smiled, said a quick "thank you," and ate. Well, I had a few bites and moved the food around my plate to make it look like I had eaten more than I had.

Mrs. Higgins would have none of it.

"Please finish it, Doctor," she said. "Ye must keep your strength up, if yer to be ready."

I frowned. "Ready for what?"

"What's comin'," she stated instead of an explanation. "Really, it's for the best. Now eat."

I looked at her eyes, so full of warmth and genuine affection, and ate some more. "I can't fool you, Mrs. Higgins."

"No, ye can't," she agreed. "So, it be best to not bother."

She put a small dish of marmalade in front of me, and I gave in and put it on my toast. It was amazing, and I had to admit, I enjoyed the sweet-sour taste of the orange goo. I finished the meal and pushed myself up from the table.

"I don't know where I'm going," I announced. "I literally don't have anything in the works."

"Well then," she beamed, "that leaves ye open for what's coming!"

"Mrs. Higgins, I have nothing 'coming.' I just—"

My cell phone rang in my pants pocket, making its odd musical tone.

"We'll see, now won't we," she grinned.

I pushed my way out of the kitchen and into the hall, hit the virtual button to answer the call, and turned toward my end of the house. "Wise."

"Leonard? Is that you?"

I smiled at the sound of the heavy German accent.

"Doctor Kohl, how nice to hear from you." I glanced at my watch. It was just past 10:00 a.m. "Awfully early out there in California, isn't it?"

There was silence for a moment as if Fritz were considering my words. Doctor Kohl had created one of the first fully accredited parapsychology programs in America. It was his teachings that allowed me to develop my psychic abilities and control them.

"Leonard, can you come out here, to California?"

I blinked and stopped my progress down the hall.

"What?"

"I haff a team vorking at Scudder House."

I recalled Fritz had emailed me about getting the funding and his desire to return to the famed haunted manse. I had politely declined his invitation to join that team.

I had no desire to return to the place of my first major triumph as a psychic. Acting as a medium, I had located a trove of gold and collectibles hidden behind a false wall in that house years ago. News reports around the country referred to me as 'the super psychic of Scudder House.'

But during that experience, I had touched something dark and malignant, far beyond my ability to handle.

I piped up. "I know. How is it going?"

"Not vell, Leonard. Could you come out? I can arrange a plane ticket for you."

I pushed open the door to my sitting room and moved to my desk to boot up my laptop. I couldn't think of anything I wanted to do less. Here I was still getting over Jyanette, and Kohl wanted me to face whatever was lurking in that house? I didn't think I would be the right person for the job.

"I don't know," I replied. "I don't think I'd be any help—"

"Leonard, I need you," he implored crisply. "This morning—" he paused, and I heard a catch in his breath. "One of my team died in that house, Leonard."

2. GOLD COAST

In the kitchen, Mrs. Higgins turned to face me with a twinkle in her eye.

"What're ye staring at me for? Don't ye need to pack?"

I frowned. "You heard?"

"Aye, Doctor. With that boomin' voice of yours, I am sure the neighbors heard. Get yourself ready and I'll drive ye to the airport."

I packed quickly, reminding myself that I would be working in the field and not in a nice, air-conditioned office. I packed jeans and rough clothes with long sleeves, which I could roll up if I became too warm. Also recalling just how cold Scudder House had been, I threw in a pair of denim jackets, one lined with faux sheepskin.

With my big suitcase and my laptop bag, in which I added a plain, blank composition book to take notes, I loaded the case in the hatchback of Mrs. Higgins' tiny car and went to my van to switch out my cobra-head cane for a folding one I kept there. I prefer the snake-topped one, but since it contains a twenty-four-inch sword, I thought it best to leave it behind, as opposed to trying to explain it to the authorities at the airport.

The folding cane is a nice creation, a series of four interlocking metal tubes held together by a thick elastic 'bungee' cord. It can fold down and fit into my leather laptop bag with no trouble, and extends to a full thirty-six inches to help with my long legs.

Dressed in a good suit, which I always do when I fly, and with all my accoutrements packed, Mrs. Higgins and I were soon off to Newark Airport.

She hummed contentedly to herself as she drove, but I couldn't let things pass. "How did you know Doctor Kohl would need my help?"

"I don't know what ye mean," she said.

"All that stuff about eating, so I would be ready…"

"Oh that," she demurred, her eyes on the road. "That was just me woman's intooition."

"You always say that," I offered.

"Then why do ye always ask?" she grinned.

It's only about a twenty-five-minute ride from Mountainview to the airport, and we were making great time as it was 11:00 a.m. and there wasn't much traffic.

Early August in the Garden State is perfect for people looking to get in their last vacation before fall. I would start my classes in three short weeks, but the idea of not having much to do until then would have made the time drag terribly.

I decided it was good for me to take this on, but I also dreaded going back to that house.

Since I had done the paperwork for TSA Precheck, I made it through the security check line in record time. Of course, they had to run a wand over my frozen leg as some pins within it made their machines go haywire. But I was polite and accommodating and would have undressed if asked. They only required me to pull up my pant leg to reveal the flesh of my knee, which made the hardened TSA agent wince.

"Wow. That must've hurt."

"Still does in cold weather," I agreed.

Soon, I found a place in the waiting area where my leg sticking out wouldn't trip any unwitting flyer, and I booted up my laptop to email people who needed to know I would be out of town.

First was my best friend and boss, Jon Baines, who, as associate dean, gets no weekday off, summer or fall. I quickly let him know I was going out of town to work on Scudder House.

I followed it with two quick missives to Bill McGee and one to my TA, Teddy Santos.

I then surfed the web while I waited and several quick responses from my compatriots surprised me.

Jon wrote:

If you get publicity like the last time, be sure to mention that you're teaching at GSU.

Jon

Cute. That was Jon, always promoting, always fundraising. McGee's had a different tone:

I trust you, buddy, but I am worried. You are in a fragile place right now. Are you going to be able

to hook up with your old sponsor while you are
there? I think you need the support.

Bill

I looked at the message and shook my head. Bill and I worked
well together on cases, and he'd helped me through a rough patch
over the last few weeks, but perhaps having him as my Alcoholics
Anonymous sponsor opened up situations I wanted to avoid.

I quickly assured Bill that I would contact my sponsor in
California. I then sent a quick email to Chuck Granger, just as
the plane was boarding.

I had a seat on the exit row in business class that Fritz had
reserved to accommodate my frozen leg, but I could barely fit.
The joys of being over six feet tall with long legs.

Six hours later, I landed at San Francisco International
Airport. With the time difference, it was only three hours after we
took off.

I dutifully walked out of the secure area and followed signs to
get my luggage. Fritz had told me someone from his team would
pick me up, so I was glancing around to see if there was anyone I
knew.

A perky Asian woman jumped and waved to me with a big
smile. As I drew closer, I realized there was something familiar
about her.

"Len!" she laughed and gave me a hug. Then she backed away
and looked up at me as the pieces clicked into place in my brain.

"Anna?" I said, and I could feel a big smile pull at my lips.
"Geez, is that you?"

"It is," she gushed. "You look so much better without the
beard!"

My hand went to my chin as memories flooded back to me. It
had been in my final year with Doctor Kohl, while I was his

teaching assistant and working on my doctorate. A new freshman had come into the class, with thick glasses and a quiet manner. To say she had been a wallflower would have been an understatement. She practically faded into the scenery. I coaxed and encouraged her, as she was bright and truly gifted in the study of parapsychology.

In the year-and-a-half since I'd returned to New Jersey, she had blossomed. I couldn't believe she was the same woman.

"What happened to your glasses?" I blurted.

"I got contacts," she explained and looked up at me unabashedly. When we first met, she couldn't make eye contact, let alone meet my gaze.

"You look great," I effused. She wore jeans and a good work shirt for the field, but she stood with her back straight and her smile engaging.

"There have been some changes since you were gone."

I nodded stupidly. "I guess so."

We started toward the appropriate carousel to pick up my luggage, and she took my arm and all but danced beside me. "It's really good to see you."

I nodded. "You, too. I just wish it were under better circumstances."

She became serious, her mood immediately dampened. She sighed. "Yeah, Joey. I feel shitty. I was so glad to see you, I forgot for a minute."

"What can you tell me?"

"Not much, and not here. We'll talk once we're in the car."

We waited for the luggage to be unloaded, and I studied her carefully. She was petite, about five foot three, and her hair was straight, black, and fastened back into a ponytail. That was a logical choice when working in the field. She had dark eyes that were taking in the open space and analyzing it. I had never noticed that she was quite shapely. I guessed she slouched so much when I knew her; I wasn't aware of her attributes.

She was a lovely young woman, and I guessed she was about twenty-four at this point. She had already earned a Bachelor of Science degree before she started studying with Doctor Kohl.

"So, why all the changes?" I asked as the carousel came to life and revolved, moving bags out to the passengers.

"I was tired of the person I was," she stated simply. "I finally stopped being a good little Korean girl and became my own person."

"Well, it's a rather amazing transformation," I told her.

"I know! Once I realized I didn't have to be seen but not heard, I — kind of — came out of my shell." She flashed me another smile. "Do you like?"

"Very... much," I stammered and felt myself flushing with embarrassment. "I mean, I always thought there was more to you than you let others see."

"It was you, Len," she laughed and took my arm again. "You really spent a lot of time telling me how good I was."

I carefully extracted myself to get my sturdy suitcase as it appeared in front of us on the carousel. I pulled it off with one arm, setting it up on its wheels. With a nod, she led the pair of us out to the parking garage.

She soon pulled open the trunk of the Honda Civic, and I maneuvered the suitcase into it.

I got into the passenger seat after I pulled it all the way back, and adjusted myself to fit in the small vehicle.

"Sorry I couldn't bring the van, but it has the generator at the site," she apologized.

"It's okay, I can make it work," I grunted.

It was necessary to cross my right leg over my left, but I got myself uncomfortably into the seat. She started the car, and we soon headed for the exit.

"Are we going directly to Scudder House?" I asked as we moved onto the highway and headed north.

"No, the police have shut it off as a crime scene. I was told to take you to the house where we're staying. Doctor Kohl needs to talk to you."

"House? How many people are on the team?"

"Seven, including Doctor Kohl," she said simply, and then her expression grew dark. "I guess it's only six now."

"What happened with your friend, Joey?" I insisted. "Fritz didn't give me any details. He just said there was a death."

She blinked her eyes to fight back tears. "It was all so awful."

"What happened?"

"Joey jumped from an upper-floor window — with a noose around his neck."

"What?" I replied, shocked.

She kept her eyes on the road, but I could see all the emotions tearing at her.

"Just like Elias Scudder," she whispered.

I faced forward, my eyes on the sunlit road ahead of us. I was familiar with the history of the house, and what a history it was.

Scudder House was a magnificent structure for its day, built at the behest of Elias J. Scudder, the last of the great railroad tycoons. It sat on a many-acred estate in a town called Brisbane and overlooked the San Francisco Bay.

The day the family moved in — a summer day in 1894 — they held an enormous party for the San Francisco elites, as well as the employees of the railroad company Scudder founded.

During the fireworks that night, Elias's youngest daughter, only five, backed up into a sinkhole that the land surveyor said could not have existed on that property. The sounds of the explosions muffled her cries, and as she lay there, the dirt closed up again and suffocated her.

Tragedy and strange events occurred at the house over and over, one of them being the death of Elias Scudder.

On the day of the stock market crash in 1929, Elias leapt from a window on the highest level of the house with a noose secured around his neck. The fall broke his neck instantly, and he had to be taken down by the servants.

That this friend of Anna's, a researcher with the team Doctor Kohl had pulled together, would kill himself in the same way was shocking.

I shook my head as we continued the ride up Route 110 and took a turn onto Bayshore Avenue, then onto San Bruno, which took us into Brisbane.

There were houses on both sides of the street, and we turned onto another smaller road, and then in front of a house, where she pulled to the curb and parked.

I slung my leather laptop case on my arm, and she opened the trunk, giving me another admiring smile. "We're so glad you could come so quickly, Len. I know that Doctor Kohl will be relieved to see you."

I nodded dumbly. "Fritz invited me to join the team when he assembled it. At the time, I couldn't commit."

She walked ahead of me as I wheeled the suitcase, and we approached a good-sized bungalow that faced the street. I struggled to get the case over the threshold, as she held the door open for me.

I finally got the case in, and it slid easily into what appeared to be the living room. A couch covered in brown crushed velvet was in front of a large flat-screen television, flanked by a loveseat and an upholstered chair, both covered with an ugly beige fabric.

The room was large, with a small kitchen and an island at the far end. A sliding glass door revealed a remarkable view of the bay to my left.

As we moved in, there was a pair of open sliding doors to my right, and I could see a bedroom with a pair of full-sized beds at either end.

"I'll show you your room," she offered, and led me to a small hallway where she pulled open a door to our right. "This is the largest bedroom."

I wheeled my suitcase in. A queen-sized bed stood against the far wall, and the walls featured a garish salmon paint. There was a small closet and a bureau with a large mirror that faced the bed. A cheap throw acted as a blanket, not that one needed a blanket in the summer. It wore a printed geometric pattern that clashed with the rest of the room.

"I would think Doctor Kohl would take this," I suggested. "He is the team leader."

"He did, but he's moved into that other bedroom we passed. There are two beds, one for the doctor and one for Liam." She gestured vaguely in the direction we came from. "I'm in the room across the hall from you with Zabella. We have bunk beds."

"Are there more bedrooms?"

"No, George and Lamar sleep on the two sofa beds, one on this level and one in the basement."

"Where is everyone?"

"Still at Scudder House, I guess. The police asked to question them, to understand Joey's frame of mind."

"I don't need to unpack. Perhaps we should join them?"

She faltered. "That's not what Doctor Kohl told me. I guess I could text him."

She retrieved her smartphone from a pocket and stepped out of the room to type a quick message.

I gazed around my temporary abode. It felt very different from when we last visited Scudder House. I'd been in Jersey for a year and three months, so I decided it had to be about two years ago. Then, we had stayed in a hotel, but I guessed it would be cheaper to rent a house with a larger team.

I was tired. For me, it was 8:00 p.m., though the clock here read 5:00. Flying is always a tiring experience, plus the rush to get to the airport had been hectic.

Anna stepped back into the room, and I turned to face her, shaking myself from my reverie.

"Doctor Kohl says to wait. He and the team are on their way back. It should only be a couple of minutes. Would you like coffee? We have one of those K-Cup machines."

"Sure," I said, and we headed back to the kitchen. "So, what is your official job as part of the team?"

"My task is to chronicle the research. I keep the diary and paperwork for the university, which is funding us."

I smiled. "You make sure to dot the i's and cross the t's?"

She smiled back. "Joey was our computer programmer, and I guess George is the electrician, because he set up the generator and the lighting."

She opened a cupboard and pulled out the box of coffee pods.

"Why did you need a programmer? Are you using new equipment?"

"No," Anna said, her voice distracted as she fiddled with the machine. "He was writing the code for the Accelerator."

She slid a cup under the spout and pushed a button. The machine hissed, a violent, mechanical sound that seemed to grate against my very bones. She turned back to me, a casual question on her lips, but the words died before they could leave.

I was already on my feet. The chair screeched back against the floor like a wounded animal.

"How do you take your—" She stopped, her eyes widening as she scanned my face. "Leonard? You're white as a ghost. Are you okay?"

Before I could answer, the front door groaned open. A group of silhouettes spilled into the foyer, their footfalls heavy and out of sync. They weren't talking; they were murmuring in low tones of people who had just stepped out of a funeral — or a crime scene.

I didn't wait for an explanation. Ignited by a sudden, frantic heat, I limped toward them to intercept the man leading the procession.

Doctor Kohl looked up, his spectacles sliding down his nose. He attempted a weary greeting, but the words withered when he saw my expression. I didn't stop until I was inches from him, looming over his small, fragile frame.

"Leonard?" he stammered, shrinking back. "What on earth —?"

I didn't give him room to breathe. I leaned down, my voice a low, vibrating snarl that silenced the rest of the room.

"How could you put that goddamn machine in the Scudder House?"

The color drained from Kohl's face. He stared up at me, eyes filled with concern.

3. HISTORY LESSON

T he problems at Scudder House did not end with the death of Elias Scudder and his dramatic jump. There was more to the story than that.

The widow had remained in the house but died within ten years, growing more paranoid with each passing season. They claimed she died of natural causes, but that didn't explain why the servants found her with her eyes wide open with terror, and how her hair had turned stark white overnight.

An unmarried daughter, Frances Scudder, took over the running of the house. In the 1940s, when people whispered about such things, rumors suggested she had liaisons with several well-to-do women in the neighborhood.

She died by leaping from the same tower her father had chosen, but she used no rope. The fall killed her effectively. She landed on the house's decorative and quite sharp fence posts, penetrated through her sex and into her heart.

The house made headlines once again.

As a trust fund maintained the property, her brother, Martin Scudder, in his sixties, took up residence. In what people now call the "Curse of Scudder House", his bed collapsed, trapping him under the mattress and pillow, which slowly compressed and suffocated him by morning.

The last resident was a nephew named Nat Hewing, who sought the sizable sum of money and valuables that he believed were hidden in the house. He sold off the furniture, the fixtures, and put holes in the walls in search of the treasure.

He lasted only two months before he attempted to light a fire in the living room, using paint thinner. Not in the fireplace, but on the large hearthstone in front of it. He set himself on fire. The house sustained no damage. Even the floor under his charred corpse was unmarked.

The house remained empty, though there were reports of strange lights and unusual sounds over the years, mostly observed from the nearby quarry. Since the mansion was in a remote location, fairly removed from the residential area of Brisbane, the residents of the town largely ignored the house and avoided it.

Two years ago, I entered Scudder House and had one of the most frightening experiences of my life. I did, however, find the hidden treasure Nat Hewing had searched for in vain.

The resulting publicity drew headlines all over the country.

Now, as I gazed at the man who taught me how to control my abilities, I was furious.

"Vhat is wrong, Leonard?" Fritz worried, surprised at my outburst. The other members of his team drew protectively around their teacher.

"You used the Accelerator at Scudder House," I bellowed. "Are you insane?"

"No, Leonard, ve did not!" he corrected me and rose to his full height. "At least, no one vas supposed to vithout other people there."

I folded my arms and glared at him. "But even taking it there, what were you thinking?"

A tall young man with long brown hair glared at me. "Don't you talk to Doctor Kohl that way!"

The African-American man next to him, who was thin and very young-looking, agreed. "Yeah, who are you to talk like that?"

Kohl put his hands up to calm everyone down. "Now, now, this is merely a misunderstanding. All of you, relax." He then turned to me and said, "Ve should talk about this in the other room, Leonard."

"No," I insisted. "I want everyone to know how dangerous that machine is." I glanced at the others, my temper still hot. "Did you tell them that people died because of it?"

Fritz exhaled deeply, and his jaw set. "No, I did not."

My outburst had surprised him, but he had no trouble taking charge of the situation. "But it vas not supposed to be used, except in controlled situations. Joseph activated it vithout anyone there."

"Wait a minute," the black guy blurted. "I thought it didn't work."

Anna spoke up. "That was our conclusion yesterday. I have it in my notes."

"Ja," Kohl said and faced me. "And it vas only to be used ven ve vere all there to make sure controls vere in place."

"Wait," I said. "Was it used?"

Kohl nodded his head sadly. "It vas the first thing I checked ven I arrived and found Joey — like that. It appears he got it vorking and attempted to use it."

I wandered over to the chair and sat on the large padded arm. I looked over at the others. "Do any of you know what that thing does? Do you understand the danger?"

The brown-haired young man looked at the others and simply said, "We were told it takes a reading of the energies in a location and amplifies them."

"Close," I spoke through gritted teeth. "It's more like sympathetic vibration. It takes the readings from all the machines, and then puts out the same frequencies found in the environment. Understand — the effect doesn't just double the ambient energies; it causes them to jump exponentially."

Fritz came over. "Joseph didn't understand the dangers, Leonard. To him, it vas just a software problem to be figured out. He vasn't a psychic. He didn't know vat it could do."

I stared at the floor. "Did you warn him?"

The African-American man stepped forward. "The doc — I mean Doctor Kohl — has cautioned all of us since the first day."

A raven-haired woman approached us as well. She was tall and spoke with a slight Slavic accent. "Doctor Kohl has told us again and again of the risks in that house." She looked at the rest of the group, turned to me, and extended her right hand. "I believe we got off on the wrong foot. You must be Leonard Wise. I am Zabella Rovensky." She pointed at the man with the long, brown hair. "This is Liam, and this is Lamar." She indicated the African-American member of the team, who nodded to me, still wary.

A heavyset young man with short brown hair and a linebacker's build stepped closer. "I'm George Humphreys, in case anyone else didn't say so."

I looked at all of them a little sheepishly. "Well, it appears you all know who I am, and I seemed to have introduced myself in the worst way possible."

Kohl moved to the center of the room. "No, Leonard, you did not. You are the only one in the room who truly understands how dangerous that house can be." He looked at his charges. "I hope ve all have a deeper knowledge now."

"I didn't even know you had an Accelerator," I admitted. I had previously seen only one, which was used at Hedden House.

"Ja, built by Doctor Haring," Kohl agreed. "I vas able to track down the team that he'd used to make it operational. Joey vas merely supposed to correct some minor problems in the software and get the machine vorking."

Lamar cleared his throat. "Joey was a bit of a show-off. I think he wanted to get it working and show us he could."

I shook my head, my gaze still on the floor. "It's insanity to use that machine in that house. It's already too active."

There was silence as they looked from one to another.

"What?" I asked.

"For you it vas, Leonard," Kohl said.

"I don't understand," I replied.

Anna spoke up. "The truth is we've been there for a week, and we have had no measurable phenomenon."

"That's impossible," I said. "When I was there—"

"Ja, that is the point," Kohl said. "Ven you vere there."

Liam spoke up. "None of us are psychic."

"Hey!" Lamar corrected.

"Sorry," Liam offered. "We have a psychic, but not at your level, Doctor Wise."

"Okay, I'll accept that," Lamar conceded, but crossed his arms with annoyance.

"First, call me Leonard or Len," I said, softening now that my panic had abated. "But let me get my head around this. You've been there a week with no manifestations?"

The young people all looked at me and shrugged.

"Pretty much," George acknowledged.

"Then today, last night, Joey activated the Accelerator and… died."

I didn't want to say "killed himself." Because in that house, there was a presence that may have taken possession of him. He may not have even known what he was doing.

George looked at the other members of the team. "We're the ones who found Joey. He was hanging off the side of the building. I… got him down."

Zabella continued the story. "Doctor Kohl told us not to go into the house. He didn't want us walking through any evidence by accident."

Lamar lifted a hand. "The police wouldn't let us in the house. They kept us in a group and asked us a lot of questions."

"The generator that powers the house had run out of fuel," Liam said. "It was all still connected from when Joey tried it, but the Accelerator shut down after it completed its cycle."

Fritz broke in. "Once the police escorted me in, allowed me to check the equipment. I noted that someone had used the Accelerator."

"Was the software like the program Doctor Haring used? Could you tell how long it had been active?" I asked.

Fritz shook his head. "Only ten minutes."

My head snapped up. "Ten minutes? It's hard to believe that was enough time for him to do it."

Liam cleared his throat. "The police agree with you. They don't believe it was a suicide."

"What?" I stood.

George moved through the group and headed to the kitchen. "Yeah, we've all been through that house. If they examine things, our fingerprints will be everywhere. The rope he used? We all touched it, I'm sure. We used it to move equipment."

Zabella started. "One of the policemen, a detective, says he wants to look into it further."

George reached Anna and asked, "We got any snack bars? We've been out there for hours and my blood sugar is low."

Anna gave a quick nod and opened a cabinet to pull out a granola bar of some type, which George tore open, his hands shivering.

"The police have secured the site?" I guessed. "Until when?"

It was Fritz's opportunity to speak up. "Ve vere told ve could return tomorrow."

Liam piped up. "They thought we could come back tonight, but…" He raised his hands like a conductor, and the entire group said in unison, "You don't go to Scudder House after dark."

I sighed. "At least that is something we can all agree on." I looked from person to person. "What do each of you do as part of the team?"

Lamar stepped forward. "Well, I'm the psychic, but I'm still trying to master what I do. I mean, sometimes it flows and sometimes…" He shrugged and sat on the brown velvet sofa.

I nodded. "Do you get flashes of insight?"

"What do you mean?" Lamar asked.

"I call them buzzes. I get these little warnings or messages of things that help me."

"Like a 'spider-sense?'" Liam offered.

I chuckled. "Well, I wouldn't say it works at superhero status, and no radioactive insect has bitten me. But those brief insights have saved my bacon a couple of times."

Lamar nodded. "I mostly get readings. Things come to me in a flood once I get on the right wavelength. I have to open myself up to whatever comes. And then it kind of hits me all at once."

"Impressive," I said, knowing how overwhelming it was to have one's mind bombarded by images and thoughts.

Liam raised his hand next. "I'm the geek. I get the machines to cooperate, and I compile the data."

I nodded. "What equipment do you have on site?"

He began to count off on the fingers of his left hand. "Spectrometer, digital recorder; full-spectrum cameras, both still and video; electromagnetic field reader, radio frequency field meter, ultrasonic motion sensors." He paused and considered for a moment. "That's about it."

Zabella strode across the room and sat on one stool at the kitchen island. "I read the data and note spikes in readings and correlate the active and inactive times at a site. I give my information to the team and especially to Anna." She smiled at her Korean roommate.

I piped up. "Anna is the chronicler; she already told me. George, what about you?"

He laughed and went on. "I drive the truck. But seriously, I'm the muscle. I move equipment and make sure that the generator keeps going. I'm also trained in first aid and CPR and have an emergency kit for wounds or anything."

I turned to Fritz. "Quite a team you put together."

Kohl nodded. "Ja, I am quite pleased vith who ve vere able to get this summer. Ve received sponsorship from the University of San Francisco again, like ven you and I vent in the last time, as vell as from other sources. Ve only have another two veeks to complete our vork."

I thought about it. "Does that mean that Doctor Janis will come around?"

Fritz sighed. "He vill be here tomorrow."

My lips tightened. When I made the discovery of a large safe hidden behind an intricate fake wall at Scudder House, Doctor Janis ran a press conference in which he made little comment about Doctor Kohl or my contribution to the find. I blew that up by telling the press I contacted the spirits of Scudder House, and the attention all turned to me, which did not go over well with Janis.

He got his revenge when he catalogued all the items found in the house and put them into a display which traveled from museum to museum called *The Lost Treasure of the Last Robber Baron.*

As part of that display, he went over his own personal history and how important the find was to the team from the University of San Francisco. He omitted Doctor Kohl, me, as well as the Southern California University of Health Sciences, which had the only accredited parapsychology department on the West Coast and the team that made the actual find.

To put it simply: Janis was an attention hog, who wanted himself to be the important part of any find. Now that a death had occurred on the site, he would become involved, whether or not it was appropriate.

"Well, thank you all for talking to me. I'm sure you all had a hard day. Perhaps I can run out and buy some dinner for everyone?"

The room erupted in cheers of agreement, and I moved to Anna. "Could you drive me? And what does everyone like to eat?"

George bellowed, "Lucky House. Let's get Lucky House!"

This met the approval of the group. I turned to Anna to see her pull a well-used menu out of a drawer in the kitchen.

"I guess it's settled then." I smiled.

The drive back to San Bruno Avenue and into the center of town was a short one. Driving up Vista Lion Avenue, I felt surprised. Considering how close Brisbane was to a bustling city like San Francisco, it maintained the look of small-town America with buildings only a couple of stories tall and varied.

As we drove up the main drag, we could easily see the San Bruno Mountains towering over the town. It was these high hills that had attracted Elias Scudder to this area. He bought the site long before they built the house, due to the breathtaking views of the bay from the mountaintop.

As we headed uphill and away from the center of town, a two-story brick building appeared to our right. The brick on the first floor was painted with bright-red paint, and we pulled into the open parking space in front.

As we walked into the restaurant, Anna spoke quickly to an Asian woman with gray hair behind the front counter. The woman smiled in recognition and went to fetch the order, which we had called in before we left.

Fortunately, Anna had warned me they only took cash. Tomorrow I would have to increase my "walk around" money by visiting an ATM, but I had more than enough for tonight.

I glanced around the room, which was small. They could only seat a few people — maybe two dozen at the best of times. The tables had bench seating painted bright red as well, which seemed to be a theme of the place.

The hostess returned with a pair of large paper bags, and she quickly totaled up the purchase, and I slipped her the cash. The woman indicated me and said something to Anna, who replied with something humorous, as the pair of them laughed.

As we got back into the car, I said, "I thought you were Korean, but that woman was speaking Chinese."

She flushed again. "Do you speak Mandarin?"

"No, but I recognized it. It appears you speak it fluently."

She relaxed. "I know five languages: English, Korean, Mandarin, Japanese, and Spanish."

"Wow! I never knew that."

"As I told you, I'm less shy now."

As we pulled away from the curb, I asked, "So, what did that woman say to you?"

"What do you mean?" she responded coyly.

"You turned red and said something back to her that made her laugh."

She shrugged. "Just a little bit of banter."

"Nice deflection. I thought you weren't shy anymore. Come on, what did she say?"

She exhaled sharply as we turned a corner. "She asked if you were my boyfriend."

"Really? Aren't I a bit old for you?"

"Len, I'm twenty-four. And you're only what? Twenty-nine?"

"Thirty-one."

"Still not really 'robbing the cradle.'"

"What did you tell her that made her laugh?" I glanced over at her with her hands on the steering wheel and her eyes staring straight ahead. She adjusted herself uneasily in her seat. She might have decided that she wasn't shy anymore, but she certainly was still easily embarrassed.

"I would rather not say." Her jaw set and her lips were tight.

I let her off the hook. "Okay. I was just curious."

"It's obvious you've been working with the police. Your questions sound like an interrogation," she related huffily.

"Wow! I didn't expect that," I told her.

"Well, I will not let you bully me." She turned down another side road.

"I'm sorry, I didn't mean to… I was just curious."

She pulled to the curb in front of the rented house and shifted the car into park. She turned to me, her eyes flashing. "I told her I was working on it."

Without a word, she got out of the car and opened the trunk as I got out. I was a bit chagrined. She was working on it? Working on what? Making me her boyfriend?

I decided silence was the best choice, but my mind raced as I went to the back and grabbed a bag of food.

My breakup with Jyanette was so fresh, and I was still pretty miserable. And here was a young woman, whom I'd always encouraged and admired for her agile mind and quick grasp of what Doctor Kohl and I taught.

Since I'd arrived, she'd certainly given me the signals that she was interested. But was I? And to what extent?

We went into the house. The group was lazing about on the furniture in the front room as we tramped to the kitchen island and set out containers of food. Everyone was pretty quiet after losing Joey, and I tried not to impose as I helped Anna set up.

Liam pulled a large bottle of white wine from the refrigerator and filled empty plastic cups and passed them around. He put one in front of me.

I stared at the amber liquid in the cup and found myself torn. This is what Bill had warned me about when he told me I was still fragile.

And here it was.

I could smell the slight acrid scent of the wine, and I wanted it with every fiber of my being.

I took a deep breath and slid the glass over in front of Anna. Then I grabbed one cup and filled it with water from the sink and put that where the wine had been a moment earlier.

My self-control wasn't completely gone, but to have it tested so easily was going to be a problem.

Liam held the cup up in the air, and we all followed suit.

"To Joey," he said solemnly.

We all clinked cheap plastic and took a sip. Lamar emptied his glass and held it out for more.

"What the hell," he said by way of explanation. "I ain't working tonight."

I looked over at him as he refilled his glass. I understood completely. Lamar was the team psychic, and alcohol was one way to shut down his abilities. With the plethora of unwanted information that constantly hit me at all hours of the day and night right after my abilities manifested, alcohol was the only thing that could shut it off.

It then became a crutch.

I used booze to shut down my second senses, and then I found I could make them function even after having a little, but it took a force of will.

So, I embraced it.

I started with a little vodka in the morning, just to blunt the input. Then a drink in the afternoon, so I could keep away everything except the most powerful impressions. Then, enough to knock me out at night so I could sleep without nightmares and mental voices from the living, as well as the deceased.

Alcohol had been my wonder drug.

But even a young man can only be a steady drinker for a while before it affects every aspect of one's life. It affected mine. I started to be late for appointments and classes, and my work became sloppy; my writing disjointed.

That's when, about two-and-a-half years ago, Doctor Kohl told me to give it up or get out of his program.

By that time, I had mastered many of the techniques I now use to stop the flow of unwanted impressions, to focus my mind, and limit the input to only what I wanted to let in.

So, I really had no excuse.

I joined Alcoholics Anonymous and met my sponsor, Chuck Granger, who worked with me and helped me, especially during those first few months when it had been hard. I not only had to break the cycle of chemical dependence on the substance, but I had to unlearn the bad habits I had developed. If I were bored, I drank. If I were tired, I drank. If I needed a pick-me-up in the morning, I drank.

That's what made it so hard to stop. It was a part of my life.

I also knew that I'd had missteps along the way. In the last year, I'd become drunk three times. Once on a date with a young woman, who ended up murdered before my eyes. The second time on New Year's in Maine, when I just didn't give a damn. The third time occurred after the hospital released me following my breakup with Jyanette.

And there it was.

The pain was like a wave that washed over me. Did I say a wave? It was a tsunami of grief, and I found my eyes were wet. I stood there in stunned silence as the young people sat about with their food containers open, using forks or chopsticks, as they chatted, ate, and drank.

A hand touched my arm, and I looked over to see Anna, her eyes filled with concern. "Len? Are you all right?"

"No," I croaked and fought to keep control. "But I'm working on it."

I glanced around the room and noticed that Fritz had not appeared when we brought dinner in. "Where's Doctor Kohl?"

Anna glanced around as well. "I don't know."

One of the large sliding doors that separated the living room from the first bedroom slid open, and Kohl came out, his hair in disarray. The room grew silent as the young people stared at him, and he walked over to me.

"Leonard," he gulped. "Ve haff a problem."

I stared at Fritz for a moment and leaned closer. "What's wrong?"

He looked around the room and then gestured me to follow him down the hall. We stepped away from the kitchen, down the short passage, and he took my arm to pull me into my bedroom.

"What is it?" I asked, my voice low.

He turned to me, his eyes wild, his voice a hoarse whisper. "I received a call from that police detective. He is certain that Joey vas murdered."

4. STRANGE APPEARANCE

"*M*urdered?*" I muttered.

"*Ja!*" he said and looked at the open doorway. He quickly walked over and shut the door. "He says he vants to question the team again."

I stood there in disbelief. The concept that one of these young people might have attacked someone, put a rope around their neck, and thrown them out of a window was inconceivable to me.

I tried to get my head around it. "What evidence does he have?"

"Apparently, there vere bruises on the face, blood under the fingernails, and scratches that appear to be from defending himself."

I nodded. "That would make any good detective suspicious. When does he want to question the group?"

"Now. He told me he is on his vay over."

I gulped. My throat felt tight, and I didn't know why. After all, no one suspected me of anything. "We'd better tell them."

Fritz nodded, and we headed back to the living room.

The group was sitting, after having refilled their glasses, and were eating and chatting. I raised my arms and spoke steadily.

"Everyone?" The group's attention turned to me. "The police detective is coming back. He needs to do some follow-up questions."

"When?" Liam said, much as I had.

"Right now. So, have no more wine." I looked around. "He'll want to talk to each of you alone. Where would be the best place to do that?"

"Downstairs," Anna spoke up. "There is another sitting room down there."

"That's where I sleep," Lamar said.

"Good. Now, I've worked with the police. They'll want to ask questions and might even ask you to come down and supply a DNA sample."

"Oh Christ," George said.

"What's wrong?" I responded.

"I found Joey. I'm the one who cut him down and tried to give him CPR." He turned to the rest of the group. "But he had a broken neck and was dead."

"And your concern is that you left DNA?"

"Well, yeah, I gave him mouth-to-mouth," George pleaded.

"Okay, well, the point I was going to make is that you are not required to give DNA if it makes you uncomfortable. And if the police arrest you, say nothing." I turned to Doctor Kohl and urged, "Do you know how to get in touch with your university lawyer?"

Fritz nodded.

"So, my point is just talk to the detective. Say what you know, but don't elaborate; just the facts. You can stop talking anytime, and you can insist that there be a lawyer if they call you in for an official inquiry."

A murmur ran through the group, but then they all looked at me and nodded.

My timing was excellent because suddenly there was a knock at the door.

George opened the front door to a man standing outside in the long shadows cast by the setting sun. He stepped in, a tall man with a slightly olive complexion. He possessed strong features: a Roman nose, large ears, and dark hair. His gaze swept the room with the eyes of a cop.

Fritz moved forward to meet him. "Detective, you've met everyone, I believe."

"Yes," he replied in a deep voice with no accent. His eyes met mine, and he moved into the room toward me. "You must be Doctor Wise. Ms. Chou said she needed to pick you up at the airport." He held out his hand. "I'm Detective Jorge Valentin."

I took his offered hand and gave it a firm handshake. "Leonard Wise. Let me know if I can be of any help."

A brief smile flashed on his face. "How often does one get help from the 'super psychic of Scudder House?'"

I sighed. "I guess people still talk about that."

"It's a small town, Doctor. It was the biggest thing that's happened in the last few years." He turned around slowly to take in the entire room and observed the young people. "A lot of folks here think they should've torn down the old place after that."

I felt my face flush, but I focused on my breath, calming myself. "It's an interesting location, from a parapsychologist's point of view."

"It's been a problem for this community for decades. People sneaking in to see the 'famed haunted house.' I can't tell you the number of times I had to go there when I was a patrol officer to help some drugged-out, smart-ass kid who scared himself silly in that house."

I met his eyes. "Did you ever see anything there, Detective?"

Our eyes locked, and if I wanted to, I could have easily slipped into his mind.

But I didn't.

I saw a momentary flicker of doubt before he said, "Not a thing." He then turned to Kohl. "Not to scoff at what you are doing, Doctor Kohl, but I'm afraid I am not a staunch believer."

He moved to the middle of the room and was the center of attention, but he neither needed it nor craved it. He merely accepted it. "I hope Doctor Kohl explained why I am here tonight. We have the initial forensic report, and I need to talk with each of you again, just to make sure I have your stories straight."

Or to poke holes in them.

Zabella raised her hand. "Is it true you think someone murdered Joey?"

Valentin's jaw became tight. "There's some unusual forensic evidence that doesn't quite match up with our first conclusions."

I suppressed a smile. He'd put forth the basic information, giving nothing away.

He went on. "We just want to make sure we have as much information as we can gather. After all, you were the ones who found him."

"It was terrible," Anna said, and all of us turned to look at her. Her eyes were glistening, and she stared at nothing. "To see him hanging there…"

A heavy silence filled the room.

"You can see why I want to follow up, clear up any misconceptions." He looked around the room sternly. "Now, shall we begin?"

He was there for over an hour and took each member of the group downstairs to question them one at a time. The group had stopped drinking. In fact, someone had put the wine back in the fridge.

Anna went first, and after ten minutes, returned looking pale and fragile. I offered her some water, but she went to the fridge, got the wine, and poured a full cup with the admonishment that she "needed something stronger."

This repeated itself each time a person went down. George went last. While waiting, he paced and clenched and unclenched his fists, not knowing what to do with his nervous energy.

"Would you sit down and stop pacing?" Zabella chided him. "You're making us all nervous."

"They're going to blame me. I'm the one who released the rope and got him down. I'm the one who tried CPR."

"We all saw you do that stuff, man," Lamar suggested. "It'll be fine."

"It would've been better if you guys had helped me," George complained.

"Sorry, man," Lamar said. "The rest of us were just so shocked and all."

I glanced back at Anna to note that she'd refilled her glass yet again. I moved closer to her and touched her arm. "Maybe you should slow down a bit."

She gazed up at me, stopped, and put the bottle down. A hand went to her head. "Maybe I should. It's been quite the day."

"I understand," was all I could manage. The bottle seemed to wink at me, and I clenched my fists to stop myself from pouring my own glass of the amber liquid.

She put the bottle away but kept the half-full glass.

Finally, the detective came upstairs. "Thank you all for your time. I know you're in the middle of research, and we should be able to clear it so you can return to that house tomorrow. But, do not discuss this case with anyone and do not leave town."

His gaze moved to me. "Doctor Wise, could I speak to you outside for a moment?"

This surprised me, but I used my cane as I followed the detective out the door.

It was like striding into a sauna as I stepped out of the air-conditioned house. My shirt was instantly wet with sweat and clung to me. I could hear the sounds of native creatures as they peeped and chirped. Bats flew overhead, occasionally appearing in the beams of the streetlights as they consumed a tasty insect.

He stepped over to a vehicle parked just down the street.

"Is there something on your mind, Detective?"

"Yes. Doctor Kohl told me earlier that you were coming, so I did a little checking, made a couple of phone calls about you."

"Anything I need to worry about?" I asked.

"On the contrary," he explained as he pulled his detective's pad from his pocket. "I spoke to a Lt. McGee at the Mountainview Police? He's quite a fan."

"We've done some good work together."

He nodded as he glanced at the pad. "He told me that. I just want to tell you to stick to what you are here to do. Do I make myself clear?"

I frowned. "I'm afraid that's about as clear as mud, sir."

"Look, I'm the only detective in a police force of ten people. Although we are right next to San-Fran, we are just a small town, and things like this don't happen here. We've had one murder in the last decade, and that caused enough problems."

"So," I urged, "what is your concern with me?"

"My concern is that I am trying to solve this case, whether it was a suicide or something else. The last thing I need is some amateur out trying to find clues or bothering me with crackpot theories."

I blinked down at the man who was about five inches shorter than me. "Look, Detective, I've been at that house before and it wasn't a pleasant experience. That's why I'm here. I'm a researcher, and this place needs to be studied."

"Well, focus on that, and I'll take care of the police work."

He pulled out a small business card and offered it to me.

"What's this?"

"If you get any of your 'insights,' don't act on them. Call me. My cell is there so you can get me at any time. No amateur heroics, got that?"

I pocketed the card. "Got it. But let me tell you one thing. There's something in that house, something bad, and it is entirely possible it could have led a person to suicide."

"Or to murder?" he pointed out.

I hissed out my breath and hung my head. "Yes, or to murder."

"I told you, Doctor, I am not a believer. It's going to come down to evidence and motive. I'm going to get answers, and some of them you might not like."

He got into the car and drove away as I stood outside in the stifling darkness.

5. LOOMING PERIL

The others were all gone from the living room when I returned except for George, who had removed the cushions off the sofa and then unfolded the bed which was hidden within.

I looked at his worried face as he brought the frame into position and prepared the bed.

"It'll be okay," I told him.

He stayed focused on his task. "Not from where I'm standing. That cop hates me."

"I don't think that's true. I think he merely dislikes all of us."

That got a grin. "Well, everyone is shutting down. We get up early here."

I nodded. "Sleep well, George."

He grunted and continued to prepare his bed. Since the door to the bedroom next to the living room was open, I looked in.

Doctor Kohl was already in bed — in pajamas, no less — and reading. On the other end of the room, Liam had shut off the small lamp near his bed and turned to face the wall. I went over to Kohl as he looked up from his book. It was a treatise with the title, *Hauntings in the Middle Ages*.

I whispered. "So, 6:00 a.m. tomorrow I assume?"

"Nein, make it 7:00," he murmured. "The sun does not come until 6:45, and I don't want to be there until it is full daylight."

"Sounds like you have this figured out." I smiled.

"Planned out," he sighed. "It has been a most trying day. Thank you for coming, Leonard."

"I hope I can help."

He nodded. "I vill be most interested in your impressions. Lamar is not bad. Sometimes, he can be quite gifted. But his vork is uneven. Perhaps I have pushed him too hard, too fast. Maybe I expected results like you and I had."

"I don't know, but there's something evil in that house, Fritz. It's more than the ghosts or the hauntings. Something primal—"

"Ve vill see vhat can be found tomorrow. Good night, Leonard."

I headed through the living room, down the hall, and opened the door to my room. There was a candle lit in a glass tube on the dresser, which surprised me. I peered around the door.

Anna lay on my bed.

She was wearing a pink babydoll outfit. Thicker pink silk covered her breasts, but a sheer, translucent fabric hung loosely past her waist. I could easily see a frilly pair of G-string panties through it.

Nothing else.

I shut the door as she rose from the bed, a bit unsteadily.

"Anna?" I questioned. "What are you doing?"

"Acting on my impulses," she said with a tone that sounded like she'd practiced it. She attempted to walk toward me while swaying seductively, but it threw off her balance and she stumbled.

I caught her and helped her upright, and she reached up and pulled her face to mine and kissed me. Her tongue touched mine, and she made a "hmmm" as she did and pressed her lithe body against mine. I could taste the wine in her mouth.

I pulled back. "Anna, you're drunk."

"Just a little." She drew close again. "But I've wanted to do this for a long time."

She moved toward me again, and I moved away until my back was against the door. I held up my hands to restrain her. "Anna, this is not the best choice."

"I wanted to show you I'm not shy anymore." She slipped past my hands to give me a peck on my lips. "That whole year you were the TA to our class, I wanted to do this."

"Anna," I said, holding her hands and attempting to sound soothing. "This is not good timing."

She considered it and frowned. "Don't you think I'm pretty?"

"You're gorgeous. You are also drunk, and I just broke up with a woman I was in love with."

"Then your fee — I mean—" She giggled. "I mean you're free. So am I!"

I sighed. She apparently had a lot more wine when I hadn't been watching. "I think you need to sleep it off."

"Good idea. Get in bed with me." She took my hand and pulled me toward the bed.

"Anna, you need to go back to your room, and I need to sleep — alone."

She frowned again as she tried to get her head around what I said. "You want me... to go?"

"I think that would be best."

"You think I'm ugly," she said, and her face became a mask of abject misery.

"No, I think you're beautiful, and you're drunk and upset about Joey and want something that will take your mind off it. Lord knows, I would love to escape for a while, but it would take advantage, and I won't do that."

"Joey," she said, and a sob slipped past her lips. "He liked me. I could tell. And now he's dead." She looked at what she was wearing. "And I'm terrible at this. I even got dressed up."

I swallowed hard. I really wanted to take her in my arms and comfort her. She truly was beautiful, and the negligee showed off every lovely curve of her nubile body. But all I could think of was the last time I'd made love to Jyanette, outside in the open with her moans and the fragrant spring air.

"You look lovely. And I'm sorry about Joey. Go back to your room, sleep it off, and things will look different tomorrow."

She looked at the floor. "You still like me, don't you, Len?"

"I like you, and I want you as well. But not like this. Not while you're drunk and sad."

She nodded and headed toward the door, weaving a bit as she went. She turned back, forced a crooked smile, and went out.

I sighed, walked over to my bed, and sat down heavily as I tried to get my pulse to a slower pace. I shook my head. Why was I being "Mister Proper" suddenly? A beautiful twenty-four-year-old threw herself at me, big time, and I said no? It wasn't as if I was being unfaithful. Jyanette had broken up with me.

And there she was in my mind's eye, lying in the bed in the hospital, one eye closed from swelling, her dark skin purple with bruises, her lips cracked and dry.

She took my face in her hands, forcing my eyes to meet hers. I saw the wreckage of her heart in that look, but I also saw a wall I couldn't climb. "Len, I want a life. I want a family. I want babies and Sunday mornings without shadows."

"I want that too," I whispered.

"But I could never bring a child into this. My mind tells me it was an illusion — the power of suggestion — but in my dreams, I can still feel that thing's thoughts inside my head. I can't live like that. I won't."

"Jyanette, I'll do anything—" I begged.

She stared at me in abject wretchedness. "Every few weeks, you show up broken, half-dead, or haunted. How do I raise a child with a man who might not come home at all? Or worse, a man who brings the monsters home with him? It would break me, Len. It's already breaking me."

"I'll just teach..." I spoke aloud, lost in the memory.

The tears came, and I let them.

I slept fitfully, a vivid dream invading my mind.

I was standing and looking up at Scudder House with its dark, foreboding stone and castle-like turrets. It was dawn, and the light was just beginning to come up as I approached the house.

A body hanging by a rope rested on the outer wall of the building. From where I stood, it appeared to be a sickening Halloween decoration.

As I drew near, I could see the face of a young man, pale white in death, his head at an obscene angle. He wore a polo shirt and khaki pants. I walked onto the cracked bricks of the circular driveway and drew closer to watch the body slowly turn a few feet above the pointed steel of the decorative fence that stood only a foot from the building.

As he spun, I suddenly noticed that his clothes had changed. He now wore an old-fashioned suit, and the hair on his head was gray. As the body slowly revolved, I could see a vest, a fob for a pocket watch, and a starched white collar, and the very dead face of Elias Scudder.

One eye popped open to show pure red, and although he hung from the noose, he somehow twisted his head to look directly down at me.

"You are the one we want," he growled menacingly as he lifted one arm toward me as a noose came down around my neck.

I grabbed the rope at my throat with both hands and pulled at it, trying to push it away as something lifted me into the air. My back hit the stone of the building, and I looked down upon the town of Brisbane and across the San Francisco Bay.

The rope drew tighter...

I burst up from my bed as my hands slapped at my throat and the empty air. I stared around the room, my breath heaving as I tried to calm down from my dream.

God, I wanted a drink!

I knew that the wine was close and so available.

Fighting the urge, I glanced at the clock. It was 5:45 a.m., a full hour before I'd planned to rise, and I knew I would not get back to sleep. I pulled myself heavily out of bed, put on a robe, and went to the nearby bathroom, which I was pleased to find currently unoccupied. I took a quick shower, shaved, and went back into my room to get dressed.

I put on denim pants and a long-sleeved work shirt made from a light fabric. I knew August in California might be hot, but I also took out a heavy denim jacket. When active, Scudder House could be so cold you could see your own breath. I was sure I had brought winter gloves to shove into the pockets of the jacket.

I headed into the kitchen to brew a cup of coffee and discovered my cold coffee from the previous night that I had neglected to drink in all the commotion.

I had brought my laptop with me and got on the Wi-Fi in the house, using the password Fritz had sent me.

My email program was soon open, and I went through the number of useless junk mail until I noted one from 'cgranger'. This one I clicked on, and his words filled my screen:

> **Len,**
> **Good to hear from you, it has been a long time.**
> **This is most fortuitous, as I am still living in Whittier, but I will be up in San Francisco this week for a lawyer's conference, and I am representing my partnership.**
> **Perhaps we can meet for dinner, and you can bring me up to date on your life in NJ?**
> **Chuck**

I looked at the message and thought about it. Bring Chuck up to date on my life? Should I include the date with the girl who died, my recent love affair gone bad, and while we're at it, how I fell off the wagon three times?

Probably not.

However, it would be good to see Chuck, and maybe his presence could kick the desire to drink out of my head.

It surprised me how strong it had been the previous night. I was aware of 'triggers' and 'high-risk situations,' as well as my own emotional distress.

It occurred to me that McGee had been right: I was just too fragile right now. About to go into a location that was my greatest success and one of my most frightening experiences, I was also an emotional basket case.

Great.

An alarm went off near the sofa bed, and George stirred. I glanced at my watch and noted it was 6:30 a.m. Time to get the team moving.

Quietly I said, "George, do you want coffee?"

"No," he muttered. "But if you could pull a can of Red Bull from the fridge, that would help."

I got him the energy drink and limped over to hand it to him. He sat up, wearing only his undershirt and boxer shorts. He took the drink gratefully, opened it, and downed it.

I could see other people move as the house came alive.

The kitchen soon bustled with activity, and I returned to my room to avoid interfering as people used the bathroom, cleaned themselves, dressed, and prepared to face the day.

At about ten to seven, I walked out to have a little more coffee. Anna was on the island and appeared only a little worse for wear. I smiled at her, and she avoided meeting my eyes.

It just kept getting better.

Soon we were ready to go, as Doctor Kohl assigned who would ride in which vehicle.

"I can go with Anna," I offered, which got a nod from Kohl and a grimace from my driver.

Soon we were in three different cars, all pulling out to head to the site.

Once the car started, Anna, with her eyes straight ahead, said quietly, "Len, I want to apologize—"

"You have nothing to apologize for," I objected.

"Yes, yes, I do," she corrected, setting her shoulders. "I've lived as a sheltered girl for so long, that I guess I went too far the other way."

"Anna, you're an attractive woman, and that's what you are, a woman, not a girl." I placed my hand on top of one of hers, which held onto the steering wheel. "I am honored that you would pick me, but I don't take advantage of drunk women."

Her voice was barely above a whisper. "I wanted you to."

"Look, we're working together. I'm getting over a serious breakup, and I need to focus on facing this house. It isn't you; it's me."

I realized how lame that line has always been. Good job, Len. Fall into clichés.

"I embarrassed myself," she pouted, not even glancing at me.

"It was only you and me. No one else needs to know about it. And I've embarrassed myself over a woman quite a few times."

"You're kind to say that. I will control my drinking more."

"That might be a good idea."

We continued the drive in silence. Although there was so much more I wanted to say, I didn't. I needed to focus on what was coming.

We banked onto Quarry Road, the engine straining as we began the steep ascent toward the jagged spine of the San Bruno

Mountains. To our left, the land simply vanished. The road's namesake — a gargantuan, open-wound quarry — gaped like a mouth in the earth. It was a desolate landscape of stripped topsoil and gray stone, a deep pit where decades of mining had clawed away the minerals, leaving behind a hollowed-out ghost of the terrain.

That property had once belonged to the Scudder family as well, a sprawling kingdom of privilege until the trustees began carving it up, selling the estate's flesh to the mining companies acre by bitter acre.

We crested the last bluff, and there it was. The house stood alone, a dark sentinel looming against the bruised morning sky.

As our small convoy of vehicles ground to a halt, the rising sun hit the glass, but the windows didn't sparkle — they glared. Each pane was nearly a century old; the glass so thick and wavy it looked like the bottom of a green beer bottle, distorting everything behind it into a sickly blur. Heavy black iron frames subdivided the glass into narrow, vertical rectangles, like the bars of a cage. The builders constructed every inch of the place — the rust-streaked stone, the soot-stained brick — with a terrifying, permanent intent.

It wasn't just a house; it was a bunker for the soul.

The surrounding grass was a waist-high sea of yellowed weeds, choked and unkempt, save for the violent scars left by the tires of the police cruisers and the heavy boots of the team.

My eyes drifted toward the turret. They had trudged through the mud the day before to retrieve what was left of the body — the thing that had dangled from the tower like a broken pendulum.

The car door creaked open, and the silence of the mountain hit me, cold and absolute. I stepped out onto the gravel, my gaze climbing the massive stone stairs toward the arched entrance. The front door stood like a mouth, dark and cavernous, waiting.

I took a deep breath and carefully let down the walls I maintained around my mind.

This was one technique taught to me by Doctor Kohl. When I came to him, I constantly received psychic input: unbidden images, unwanted awareness, and even other people's thoughts. That's why I hate crowds — so many minds all emanating thoughts like a broken earthenware vessel leaks water.

Of course, alcohol shut it off.

Fritz taught me techniques to shut my mind away, wall it from the constant psychic chatter. It took practice and an act of will, but I'd mastered it.

Now I was carefully lowering my mental protections. The last time I had been here, the house overwhelmed me so deeply that an entity or entities took me over, and Fritz recorded me saying some interesting things. Meanwhile, I had no recollection of what I did or said.

Not an experience I wanted to repeat.

Today, as I reached out, I felt nothing. This was even more unusual, since there had been a death here just yesterday. I stood there, confused, as the other vehicles pulled up and the team got out.

Doctor Kohl immediately came up to where I was standing. "Vhat are you getting, Leonard?"

I turned to him and frowned. "Nothing."

This shocked him. "Vhat?"

"I know," I replied. "If this were like the last time, I should be doubled over and incoherent. But I've let my barriers down and I'm getting nothing."

"How is that possible? There vas a death, the Accelerator had been on—"

"I expected to be overwhelmed at the bottom of the street, but now that I'm here, I'm fine."

"Perhaps this explains vhy Lamar vas unable to get any impressions?"

"I can't understand it," I asserted. "Maybe if we go inside?"

George had driven the white van and pulled it up close to the house. He now opened the back and attached a thick electric cable to a large generator that stood in the cargo area. He pulled a cord and the generator jumped to life.

"We have power, Doctor Kohl," he announced.

I looked up at the house and the yellow tape that read "POLICE LINE DO NOT CROSS," which had been blocking the door, but now lay broken and on the ground.

Lamar came over to me. "You getting anything?"

I smiled and shook my head. "Not a thing."

He looked puzzled. "That's kinda weird, isn't it?"

Kohl spoke up. "Now you understand vhy I vanted the Accelerator, Leonard. I thought it might help."

"It worked too well yesterday," I warned. "And I have no desire to end up like Joey."

"Amen," Lamar agreed.

The two women stepped past us and into the house. Anna turned to look at Fritz and said, "I'll get the machines operating, Doctor."

He nodded, and we followed her into the house.

The interior was a preserved pocket of stagnant air and decaying grandeur, exactly as I recalled. Vaulted ceilings rose into the gloom; the height made the corners disappear into shadows.

The dark oak woodwork, once a symbol of opulence, was now a map of neglect — scored with deep scuffs and jagged scratches that looked uncomfortably like fingernail marks. Hanging over the thick, distorted window glass were the skeletal remains of velvet curtains, so frayed and heavy with dust they looked like the molting skin of some great, dead beast.

In the center of this room, the team's gear looked like a high-tech invasion force. Cheap folding tables and scarred desks held the cold, glowing eyes of laptops and other equipment. I cataloged the hardware with a practiced glance: spectrometers for measuring the chemical shift in the air, EMF readers already twitching with invisible currents, and thermal arrays designed to catch the "cold spots" before they moved. It was a masterpiece of clinical efficiency, a stark contrast to the chaotic energy of the house.

Anna moved through the center, drifting from station to station, her fingers dancing over keyboards and toggling switches. One by one, the devices hummed into a low, dissonant chorus of electronic groans.

My gaze drifted away from the blue light of the screens, scanning the perimeter of the living room until it paused at the fireplace. My heart did a slow, heavy roll in my chest. There, mounted above the soot-stained marble of the mantelpiece, was the mirror. The glass, pitted and clouded with age, but a message remained above it.

GET OUT.

Violent, dripping red spray paint formed words that felt too bright for the room's muted decay. In the dim light, the pigment looked wet, like fresh blood screaming against the silvered glass, a final warning from someone who had seen exactly what was coming.

"Anything?" Fritz whispered to me.

"Only a creepy feeling," I replied, my eyes on the message. I took the denim jacket I was carrying and threw it onto a folding chair near one workstation. "Where is the—"

I stopped when I saw the coil on top of the small makeshift box, which resembled nothing so much as a prop from a 1950s science-fiction movie.

The Accelerator.

I walked over to it. There was a laptop connected by wires to the box. I looked at the screen, which was still booting up.

Anna still walked around the room, flipping switches and making sure the machines were operational.

"Anyone know how to activate the Accelerator, other than Joey?" I asked.

Fritz looked at the machine, then at me. "Liam vas instructed how to use it by Joseph. I vanted to make sure several people on the team understood how it vorked."

Lamar piped up. "I'll get him. He's doing the EMF readings around the outside of the house." He walked out of the door.

"EMF readings outside?" I asked Fritz.

"Ja, ve do them twice a day, in the mornings vhen ve start, and then evenings before ve leave."

I nodded. "Tracking the data for fluctuations?"

"Leonard, I have to admit, ve've had very few variations over the last veek."

Liam came in with a small EMF reader in his hand. "What's up? Lamar said you needed me?"

I turned to the brown-haired young man. "Did Joey show you how to work the Accelerator?"

"Basically," Liam said, moving to the laptop connected to the machine. He focused on the screen as his fingers tapped the keyboard. "I was there the day the team at the University of Maine went through the program."

I studied the young man. "I've only seen it once in Maine, and this interface might be different. Can you activate it?"

Doctor Kohl cleared his throat. "Len, are you sure you vant to do that?"

I looked over at Zabella and Anna at one station running data, and then glanced at Lamar and Liam, then gave Fritz a reassuring nod. "I think so." I turned my attention back to Liam. "But we want to set it for a very short time. Thirty seconds would be my choice."

"Really?" Liam frowned. "As short as that?"

"How long did Joey set it for?"

Liam tapped away at the laptop keyboard and brought up a custom program. He studied the data. "He set it for ten minutes." Liam peered up at me.

"And he ended up dead," I warned, my eyes intent.

Liam blanched for a moment, swallowed hard, and then said, "Thirty seconds it is."

As he continued to type away, setting the device to work, I turned to Lamar. "Lamar, you've learned the techniques to shield your mind?"

He nodded. "Yeah, why?"

"Trust me. Focus your mind and put up any barriers you have," I suggested.

He could tell I meant it. "I will."

I turned to Liam. "Okay, do it."

He hit a keystroke and smiled at me. I heard a hum as the accelerator prepared to amplify the residual energy in the room.

Everything went dark.

6. PHANTOM SURPRISE

The next thing I knew, I was on the floor with Fritz standing over me. I was freezing.

"Leonard?" he said. "Are you all right?"

I sat up, shivering as I tried to clear my head. "What happened?"

Anna handed me a bottle of water. "You and Lamar collapsed the moment the Accelerator came online."

George looked into my eyes. "Can you stand?"

I nodded. A major headache pounded behind my brow. George offered me a hand and helped me up. I looked over to where Lamar had been sitting on a folding chair to see Liam assist him to his feet. He kept his head down, and what had happened affected him as strongly as it had affected me.

"What did you see?" Zabella bubbled with excitement. "Any impressions or revelations?"

I shook my head. "No, nothing. Lamar, you get anything?"

Lamar was being held upright by Liam. He raised his head toward the sound of my voice and opened his eyes.

He narrowed his eyes, which appeared cold and hard. In that instant, I knew that the real Lamar was far away. An evil grin broke out on his dark face as he looked around the room at the others.

"You are all dead," he rasped. Liam let him go and stepped back. Lamar glared around the room.

His body crouched as the power of whatever possessed him pulled him down into a feral position. "I mark you," he grunted in a gravelly voice, not his own. His arm extended in slow motion, and his index finger pointed at me. "You! You are the one we want."

I attempted to reach out with my mind, but I couldn't get a reading. I tried to focus on the energy that was controlling Lamar, but the only input I could detect was with my normal five senses.

Lamar took a lurching step toward me, and I felt George move protectively to block him. I shook my head, and he moved back. I allowed my mental walls to come down, which was a danger if this was indeed an entity possessing him. It meant I could be open to its influence if it wanted me as a host.

"Why do you want me?" I demanded, speaking in measured tones directly at Lamar.

He faced me, but I didn't meet his eyes. Instead, I focused on his forehead. One of my talents is to use eye contact to slip into other people's minds, and I didn't want whatever this was to use the same trick on me.

"You were the one who was here," he croaked. "We have waited for your return."

With that, his eyes fluttered shut, and his body went limp. Liam shot forward and caught him before he could collapse to the floor.

Lamar exhaled loudly and straightened up without help. He raised his head and opened his eyes, but the strange look was gone. "What the hell?" he complained, and his hand went to his head. "Man, that machine gave me one bad headache."

I felt everyone in the room relax. Doctor Kohl took Lamar's chin in his right hand and looked into the young man's eyes. "How do you feel? Did you get any impressions?"

"I feel lousy," Lamar said, realizing the group focused on him. "Hey, I'm okay. Why is everyone staring at me?"

"You just threatened us," Liam snorted. "You don't remember that?"

Lamar looked back at the chair he'd been sitting in. "Last thing I recall, I was in that chair and the machine hummed."

I closed my eyes for a moment and put up my mental barriers as the others told Lamar the things he'd said and done.

Kohl came over to me. "Vat did you get, Leonard?"

I shook my head. "Nothing. I even dropped my mental walls to get a reading on Lamar."

Kohl hissed out a breath. "That vas risky."

"I know, but I still got nothing. I have to tell you, Fritz, this is not the way it was at Hedden House when the Accelerator was active."

"Did you black out then as well?" Fritz said, and his hand went to the back of my head. I felt a slight pain where he rubbed a growing lump. "You hit your head, mein freund."

"At Hedden House, it made the phenomenon very active. Overwhelmingly so. I don't know what we just experienced."

"Wait a minute." Lamar moved to the center of the room and raised his hands. "Are you all saying I was possessed? By some thing?"

I stepped toward him. "It wasn't you, but it wasn't any kind of entity I've dealt with before."

Zabella moved to one of the open laptops around the room. "Let me compile the data, see what the readings were like when the Accelerator was active and Lamar went all Exorcist on us."

"That was pretty intense," George said, a small smile appearing on his face. "Lamar, you weren't just pulling our leg or anything, were you?"

Lamar looked stricken. "I would never do that."

George shrugged. "I thought I should ask."

I limped over to Zabella, who spun the laptop so I could see the screen.

"Are you able to track all the readings on each machine?" I asked, as I glanced from workstation to workstation, as the different machines clicked away.

"Yes," Zabella explained. "It made sense for each workstation to access the data in real time. Then, when we shut down here, we move the data to the cloud and analyze it at our leisure."

"How does it send the data to the cloud servers?" I wondered.

She pointed to a large router sitting on one of the nearby tables. "Cellular router. The cell towers are so close, literally right up the mountain from here."

I shook my head. "Amazing. This is so far beyond anything I've ever seen…"

I glanced over to see Fritz talking with Lamar, who was adamant in telling my mentor that he had no recollection of the recent events.

I turned back to Zabella. "What are the readings from when we activated the Accelerator? Was there a spike?"

"I'm working on it," she told me, her eyes fixated on the screen. "It's odd. Maybe the data got corrupted."

"Corrupted?" I frowned. "By what?"

She shrugged. "I don't know, but it looks like there wasn't a spike of any kind."

I exhaled heavily and hobbled back to Kohl and Lamar.

Lamar was talking as I drew near. "I can't explain any of it, Doctor Kohl. All I know was that I was sitting in that chair, then I was standing and you were all staring at me."

Fritz turned to me. "Any other impressions, Leonard?"

"My story is the same as Lamar's. I was standing, I heard the hum of the Accelerator, and then I woke up on the floor."

A line appeared between Fritz's brows. "So strange. And vas there data from vhen this occurred?"

"Zabella says there wasn't a spike. In fact, she noted no changes of any kind."

Fritz's frown deepened. "This makes no sense. In all the years I've studied, every place where there has been a phenomenon—"

"Professor?" Anna stepped forward. "I believe the data might be hidden."

"Hidden?" I repeated.

"Yes," she declared, her voice confident. "As Zabella was telling Doctor Wise, we can observe the data from every workstation with any of the machines. I was looking over the same data as she was, but I think the results might be hidden."

"Please, clarify," Fritz insisted.

"The Accelerator uses the other machines to get a baseline, which it uses to create vibrations at the same frequencies that are detected."

"Ja," Fritz agreed.

"What if the frequencies are so low they don't register? Or what if they exist at a unique frequency our programs weren't designed to detect?"

Fritz and I exchanged a glance.

"I don't know," Kohl said, rubbing his chin. "If the frequencies are undetectable, there vould be nothing for the Accelerator to use as a baseline."

"Perhaps it could be readings we count as background noise," Anna suggested.

I pressed my lips together. "Of course! Fritz, did the team calibrate the machines so that they negated any background vibrations?"

"Yes, of course, the first day," he proclaimed, contemplating what I'd asked. "That is vhat Joey did, as ve set up the machines."

"Liam," I snapped, and the young man turned away from his own computer station to look at me. "Can you remove any background noise limitations on the data readings?"

"What?" he demanded and walked over with a puzzled look on his face. "It took Joey and me days to figure out the calibration…"

"I know," I assured. "But whatever affected Lamar might hide in those background vibrations. That would explain why we didn't see a spike in the readings. If the program ignores certain vibrations—"

He shook his head. "It doesn't work that way," he sighed. "But I can keep the current settings as a baseline and reset. Give me a couple of minutes."

He moved back to his laptop and started working feverishly.

"An entity that hides itself?" Fritz said to both Lamar and me. "Usually, if there is a trapped entity, it vants to be discovered."

"That's what you taught us," Lamar surmised. "You also taught us about residual haunting, where a traumatic incident leaves an energetic imprint on a location."

I smiled at the recollection of studying the same theories. "Like an old film loop repeating and repeating, but only for someone sensitive enough to experience it."

Kohl looked at us both with pride. "I taught you both vell."

I cleared my throat. "But I've been here before. Back then, just being in the house was an overwhelming experience. There was nothing hidden. Quite the contrary; it was aggressive, the same way Lamar was when whatever that was possessed him."

Lamar joined in. "I read the reports of that encounter. And, Len, you were unconscious that time as well."

"Yes, an entity or entities took over, and I remembered nothing," I reported.

"Much like vhat happened to Lamar today," observed Kohl.

I nodded. "It could be the same entity. This house has a history of strange occurrences—"

"And a high body count," Lamar announced. "Could whatever got inside me have done the same to Joey? Could it have made him kill himself?"

I turned to Fritz. "Was Joey a sensitive? Did he have any inherent psychic ability?"

Fritz mulled this over. "To be honest, Leonard, he vasn't one of mine. He vas Doctor Janis's student."

"Really?"

I heard a vehicle approaching up the lonely road leading to the house. I was concerned that it might be the police detective here to take another look.

The others heard the car, and all raised their heads. I headed for the door. "Liam, keep working on that. I'll check on our visitor."

"Ve'll check," Fritz agreed as we stepped outside.

A minivan was coming up the hill. I gazed over at the quarry, noting the rumble of machinery in the distance as huge earthmovers thundered through the multiple roadways carved into the earth.

"Vibrations." I gestured, and Fritz looked over at the quarry as well. "I would imagine that those trucks would create a high level of background vibration."

Kohl studied the movement of the trucks, then nodded. "I agree."

The minivan pulled closer, and I recognized Doctor Janis, his balding pate reflecting the sun as the vehicle drew near. In the passenger seat was a beautiful blonde woman. They parked, and the pair stepped out.

Janis looked the same as I remembered: thin and studious with heavy-framed glasses, perhaps a little balder than at our last encounter. He wore a long-sleeved work shirt and khakis with a heavy pair of hiking boots.

A bit much for an indoor location in the heat of summer.

The blonde was stunning. About five-eight with blue eyes and pale skin that suggested a Scandinavian heritage. With thin hips and a chest that I was certain surgery had augmented, she also wore sensible clothes for fieldwork: a long-sleeve linen 'bush' shirt in a light-brown color, with a pair of jeans that looked like she'd been poured into. She was also wearing hiker's boots and a small vest, and gave more of the appearance of a supermodel at a fashion show than a researcher. As she drew near, I could see that she was wearing full makeup, including eyeliner.

"Henry," Fritz greeted them. "Good to see you." He turned to the young woman. "And, Haley, nice that ve got you out here."

"I wouldn't miss it, Doctor Kohl," the woman replied.

"My God, it's hot here in the hills," Janis said and glanced over at the quarry. "How can you work with all that ruckus?"

"It may have interfered with some of our equipment," I proposed. "Nice to see you, Doctor."

Janis eyed me suspiciously. "You as well. And aren't you a doctor now?"

"Yes, the university accepted my dissertation since we last met."

"And teaching at GSU as well?" Janis said.

I noted that he'd done his research. "Yes, for over a year now."

"Very nice." He turned to his attractive companion. "This is Ms. Wolder. She is my assistant for the summer."

She turned with a dazzling smile, which showed perfect teeth. There were a lot of attractive young ladies who came to California to get into movies, and this had caused a real shift in the gene pool.

"Pleased," I said and shook her hand as she stared up at me. "I'm Leonard Wise."

"Yes, I bet you are!" she gushed. "The super psychic of Scudder House." She gave her wavy blonde hair a toss that would have looked false on anyone else, but it gave her a flirty quality that seemed totally natural.

"That's not the title I prefer," I replied sardonically.

"Or one that is accurate, really," Janis said as Ms. Wolder eyed me. "So, bad stuff, Fritz, the suicide. Reporters have been hounding me all day."

"Ve are trying to get back on track, Henry. There are things ve do not understand, and ve are trying to correct them."

"I have to tell you, we don't need any bad publicity right now. The city of Brisbane is desperate to tear this place down."

"What?" I blurted.

Janis nodded with a backward glance at me. "They consider it an eyesore, and they feel it attracts a lot of 'ghost-hunters.' Now with a death, the council is calling a meeting tonight to discuss demolition."

During this talk, my attention was on Janis, but I noticed in my peripheral vision that Ms. Wolder had not taken her eyes off me and kept looking me over.

"This is terrible," Fritz said.

"Yes," Janis sighed. "So, I recommend you try to get us something we can use to stop it."

"Doctor Kohl," a quiet female voice said behind us. We turned to see that it was Anna.

"Yes?" Fritz said and turned.

"We compiled the data and are ready to run it with the new parameters," she said, and then looked over at Ms. Wolder. Her expression darkened, and I could see her grow tense.

"*Ja, das ist gut,*" Fritz offered, and he turned back to our guests. "Please come in out of the sun, both of you."

As Janis and Kohl headed up the short porch steps, I met Ms. Wolder's eyes.

"Nice to meet you, Doctor Wise," she purred, again taking my hand for another shake.

"Please, call me Len."

"I will. And you should call me Haley, like the comet," she said in a sultry tone as she released my hand and moved past me.

Amused, I watched her head up the stairs while Anna stared at her with such contempt that I wouldn't have been surprised if Haley had burst into flames.

Like the comet.

I headed up the three steps, a slower process with my frozen leg. I have to take one step at a time and pull my leg up behind me. This is when my cane makes a tremendous difference. Anna stood on the porch and seethed.

I smiled, and she glared at me. "Calm down, she's harmless."

"I heard her coming on to you," she hissed. "And she is an enormous ball of useless gas — like the comet!"

"And I'm not interested in playing along," I said, then I added, "With anyone!"

Chastised, she turned and stormed into the house. I followed at a safe distance.

Anna moved to the nearest computer station and pulled up the data while Janis looked disapprovingly around the room.

"Look," I said and pointed at a graph that appeared on the screen. "There was a definitive spike during the use of the Accelerator."

"Yes, it seems I was right, Doctor Wise." Anna flipped her hair, raising an eyebrow at me as she mimicked Haley's flirtation.

I couldn't help but smile. "Hidden data. The machines dismissed it as background vibrations."

"Now that I've seen the quarry when it's busy, I can understand that," I responded, hoping we could focus on the task at hand instead of our hormones. "Those trucks are creating a great deal of vibration that comes up through the mountain. Joey must have set the machines to disregard it."

Liam walked over. "You mean we set the background elimination too high?"

"Exactly," I maintained. "But I don't think it was your fault; you were following protocol. It's just with the quarry next door; the settings were overcompensating."

Liam looked at me glumly. "Do you think it could've cost Joey his life?"

I stared at the computer screen. "I don't know about that. But I know this house. Something in it persuaded him to kill himself."

Janis frowned. "Do you really think that's what happened?"

I shrugged. "It's either that or someone killed him."

Janis glared at me and glanced around the room at the team, then spoke haughtily. "Really, I think we should keep such suppositions to ourselves, Doctor Wise."

I spoke in a quiet tone. "It's better if the team is aware of the dangers here. We think it might just be the phenomenon, but there could be an actual person. I seriously doubt it would be a member of the team."

Fritz frowned. "You think some stranger killed Joey?"

"It's a possibility," I insisted. "At this time, I am not ruling out anything."

We all turned back to the computer, and Fritz said, "How high a spike vas there, Anna?"

"Low enough for previous settings to ignore, but higher than the new baseline."

She pointed at a graph that showed the specific timeline. It was plain to see that there was a slight spike that lasted ten minutes.

I shook my head. "That really is a tiny spike. Negligible, in fact. Can you show the thirty seconds we ran this morning?"

Anna hit a few keys on the laptop, and a different graph appeared.

"Is that higher?" Janis asked.

I grimaced. "It's the same, yet that was enough to knock me and Lamar unconscious."

"What does it mean, Doctor Wise?" Haley asked, turning her bright-blue eyes to focus on me. Anna pursed her lips in annoyance.

"The Accelerator amplifies whatever vibrations it detects. If it is an entity, that would give it a lot of raw power. Yet so little is being detected by the equipment." I glanced around until my eyes focused on Liam. "Are any of the cameras in the laptops set to record this room?"

He shook his head. "No. But if you want, I can arrange it so all the cameras are recording."

"No video?" Janis huffed. "Seems like you were unprepared."

"We've been setting up equipment all week," Liam argued. "So far, with little results. It didn't appear that video was necessary. How did I know Joey was going to—" He stopped speaking, aware of what he was saying.

"Well, to business," Janis clarified and stepped to the center of the room. "I am here to tell you that, because of the death of Mr. Thompson, the University of San Francisco will shut down this research location at the end of this week."

"Vhat?" Doctor Kohl sputtered. "Henry, ve vere supposed to be here all of August! It took years to set up the funding—"

Janis held up his hand. "I am afraid I have little to do with it, Fritz. You can do research until Friday, but as of Saturday, you must begin loading out. We will compensate all of you for your time, but the risks are simply too high. Ms. Wolder, let's allow them to get back to work."

Doctor Janis and Ms. Wolder headed for the door, followed by Fritz and me.

As they walked down the stairs, Fritz called out, "Really, Henry. Can ve talk about this? Perhaps if I speak to the grant committee—"

"Fritz, it's out of my hands," Janis said as he opened the back of the minivan and pulled out a backpack. "The word came down from the trustee of the estate."

Ms. Wolder turned around, and Janis held out the backpack as she slid the straps over her shoulders. She then picked up a backpack as Janis turned his back to her.

She then did something curious. She pulled out the small bottle for water that hung in a web pouch on the side and replaced it with a similar bottle she pulled from the back of the van.

She then held the backpack against Janis as he pulled the straps in place.

"There must be something ve can do, Henry," Fritz raged. "If you are right and the town vants to demolish this house, they could lose irreplaceable data."

"You have the rest of the week, Fritz," Janis sighed as he closed the back and locked the vehicle with the fob. "Now if you'll excuse me, there is a fascinating crystal cave I promised to show to Ms. Wolder."

The girl flashed one of her dazzling smiles, and the pair of them headed off toward the nearby forest, just beyond the clearing of the house.

Fritz stood in stunned silence.

I now understood the reason for the long sleeves and heavy boots, despite the August heat. They never intended to work the site with us; they'd always planned to head out into the woods.

As they wandered off, I looked up the mountain to see a trio of large antennae on a bluff near the top. They were the classic design: ironwork frames that reached toward the sky with smaller attachments sticking out at all angles. It surprised me they weren't 'disguised' as trees, as some cell-phone towers are in New Jersey. Builders construct those with green 'branches' attached to a thick brown 'trunk.' The illusion breaks when you see the door that accesses its inner workings built into the side of the "tree."

Doctor Janis and Ms. Wolder disappeared into the greenery and dappled sunlight as Fritz and I watched them go.

"Now vhat do ve do?" Fritz asked me.

"I have an idea, but you won't like it."

"And that is?"

"We work here at night."

7. UNSEEN THREAT

"N ein, nein," Doctor Kohl repeated as we stepped back into the house. The morning heat was becoming oppressive.

From what I'd read on the flight across the country, Brisbane, California, is a very temperate location. Even in the summer, the temperature only gets to the high seventies or low eighties.

This year they were having a heat spell, and already it was in the nineties.

"You have to admit it's the most logical choice," I insisted.

"No, it is a ridiculous choice," Fritz countered.

The rest of the team was aware of Fritz and me arguing as we entered the house.

"Wait," Lamar spoke up. "Are you thinking about working the site at night?" He faced me. "I thought you were the one who said we shouldn't do that."

The rest of the group moved away from their workstations to gather around us.

"I did. In fact, when Doctor Kohl said he was returning, that was one thing I strongly advised. I mean, this is a research situation at a very active site."

Liam cut in. "But now you feel differently?"

I sighed. "Last time Doctor Kohl and I were here, we didn't have nearly as much equipment — just a digital recorder and an electroencephalogram."

"Ve didn't have the budget for much else," Kohl agreed.

"Plus, I think it must have been the weekend, as the quarry wasn't sending up a lot of noise and vibration like they're doing now."

"But the last time you were here was during the day," Anna added.

"It was supposed to be. But it took longer to set up and get the generator going. I started my reading while the sun was setting."

They all stared at me.

"Plus, last time I was here, there was a heaviness to the house. This room, for example, the psychic weight was almost crushing."

"And this time you say it isn't?" George asked with suspicion.

"It's like a completely different house," I attempted to explain the surprising change in the 'feel' of the place. "From what I can tell, there is very little I can sense at all."

"Except vhen the Accelerator was active," Kohl pointed out.

"Yeah," Lamar said. "And both of us going unconscious at night might not be the best choice."

"As well as possible demonic possessions," Zabella remarked, with a poke in the ribs to Lamar.

"The point is," I said, "if we are going to make any kind of breakthrough, we are going to have to work at night, when the house is the most active."

"But the dangers, Leonard—" Kohl fretted.

"We should be fine, as long as we don't use the Accelerator. In fact, I would advise that we disconnect it completely. Just shut it down."

"What?" Liam fumed. "We spent the better part of last week getting that thing functional."

"And it got Joey killed," I stated.

They couldn't meet my eyes, and all looked down at the floor.

"If ve are going to do it," Kohl affirmed, "ve need to make plans."

George lifted a finger. "Well, first thing I need to do is a gasoline run at some point. The fuel for the generator is getting used up pretty quickly. I'll take the empty fuel cans and get them filled."

"Food would be a good choice too," Liam requested.

George pulled out a small pad and the stub of a pencil and made notes. "Anything else?" He looked around and no one responded. "Okay, food, drinks, and gas."

"Usually in that order," Lamar quipped.

"I'm going to meditate and see if I can bring myself down to a level where I can detect what is going on in the house," I said.

"Is that a good idea, Leonard?" Kohl asked.

"We could run an EEG," Zabella suggested. "We have a cap with the electrodes. You only need to put it on."

Lamar looked at Kohl. "It could also help us make sure he doesn't go too deep."

I shrugged. "It's worth a try."

Zabella nodded. "We can track your brain waves, and the other machines will track the surrounding data. It would help to see if there is a correlation."

"It is a sound approach," Kohl sighed. "If you think you have things in hand, I vill help George get fuel and food."

"I think it's our best course of action," I assured him. "Besides Fritz, it's daytime. What could happen?"

"In this house, Leonard?" Kohl looked at me with his eyebrows raised.

Everyone moved into action. George headed out the door as Fritz grabbed the keys to one of the rented cars. Liam turned to the machines to include the EEG in the data stream. Anna went through plastic storage bins to find the EEG cap, and Lamar assisted Liam in getting the electroencephalography machine set up with the laptop. As they readied the equipment, I reflected on how hot the room had become, even indoors. The last time I had been here, it had been so very cold, especially in the basement.

Despite the heat, a chill went up my spine as I recalled the underground space with its sandstone walls and brick archways. Would I be willing to go back down there if necessary? Would I be willing to return to the location of my greatest triumph, that dark place shut away from the sunlight?

I certainly didn't want to.

Anna had located the cap, and Lamar hooked the wires to the small box that would amplify the readings and interface with the computer. Liam was checking the program to make sure it would work with the software that tracked all the machines.

The technical side of things, I didn't understand at all.

That's exactly why Teddy Santos is my teaching assistant. Not only is he truly getting a grasp of what I teach, but his main background is in computers. So if I need anything that uses interfaces or apps, I just get him to do it.

I grew up in the 90s, so I wasn't used to having a smartphone grafted to my palm day and night like many millennials. Then again, my study for years has been controlling the mind and the realm of the spirit. I had other things to focus on, and increasing my followers on TikTok wasn't one of them.

Anna held up the unattractive yellow headpiece and nodded for me to sit down. I sat in a folding chair, my right leg sticking out at an angle. She delicately ran her hand over my head and whispered, "You have really nice hair, Len."

"Keep doing that, and you'll put me to sleep," I murmured with my eyes closed.

I jumped when something wet was slapped to my head.

"Hey," I bellowed.

"I thought you wanted to wake up, Len," Anna giggled. "Relax, it's just a saline solution to improve the scalp-electrode conductivity. It'll dry out of your hair when we're done."

"You could have warned me," I grumbled.

"What fun is that?" she teased and continued to rub the solution into my hair, massaging my scalp as she did.

I had to admit, once past the initial shock, it was nice to have her rub my head, and the solution was cool on this hot day. Her touch was soft and sensual, and ideas of her touching other parts of me ran through my mind.

She then carefully pulled the cap onto my head, adjusting the electrodes as she went to get the best contact with the skin.

I understood her choice of saline solution. Newer EEG caps use it, and it cleans up much better than the conductive gel that was the preferred interface even a few short years ago. When

Doctor Kohl and I were last here at Scudder House, we used an older machine and needed to place the electrodes one at a time with adhesive pads, as well as use the gel, which took a lot of shampoo to get out of my hair.

She finished getting the cap in place, fastened the elastic strap under my chin, and gave my shoulder an affectionate squeeze.

I opened my eyes and glanced over at Liam. "How do I look?"

Lamar spoke first. "Like an extra in a bad sci-fi movie."

I grinned. "I have finally achieved my goal!"

Anna met my eyes. Hers were bright and excited. Apparently, she'd enjoyed the contact of touching my head as well.

Liam was at the laptop and spoke with his eyes on the screen. "I'm adjusting the bandwidth and sampling rate. Len, can you close your eyes and try to relax your mind?"

Lamar snorted. "You mean the stuff Doctor Kohl makes those of us in the 'gifted' program do every day? I think Len can handle it."

I smiled at the banter and closed my eyes. I focused on my breath to put myself in a light, meditative state.

My mind flooded with what we call 'cloud thoughts.' They are the simple things we worry about every day. When you learn meditation, it is the brain's way of distracting you from your goal. As you try to calm yourself and be at peace, your brain is very busy trying to make you focus on other things and remain active.

Knowing what they were, I just observed them, like clouds, and let them float away.

"Good," Liam noted as I sat unmoving. "Okay, Len, we're tracking. Do what you do."

I nodded my head gently, not wanting to break my meditation, and went deeper, focusing on my breath and allowing my mind to relax.

This form of meditation is one part ancient teaching, one part self-hypnosis, and one part breath control. As I drew myself down to a lower level of existence, I experienced colors, smells, and other stimuli. Again, the brain's attempt to distract.

I perceived the surrounding room through my mind's eye, seeing the room, yet now it was in hues of grays and blacks, almost like an old movie. I could imagine the position of each person. Anna had moved to a laptop to follow up on the data as Lamar stood and watched me carefully. It was his job to move in if I stopped breathing, which can sometimes happen if you go down too far.

Doctor Kohl trained all of his students in these techniques, and also how to watch out for each other when any of us attempted deep meditation.

I could hear the murmur of voices, but I stayed focused on my breath and the energy of the place.

"He's pretty far down," Liam said. "This is amazing."

Zabella spoke up. "Look at the correlation with the other machines."

"All of the other measures are climbing," Anna said in a harsh whisper.

I could sense it. The house was indeed becoming active around me. I could feel other people, other beings, whether memories or entities, become cognizant as if awakening.

And something else.

I wasn't deep enough to reach it, but it was there, deep down, and it knew that I could sense it like a shadow glimpsed from the corner of one's eye.

I wavered there for a moment. To go too deep held dangers, as well as made me more vulnerable. Whatever it was, it was comfortable in this lower level of existence, and I would be an intruder. It would have the home-field advantage.

And then something pulled at me. At first, I believed it was a 'cloud thought' or some other distraction. I heard a woman's voice as she yelled for help, but it was only in my mind.

I relaxed and allowed my mind to be pulled to the sound, and all at once I was outside, in the woods. Everything had the odd sepia tone that I get when I perceive a vision.

The person calling out was Haley Wolder.

She stood near the mouth of a small, tubular cave, and in the cave I could see the sparkle of crystals. Even with the color removed, they glittered in the sun.

She stood in the very outfit I'd seen her in a few minutes earlier, but at her feet lay Doctor Janis, unconscious.

She looked right at me and spoke. "Help me."

This was impossible. She was looking right at me, but I wasn't there. I was in a chair inside Scudder House. If I were perceiving her, if I had projected my astral self to her location, she could not see me. And then I realized what it was, and that pushed me out of the vision and up through the stages where I had lowered my mind.

My eyes shot open, and I gasped for breath, as if I had just run a marathon.

Lamar put a hand on my shoulder. "Len, you okay? Why'd you jump out of your meditation like that?"

"Doctor Janis," I wheezed, surprised that I felt as if I'd been holding my breath.

"What about him?" Lamar asked, concern etched on his dark face.

"He collapsed — in the woods." I gulped and attempted to stand.

"Len, no!" Anna yelled and stepped behind me to grab my shoulders and push me back to the chair. "We have to remove the EEG cap."

I sat and tried to calm myself.

"What did you see?" Lamar questioned as Anna carefully undid the chin strap and began to gently remove the electrodes touching my head.

"They were near a cave, and Doctor Janis was on the ground with that girl with him."

"The good-looking blonde?" Lamar wondered.

"Yeah," I told him as the cap finally came off. I stood to my full height as Liam took the cap from Anna and shut down any connection.

Zabella had stepped away from her workstation. "Where was this, do you know?"

"It was near a cave full of crystals," I explained. "It was like a hole, a tube going through a large rock face."

Zabella nodded. "I know where that is. I can lead us." She glanced at my leg and accompanying walking stick. "The ground is very unsteady. I think you should stay."

Anna looked over. "I can't go. There's poison oak everywhere, and I'm really sensitive to it."

Liam had joined the surrounding huddle. "Are you sure of this, and the location?"

"Completely!" I responded.

I also knew something else I didn't choose to share. This woman, this Haley-like-the-comet, was a psychic.

8. SHADOWY PRESENCE

Zabella, Lamar, and Liam wisely put on nitrile gloves to help protect them from the poison oak. With their long sleeves and long trousers, I assumed they should be safe. Zabella grabbed a first-aid kit and a blanket, and the team headed out.

Anna was examining the EEG cap, and after the others left, she walked over to me and rubbed her hand in my hair.

"What are you doing?" I asked.

"Fixing your hair. It's a mess. This will help it dry," she explained as she tried to arrange it. "You went to a lot of trouble to be alone with me."

I chuckled, which earned me a winning smile from Anna. Then I got serious. "Anna, you're a beautiful woman…"

"I feel a 'but' coming," she replied.

I smiled again. "Yeah, I guess so. I won't deny that I am attracted to you, and I certainly liked you back when I was teaching—"

"Almost reached the 'but,' have we?"

I exhaled heavily. "But, I just went through a nasty breakup and emotionally I'm all over the place. I couldn't offer my best self to anyone right now."

She came around in front of me and knelt so we were at eye level. "Len, I understand. I'm not looking to get married and settle down. I just wanted to let you know I was interested in having a physical relationship."

I gazed intently at her. "For what purpose?"

She shrugged and smiled. "Well, actually, I was hoping to get laid."

Her very proper manner, counterpointed with this simple declaration, made me laugh out loud. It felt good. It was probably the first time I had reacted with such a pure, hearty expression of humor in months.

Since I was still sitting, Anna opened her legs, straddled my lap to face me, and slid closer. She leaned forward to kiss me, and I didn't resist. In fact, I returned it with equal passion. It was a pleasant kiss, and I ran my hands over the smooth contours of her hips and lower back as she murmured in approval.

She leaned back and sighed. "That was nice."

She pressed herself against me, and I groaned, which made her smile turn lusty. "I think the parts of you that are not attached to your emotions are interested."

"Very." I suppressed another groan.

"So, tonight, might you be my genie and make my wishes come true?"

I chuckled again. "I don't see how I could say no."

"Not with that thing poking against me," she teased merrily. She stood, stepped carefully over my paralyzed leg, and walked back to Liam's computer station with a smug smile on her face. "You had me worried after last night. I thought I'd lost my touch."

I shifted uncomfortably and tried to get my aroused state under control. "Your touch — and the rest of you — is fine."

"Well, it's a blow to the ego when willingness and lingerie get rejected."

"I'll try to make up for it," I said, and I gingerly got to my feet, now that my raging hormones had quieted a bit.

She frowned at the computer screen. "Look at this, Len."

I moved behind her to look over her shoulder. A graph showed different colored bars rising from the bottom of the screen.

"You see these?" she explained and gestured at the readout. "It shows that as your mind went deeper, all of the readings from the other machines went up."

"Really?" I marveled. "I think I can understand that. It felt like as I went down lower, something became aware of my presence. As if to — I don't know — meet me."

"Well, this big jump here is when you came awake." She indicated a blue bar that jumped high above the others. "And these are the other readings once you were conscious."

"They all went down again," I murmured, looking at the lines on the screen.

Anna's phone rang. She pulled it out of a convenient pocket near the knee of her work pants and answered.

She listened for a moment. "All right, we'll be ready, Zabby."

"Zabby?" I questioned as she ended the call.

"Short for Zabella," she shrugged. "She likes it." She became serious. "They found Doctor Janis right near the crystal cave like you said. Fortunately, it's not too far from here."

"What happened to him?"

"They don't know, but he's unconscious. Zabella helped the guys make a stretcher out of the blanket she took and two branches."

"Wait, how does she know how to do that?"

Anna's eyebrows went up. "Zabby's been involved in some serious survivalist stuff. Anyway, they are carrying him out and want us to call an ambulance."

She turned away from me and back to the phone as she punched in 9-1-1.

I had the oddest feeling. Janis had collapsed while I attempted to contact whatever was in the house. He had been part of the team that had been here the last time when I found the hidden treasure. In fact, it was because of him that Doctor Kohl and I had come to Scudder House at all.

The timing of when he collapsed and Haley's telepathic distress call, which distracted me and broke my concentration, was suspicious. It was almost as if everything prevented me from reaching my goal.

I didn't think the house could frighten me any more than it had in the past.

It just did.

The ambulance pulled up the winding driveway, and two paramedics jumped out and came to Anna and me as we stood in front of the house. One man stopped, looked up at the structure, and whistled.

"Pretty amazing place," he commented.

The other man was all business. "Who's injured?"

I stepped off the porch and attempted to explain. "A man in the woods is the injured party. They should be—"

Just as I turned to face the spot where our comrades had disappeared, the group broke from the woods. Lamar was in the front holding a pair of tree branches. The sticks traveled through a cleverly prepared blanket, with the middle supported by Zabella on one side and Haley on the other. Taking up the rear and holding the other ends of the branches was Liam. Lying on the makeshift stretcher was Doctor Janis.

The emergency workers pulled their gurney out of the back of the ambulance and wheeled it to meet the group. They quickly took charge of the operation and transferred Janis from the provisional litter to the gurney and rolled it toward the ambulance.

"What hospital are you taking him to?" I asked quickly as they stepped into the open back of the vehicle.

"The Zuckerberg in San Fran. It's only about six miles away," one man said, as the pair moved the gurney into the back of the ambulance with well-practiced ease.

As his partner put an oxygen mask over Janis' face and checked his vitals, the other man, tall with dark hair, called out, "Who was with him? Is there a spinal injury?"

I nodded without thinking. My medical training told me that spinal injuries were dangerous, especially if you try to move a patient. It could easily kill him.

"No," Zabella assured. "And I checked him carefully before we tried to move him."

Haley ran over to the man. "He was fine and just collapsed. I — caught him, so he fell pretty gently. Didn't hit his head or anything. He just fell unconscious, I don't know why."

The emergency worker nodded, closed the back doors, and ran up to the driver's side to jump in. The vehicle moved off with the lights and siren going.

I turned to Haley. "Do you know what happened?"

She shook her head sadly.

By now, Lamar and Liam had joined us. "Do you think it was the heat?" offered Liam. He was still breathing hard from carrying Janis on the litter, and sweat gleamed on his head.

"I honestly don't know," Haley proclaimed.

I turned to the group. "There's some strange data from my meditation. Anna, would you show them please?"

She nodded, and Liam, Lamar, and Zabella followed her toward the house. Haley started to go as well.

"Not you," I ordered, and Haley stopped. I approached her warily. "Does Doctor Janis know?"

"About what?" Haley demurred.

"About your gifts? Does he know you're psychic?"

She gave that amazing supermodel smile again. "I don't know what you mean."

"I believe you know exactly what I mean," I challenged. "I was unaware there would be a third psychic assigned here."

"No one exactly assigned me," she murmured defensively. She glanced at the others who had stepped into the house. "I was led to work with Doctor Janis this summer."

"Well, that's all very convenient, you showing up and interrupting my meditation when you did," I proclaimed.

"I'm sorry about that, but it was an emergency."

"What are you not telling me?"

She exhaled in exasperation. "Doctor Wise, there are others who have an interest in this house."

"Such as?" I demanded.

Haley glanced to make sure the others were not coming out of the house. "Have you heard of the McCord Psychic Institute?"

"I'm familiar with it, peripherally," I told her. "The 'school' is based in Berkley, follows the teachings of an 'aura-reader' named Lewis McCord, who also ran a new-age church. They combine psychic practice with mostly Christian theology."

"That's true, but you can learn to hone your abilities there," she announced triumphantly. "I did."

"I thought it was some kind of cult."

She considered this and didn't seem offended. "It can be. Doctor McCord is certainly a cult-like figure, and there are those who worship him." She drew closer to me. "That doesn't mean that there aren't people who do good work."

I looked at her but avoided making eye contact, which meant I stared at the tip of her nose. "So why are you interested in Scudder House?"

"Same reasons you are. Dark history, psychics affected anytime a reading was done," she said. "Can we go inside? It's hot out here."

"It's hot in there as well," I reasoned. "But I want to know how you got involved. Doctor Janis said you were working with him this summer."

"I found out that Janis was involved in Scudder House, so some people I know got me the interview for the position."

"And with your blonde hair and good looks, you had no problem getting him to hire you."

A smug smile appeared on her face. "He doesn't mind a good-looking woman nearby. It also helped that I could read what he wanted and what he was looking for."

"You used your abilities to trick him."

"Oh, don't get all high and mighty with me, Doctor Wise. I've heard rumors of your exploits in New Jersey."

I looked away. She had a point. In my work with McGee, I had often peeked into other people's minds and sometimes forced them to tell me things. "I use my abilities to save lives, not trick people into giving me a job."

Her mouth became a hard line, and I could see the flirty persona drop away. "If I wasn't here today, Doctor Janis might've died. So I saved a life as well, Doctor."

"Well, I will talk to Doctor Kohl, and I assure you, you will not be a part of this team."

The smug smile returned. "Don't be so sure."

At that moment, a vehicle pulled up the road and came to a stop nearby, driven by George with Doctor Kohl riding shotgun.

The pair came out, and I raised my hand to Fritz.

Fritz took one look at my face and asked, "Vat's wrong?"

"Doctor Janis collapsed out in the woods," I told him as he drew near.

"*Mein Gott!*" Fritz exclaimed. "Is he all right?"

By now, George had walked over. He went straight to Ms. Wolder and spoke to her in low tones as if the pair were familiar with each other.

"We got him out," I clarified. "Zabella made a stretcher out of a blanket and some branches."

"She is quite clever," Fritz acknowledged with a nod. "Her survivalist skills were one reason I vanted her on the team."

I glanced over at Haley, who was still whispering to George, and went on. "An ambulance took him to a hospital."

Fritz's expression darkened. "Vhich one?"

Haley stepped away from George and spoke up, as if she'd been waiting for her cue. "He is going to the Zuckerberg in San Francisco." And then, as if planned, a single tear fell from her eye. "Oh, Doctor Kohl, I don't know what I'm going to do."

Fritz opened his arms, and Haley moved into them. She turned to Fritz and gave George a wink.

I felt my blood pressure rise. She was manipulating Fritz and letting George know she was doing it!

"I was supposed to help Doctor Janis work on the house with all of you," she sniffed, sounding like she was fighting to keep her emotions in check.

"That's all right, Haley," Fritz said, and released her from the hug. "You can vork vith my team. One more person vould be a help."

George nodded. "That would be great, especially if you can drive Doctor Janis' van. We need more vehicles."

Fritz said, "Come, come, let us get back to the task at hand." He turned to the big, young man. "Are you all right moving the gas cans, George?"

"I got it, Doc!" George boasted.

Fritz went to the back of the vehicle and grabbed a pair of paper bags; I assumed they held food. Haley grabbed one bag, and the pair of them walked toward the house. I stood there, annoyed at how easily she twisted Fritz around her little finger. Then again, wasn't that what she'd attempted to do with me?

What happened to my nice, stable life, with my classes, the house with Mrs. Higgins, my girlfriend, and the occasional consultation with the police?

Now I was at a research site with my abilities not responding as I expected; I was working with a team of well-meaning but inexperienced people; and dealing with a female psychic who had questionable loyalties and a hidden agenda.

So far the only bright spot was Anna. She certainly had changed from that mousey girl I had in class a short year and a half ago.

And tonight promised the delights of her charms.

So why was I terrified?

I had been close to touching something in my meditation — something deep and hidden. Then, Haley startled me out of my trance with her emergency call.

And while on the subject, where was she when Joey died?

I shook my head and trudged back toward the house.

9. SPIRITED RESISTANCE

There was a flurry of activity as I limped through the door. Liam and Zabella were setting up lunch from bags that Fritz and Haley had carried in. I suddenly felt unexpectedly tired.

I moved to the bag and extracted a bottle of water and gulped it down. Psychic experiences drain moisture from the body, and I needed to hydrate.

Anna was at one workstation, glaring at Haley. She certainly found Haley's presence annoying. I would like to ask her why. Perhaps she could elaborate on any knowledge she had of the tricky Ms. Wolder.

Fritz was standing at a different workstation with Haley looking over his shoulder and asking about the data parameters. Fritz answered in simple terms, showing his broad knowledge of not only parapsychology but the function of the individual machines.

I cleared my throat, which made them both look at me.

"Fritz," I started, "I think working at night is a good choice. But not tonight."

"Vhy?" he asked innocently. "Do you have plans?"

I must have flushed deep red, because I saw Haley slyly glance at me knowingly.

"Uh, no. But today has been stressful. We should finish up our work by sundown and clear out. Then structure our day so we arrive for sundown tomorrow."

Fritz nodded. "Ve can do that."

Zabella called out. "If you want lunch, get it now."

"Ah," Fritz said. "I've been smelling that since ve bought it. Excuse me."

He walked away, and I met Haley's eyes.

"Please, Doctor," she muttered to me quietly. "Don't get all testy because you didn't get your way."

"It's your way I'm worried about," I complained. "What can you tell me about that crystal cave?"

She frowned. "I'm sorry?"

"You and Janis went to the crystal cave, and it seemed like a big deal. It's also where he collapsed, and you reached out to me mentally. Anything special about it?"

"No, it's just one of the local sites. Most people can't find it because it's in the hills, and there is a lot of brush and poison oak."

"From my vision, it appeared like a tube carved into the mountain."

"That's pretty much it. Whoever did it dug it by hand, probably with a pickaxe, looking for gold."

"Why would they cut into a cave full of quartz?"

"You don't know? Well, I grew up in California. The miners would often look for quartz because it was a sign that there was gold nearby. Often they found gold pushed right into the quartz itself."

I raised my eyebrows. "I didn't know that."

She touched my arm. "See, I'm making you smarter already." She glanced at Anna. "What's the problem with your girlfriend?"

I saw Anna look over at us with a desire to kill. Fortunately, Haley was its target.

"She's not my girlfriend; she's my teammate and a friend."

This got a deep-throated chuckle from Haley. "Not from where I'm sitting. I'd keep my eye on her if I were you."

"Actually, I intend to keep an eye on you," I warned. "Anna has been very upfront with me. You have only tried to manipulate me since we met. And I saw what you pulled on Doctor Kohl."

She moved close and spoke quietly. "Look, you need me on this. Maybe I pushed myself in, but you're going to need my help."

"We'll see," I snapped, and walked off.

I was very annoyed and getting more so. At the Mountainview Police Department, most of the cops accepted me. Even if they didn't believe in what I do, they tolerated me. I have one detractor, Sergeant Tice, who belittles me every chance he gets. I wondered if I came across as the annoying know-it-all like this woman. If so, I could understand the reason for his dislike of me.

Even if she has a gift, I don't need someone to get all mystical and cosmic woo-woo on me.

I wandered over to Anna, who was fuming.

"What's wrong?" she sassed quietly, her eyes on her screen. "Your girlfriend getting too busy for you?"

"She thinks you are my girlfriend," I whispered.

"I do have the previous claim. I don't recall you complaining when I was kissing and rubbing up against you."

"I have no interest in her, Anna. You have punched my card and I'm yours if you want me."

"I'm going to punch her card if she doesn't lighten up on the flirty slut routine."

"Down, tiger. She may have bewitched Doctor Janis and Doctor Kohl, but I'm immune." I noticed a slight rise in one bar on the screen. I pointed at it. "Hey, what's that?"

She frowned and looked at the screen, then called out loudly, "Liam, Zabby, do you see the EMF registering on the comparative screen?"

Zabella was eating a wrap at her station, but her hand flew to the mouse, and she stared at her monitor. "Yeah, I see it."

"Give me a minute," Liam said through a mouthful of sandwich. "I got it. Let me focus on just the EMF readout."

"Nobody move!" Anna ordered loudly. Everyone in the room froze in place, except Haley, who twisted her head one way and then another in surprise. "You too, missy."

Haley stopped where she was and didn't move a muscle. Liam was opening different windows on his computer screen frantically. "We've got EMF movement. I'm trying to focus on the location."

I thought about shutting my eyes and opening my mind, just as I glanced over to see Haley was already doing it. She lifted her hand as if trying to reach out and sense the movement of the energy.

Lamar was doing it as well. He had shut his eyes tightly, and I could sense him as he attempted to use his psychic gifts to find the source of what was causing the machine to react.

Danger…

That's when the buzz hit me in the back of my brain, and it was suddenly clear to me what was about to happen.

"No!" I yelled. "Don't reach out. Don't let it in."

I slammed every bit of my training into creating the barrier around my mind, and I took two quick steps toward Haley to smack her hand with my cane, which broke her focus. She pulled her hand back in pain and opened her eyes to glare at me.

"Walls, put up walls!" I screamed to Haley and tried to get to Lamar, but I wasn't fast enough.

Lamar let out a scream and grabbed his head as I felt a wave wash over me. Did I say wave? I meant tsunami, tidal wave, an unstoppable force that crashed into my mental barriers and pushed them aside as if they weren't there at all. I tumbled to the ground, and I heard Haley scream as well.

I lay on the floor, and a moment later, it was as if nothing had happened. The pressure that had been inside my head, which I felt could have easily turned my brain tissue into farina, was gone as quickly as it had arrived.

I sat up as Liam and Anna came over to me, both with worried expressions. I glanced over to see George help Haley get up, and Fritz was with Lamar.

"What the hell was that?" Haley said, half yelling and half stunned.

"That," I croaked, "is what we are facing."

Neither Lamar, Haley, nor I was truly damaged, and we soon were sitting in folding chairs. Meanwhile, Anna, Liam, and Zabella reviewed the readouts from the machines at their individual stations.

George headed outside to check the fuel in the generator, and Doctor Kohl paced in front of us.

"Leonard, I don't see how ve can risk doing research at night," he finally asserted.

All three of us were nursing bottles of water, and if the others were like me, they were trying to push past a throbbing headache.

"I understand the dangers," I croaked. "But during the day, whatever we experienced can simply hide from us."

"It vasn't hidden now!" Fritz snapped. He stopped pacing and exhaled, obviously frustrated by the turn of events.

"How can it do that?" Lamar bleated. "Just not be here at all and then — WHAM!"

"I don't know what this is," I maintained. "I am aware of entities here, but under it all, there is something else."

"Oh, that's useful," Haley hissed, caressing the bridge of her nose with her free hand.

"It's what I've always felt in this house. Something underneath that's aware and… hungry."

Fritz snorted. "And you vant to face it at night, vhen it is the strongest?"

I went on. "That's why I want to take tomorrow to prepare. The problem is that being here weakens my mental defenses."

Lamar shook his head. "I don't see how you can defend against something like that."

"It only affected people with psi abilities," I pointed out. "Everyone else was unaffected."

Fritz turned to Haley. "I vould guess there is something you vish to tell us, Ms. Wolder."

She looked up at Doctor Kohl with an annoyed expression. The mental hit she had taken affected her. She no longer seemed able to maintain her flirty, model look. In fact, bags had appeared under her eyes as if she had missed sleep for a night.

Finally, she nodded. "I'm a psychic and I've had training. Doctor Janis didn't know."

"And vhere did you train?" Fritz insisted as he folded his arms.

"She's from the McCord Psychic Institute," I offered, and Haley glared at me. "He was going to find out anyway. You shouldn't have kept it to yourself."

"The McCord Institute?" Fritz railed. "Ve didn't allow them to join our study, so they send spies?"

"I'm not a spy," Haley barked back, then more quietly she added, "I'm a researcher. We wanted to be part of the research on this house."

"Ja," Fritz jeered. "Your institute sent many people here over the years. I believe people from the Institute came searching for the valuables. Possibly, for your own enrichment."

"I don't know about any of that," Haley objected. "But we knew that you and Doctor Wise found them. We didn't want to miss out if there was another major success."

Fritz shook his head and moved to the window. I glanced over at Haley, who gave me a dirty look. I don't know what she was mad at, as I had no reason to keep her secret, and I know where my loyalties lie.

Fritz exclaimed. "Very well. Anna, Zabella, Liam, please start the shutdown process."

Liam cleared his throat noisily. "But, Doctor Kohl, we still have hours of sunlight—"

Fritz shook his head. "I know, but I have to get ready to go to that town council meeting tonight. They are considering ending our research, ordering the house condemned."

"If they do," Haley said. "How soon could that happen?"

"If they get their vay? Tonight," Fritz asserted. "Ve vill have to get our equipment out as soon as possible." He turned to face our tall female team member. "Zabella, I vant you to come mitt me."

Zabella nodded. "I can compile any data you need from the cloud records."

"Das ist gut," Kohl said. "Now, ve have a new rule. No one is to go to this house alone. And for our 'gifted' friends," Kohl turned to the three of us in the chairs. "You vill be vith a non-psychic if you come here. If something like vhat just happened occurs again, it is best if two psychics aren't the only ones here."

"Smart precaution," I sighed.

Fritz went on. "Start the backup and shutting down. I vant to leave in one-half hour. I vill go talk to George."

Fritz headed for the door as Haley leaned back with her arms folded.

Lamar leaned toward her. "Well, at least he didn't throw you off the team."

"Yet," I countered.

This made her stand up and look down at the pair of us. "Don't you condescend to me. You male psychics always think you're better than the women. Let me tell you, there has been a history of prominent women psychics that goes back hundreds of years."

"Slow down," I said quietly. "No one is trying to berate you, and I will not say you don't have abilities. But you got here under false pretenses."

She sat back down in a huff. "You're going to tell me you've never used your talents to get somewhere you weren't supposed to be?"

I sat back. "I can't deny that I have. But I was working for the police most of the time. And my motives were pure. I was trying to save lives."

"He's got a point," Lamar added. "I mean, what are your motives? You afraid there'd be a big manifestation and you'd miss out?"

"I thought I could help," she sulked. "And now they might condemn this house. I feel bad for those trapped spirits, the former residents."

"Look, one person has died and all three of us have been pretty ineffectual," I concluded. "I think we need to come at this from a different angle."

Lamar chuckled. "You mean not let this entity shove a wrecking ball into our brains?"

"That would be a good start," I muttered.

I turned my gaze toward the thick, distorted glass of the window. The interior of the Scudder House had plunged into a deep, unnatural chill — a predatory frost that had settled into the floorboards the moment our "adversary" made its presence known.

In the grim silence, a dark thought flickered. *Well, it's cheaper than air conditioning.*

If we could just provoke the entity a few times a day, we might keep the house at a steady sixty-eight degrees.

It was a gallows-humor joke, the kind that keeps your teeth from chattering when you're staring into the dark, but it sparked something sharper in the back of my mind.

An idea took root. We had been playing the victim — reacting, flinching, and documenting the bruises. It was a lopsided conflict, a psychic guerrilla war where the entity struck from the shadows and retreated into the walls before we could swing back.

But what if we stopped waiting for the next blow?

If this thing wanted to hide in the cracks of the Scudder estate, fine. We just needed to stop being the prey and start being the hunters. It was time to stop recording the haunting and start flushing the thing out into the light.

10. WOEFUL WRAITH

We were soon driving back to the rented house; I was riding with Anna again, the others in the two rented vehicles, and Haley drove Doctor Janis' van to go visit him in the hospital.

"Want to go out to dinner?" I offered as Anna drove.

"Won't that make everyone gossip?" Anna asked playfully.

"And you don't think everyone already knows that you showed up in my room in a negligee?"

She sighed. "You're probably right."

"I've worked with research teams. There is very little you don't know about the others. Who likes who, who is sleeping with who —"

"Whom."

"And which people hate each other," I told her with a telling glance.

"I doubt I was subtle in my dislike of Haley."

"Subtle? A billboard with 'I HATE HALEY' in five-foot-tall letters would've been less obvious."

"Okay, duly chided," she grumbled. "It's just that I spent so many years being quiet and respectful."

"I remember you in the classes I covered for Doctor Kohl. You always knew the answers, but you didn't want to draw attention to yourself by volunteering them."

She smiled at the memory. "You never let me get away with that."

"I was fully aware you knew the material."

"I remember the day it all changed for me. You finished the class and asked me to stay. I wondered what I had done to get into trouble."

"I guess the only time you were ever called to the front of the room was because you were in trouble?"

"Only once or twice through all my schooling. Quiet and respectful and all that."

"I can believe it."

She turned a corner while she was speaking. "You told me how good my work was and to praise my insights."

"I remember."

"But then you told me if I really wanted to make a difference in the field, I would have to assert myself."

"Well, you've certainly taken my advice."

"I wanted to kiss you," she admitted, a slight flush coming to her face.

"That I didn't know," I said and smiled. "You seem to have no trouble kissing me now."

"Well, you're no longer my teacher." She grinned with a twinkle in her eye. "And I have learned that I have to assert myself to get what I want."

"And what do you want, Anna?"

She stopped the car near the house, neatly pulling to the curb. "What I want is a shower. And then I want to go out to dinner with you." She turned to me, her eyes aflame. "Then I want to spend the night in your bed."

She leaned toward me and gave me a sensual kiss. It wasn't for long, but it was full of promise and desire.

"Do I get to be there, too?" I teased.

"Yes, even if I have to tie you down to have my way with you."

"Kinky."

We both got out of the car, she much faster than I, because I needed to twist and unfold myself. We walked into the house, and she headed for her room and then the shower as I waited in the living room.

The others came in shortly after. Fritz was on the phone but ended the call as he stepped into the room.

"Any word on Doctor Janis?"

"He is still unconscious," Fritz worried. "The doctor says they can't find anything wrong. They've started a battery of tests."

I considered this in silence. Again, the timing bothered me. I was at a very low level in my meditation and closing in on the consciousness I detected at Scudder House. Could this entity have affected Doctor Janis, so far away? Or was it just a spectacular coincidence?

I headed to my room, sat on the bed, and focused on my breathing. I was certainly far enough from Scudder House to meditate without concern, and perhaps I would get some insights.

I was descending, the weight of the day sloughing off as I sank into the velvet dark of my subconscious. I let the surface-level thoughts — the scuff of the floorboards, the hum of the house — drift away like smoke, prying the doors of my mind wide open.

Leonard...

The name didn't come as a sound, but as a vibration, cold and familiar. Haley's image coalesced in my mind's eye, sharp and uncomfortably vivid. She was sitting on a stone bench, her eyes closed, her posture too perfect, too still.

Long-distance mental communication wasn't just a parlor trick; it was a grueling, high-level discipline I'd only touched a handful of times in my career.

To reach across the miles and weave a conversation with someone else's subconscious required a reservoir of focus and a specific, brutal kind of training — the kind that broke most people before they mastered it.

I suddenly had a new awareness of Haley's abilities.

Get out of my head, I projected, my mental voice echoing in the hollow space. *I'm meditating...*

A slow, predatory smile pulled at her lips. *I'm at the hospital. You're not planning on returning to the house tonight, are you...?*

Why...?

I just don't want to miss anything...

The word "anything" felt heavy, laden with a subtext I couldn't quite grasp. Exhaling, I focused on my breathing and maintained the connection. I needed to know what she was holding back. I shifted my focus, pushing into the static of her periphery.

Was there anything unusual before Janis collapsed...?

I felt her mental walls slam shut, a jagged spike of defensiveness that confirmed my worst fears. She wasn't just being evasive; she was guarding a secret. I didn't pull back; I pressed harder, seeking a leak in her mental armor.

Suddenly, I wasn't in my room anymore. I was standing in the woods, the air smelling of pine and damp earth. Doctor Janis was beside me, his voice a distant, droning hum of academic trivia. But my focus was elsewhere — to a woman's hand, slender and steady, pressing a bottle of water into Janis's palm.

Nothing out of the ordinary, Haley's voice whispered, but it felt strained.

The water bottle... I countered, seizing the image. *Why are you obsessed with the water bottle...?*

Another flash hit me, violent and disjointed. Janis falling forward, his limbs turning to lead. A pair of woman's hands — the same hands — reached out, catching him with a grace that felt practiced, as they lowered him to the mossy ground.

My inner eye zoomed in on the empty bottle discarded near his backpack. It was just plastic and labels, yet in the theater of Haley's mind, it glowed with significance.

She yanked the memory away; the woods vanishing into a swirl of gray mist. The suspicion in my gut turned to a dull ache. She was hiding something.

What are your plans for this evening...? she asked, her "voice" carried a new, sharp edge.

An image of Anna in that silk negligee — the way the lace caught the light — leaked from my subconscious before I could kill it.

Oh, Haley purred, the sound dripping with a sudden, toxic sweetness. *You're going to be with that girl. I knew she was more than just a friend…*

The intrusion felt like a physical violation. *Get out of my head…*

Enjoy your date, Leonard…

A wicked, triumphant grin flickered across her phantom face before she severed the link.

I snapped back into my body, my eyes flying open in the darkened room. My skin was damp with a cold sweat, and my pulse was a frantic hammer.

I stood up and headed to the bathroom to splash cold water on my face. I stood there, the cold water still dripping from my chin, and I was forced to reckon with a terrifying new reality: I hadn't just underestimated her. I had been blind to the fact that Haley was operating on a psychic plane far beyond anything Doctor Kohl or the University had ever prepared me for.

I shoved the confusion aside, trying to focus on the evening ahead, but as I looked in the mirror, I couldn't shake the image of those hands catching Janis — or the feeling that Haley was playing a different game than I had realized.

Anna took a sip from her glass of white wine as we sat in *Californios* in the Mission District of San Francisco. The trip had only been about six miles from Brisbane. We now sat at a table looking at the dark-lacquered walls, the chandeliers overhead, and shelves of cookbooks decorating the room.

Anna and I stared at each other across the table. She picked at the remains of her tostada, a dish piled high with guacamole and truffles, while I took another bite from an empanada made with jicama filled with pumpkin and a hint of lime.

The food was pure California. Mexican dishes taken to an art form with unusual combinations that were prepared carefully and deliciously.

The restaurant was a trifle expensive for a first-year college professor, but I figured we'd be eating takeout every other night.

"You certainly know how to show a girl a good time," Anna said with a lifted eyebrow.

"I try. Especially when she is the one driving."

"Well, with your leg and all. How do you get around in New Jersey?"

"I have a specially equipped van — a gift from a grateful client."

"What did you do for him?"

"Them; an older couple. I revealed who murdered their son and how."

Her head shot up from her wineglass. "Really?"

I shrugged and tried to look clever.

"Wow, you are really doing what Doctor Kohl has always dreamed of. A parapsychologist out solving crimes, helping people, stopping bad guys."

"It almost got me killed," I warned.

"How?" she questioned, her eyes bright.

"A police officer shot me."

"What?"

"Don't worry, I was wearing body armor. Still, it hurt like hell and bruised a couple of ribs."

"Wow! I guess a haunted house is really a step backwards for you."

"I don't know," I said as I speared another forkful of food. "I think I end up where I am needed. At least, I'd like to believe that."

She reached out to touch my hand. "Well, I'm glad you're here. If for nothing more than to act out a long-held fantasy of mine."

And there it was. This lovely young woman sat across from me at the table, wanting me, encouraging me, and yet images of Jyanette filled my mind. Our first date with me talking and her smiling, her bright teeth in contrast to her dark skin and painted lips. The way she would look up at me, sated and happy with half-closed eyes after lovemaking.

It was so sudden, I literally felt as if the floor had fallen away and I was hanging in midair. There was a pain in my chest, and I struggled to hold back tears.

Anna could easily sense the change. "Are you all right, Len?"

"Yeah," I croaked and stood up with the help of my cane. "I just need to use the men's room."

I hastened away, my eyes wet and my head down as I went into the nearby men's room to throw water on my face and try to get the memories out of my head.

I used the facilities and soon was back at the table.

Anna looked up at me as I sat with eyes full of pity. "You sure you're okay? I'm sorry if I put too much pressure on you."

I leaned back in my chair. "Just what I need, more pressure to perform."

She picked up her glass of wine and finished it. "You'll do fine. Maybe you need to surrender and let someone else take over."

I shook my head. "If two years ago someone had told me that Anna Chou would say something like that, I would have told them it was impossible."

She spoke simply. "Shall we find out just what is possible?"

I signaled the waiter for the check.

Soon we were back in the car and on our way to the rented home. I was still brooding about Jyanette and annoyed at myself for doing it. She broke up with me, and Anna wanted me. Why was my brain getting in the way? Why did I feel like I was cheating?

"Len?" she volunteered as we pulled to the curb near the house. "I don't want you to think there's any pressure on you to do anything. I've been so wrapped up in what I wanted, it might be inconsiderate to you, to your feelings."

"My feelings?" I replied. "I've been feeling like half a man for months."

She nodded knowingly.

I went on. "I've had little luck with relationships—"

"I know about your fiancée."

"And my recent breakup. I guess I've been in mourning." I met her eyes. "To be honest, you're the first woman I've gone out with in months."

Her hand went up to touch my face. "I want you to know you don't have to prove anything to me. When I met you, I was so scared of you, so scared of how I felt around you. Len, I want to be with you tonight."

Her lips met mine, and my doubts fell away.

I pulled back gently. "Miss Chou, may I show you my assigned bedroom?"

"I would be delighted to see it," she responded playfully.

We stepped out of the car, and I took her hand as we walked to the door, which she opened with a key.

George was lying on his open sofa bed and looking at a laptop. "Hey, how was dinner?"

"Very nice," Anna beamed. "Going over readings?"

"Just surfing the 'Net.'"

I peeked into the open doorway of the nearby bedroom. "Everyone here?"

"No, they all went to that town meeting," George reported without looking up from his laptop. "The town still wants to tear down Scudder House."

"Ah!" was all I could think of to say.

"Just me and Zabella stayed." George's eyes never left his screen.

"I thought Doctor Kohl wanted Zabella there."

George shrugged. "She downloaded the data and Liam took it. She felt he'd be better talking to a group."

"Thanks, George," Anna said.

We headed quickly down the narrow hall, and Anna pushed open the door to her own bedroom. "Zabby?"

There was simple furniture in the small room and a pair of bunk beds, one on top of the other with a ladder up to the second level.

Zabella was sitting on the lower bunk and looked up from a tablet computer. "Yeah?"

"You know where to find me," she hissed.

Zabella gave a pair of thumbs up, and Anna quietly closed the door.

Like I'd said, you work with a team and everyone knows what you're doing and with whom.

I didn't care. The months alone, my failure at Scudder House. I wanted — needed — a release.

We got into my room, and Anna lit a candle as I shut off the lamp.

"Well, here we are," she said, and without hesitation strode toward me.

I pulled off my jacket and threw it into the chair. "Yes, here we are."

She took my shoulders and gently pushed me into a sitting position on the bed. "I hope you don't mind, but you're a foot taller than me."

She leaned forward so we were eye level and pressed her lips to mine. Our mouths opened and our tongues danced, which totally aroused me.

Anna stood, her movements fluid and deliberate in the amber glow of the candle. She reached back, the zipper of her dress a sharp, metallic whisper in the quiet room, and let the fabric pool around her feet like a discarded skin.

She stepped toward me, silhouetted in lace and soft light, the distance between us evaporating until I could feel the radiant heat of her skin.

We collided with a hunger that bypassed thought. Every touch was a reclamation — fingertips tracing the curve of a hip, the smooth expanse of a shoulder, the frantic beat of a pulse beneath a jawline.

When my hands found the firm, yielding reality of her, a shiver raced through me. There was only the scent of her skin, the taste of salt and desire, and the low, broken moans that escaped her as I traced the path of her ribs with my lips.

The longing blazed into something incandescent. We moved as if trying to merge into a single entity, a desperate, beautiful struggle against the isolation of our own minds.

First, she took control, moving above me with a fierce, rhythmic intensity that stole my breath. Then we shifted, a tangled knot of limbs and heat, as I drove into her, seeking the center of the storm we'd created.

It was the ancient, frantic dance of the animal and the divine — a cycle of giving and taking until the world outside the bedroom door ceased to exist. When the end came, it wasn't a fade, but a sudden, blinding fracture. Nerve endings ignited, a white-hot flash that sent us both spiraling into a breathless, heavy bliss.

We lay there for a long time, tangled in the damp sheets, our chests heaving in synchronized rhythm. The silence of the house pressed in around us, but for the first time since I'd arrived, it felt distant — unable to touch the sanctuary of the heat we still shared.

"My," she sighed, "you work well under pressure."

"Thanks," I panted. "You're not bad yourself."

We lay there and watched the shadows on the ceiling made by the candle flame as our breathing slowed and our eyelids grew heavy. She cuddled close and whispered, "Can I stay the night?"

"As long as you like," I assured her. It felt good to have her lithe body against mine, the bare skin touching and reassuring me.

She giggled.

"What?"

"I haven't slept naked in a very long time. And not with a man for an even longer time."

"I feel bad for other men. You are quite a catch."

"Aren't I?" she whispered smugly. "I hope you don't want to talk for long, because I need to snooze after all that."

"Me, too," I sighed.

And we both drifted off to sleep.

I was following someone. At first, I didn't know who, but a part of me kept saying, *"This is a dream, don't worry."*

I couldn't see much, just the beam of a flashlight on the ground lighting the path ahead.

The beam shone on a white van that looked very familiar. A feeling of dread grew in me. The light returned to the earth and a path. Suddenly, there was a driveway of dark-red, cracked ceramic tile — very old. The light rose and shone on a black iron fence and a stone building.

Scudder House.

This was a dream, nothing more. It had to be. No one would go to Scudder House in the middle of the night by themselves. That was insanity, even if you didn't believe ghosts haunted it.

I saw a hand fumble with a key to open the door. I was sure that no one other than the team had a key, and only one at that!

The flashlight swung around the living room, over the dark workstations, and flashed for a moment on the mirror with its painted letters that warned "GET OUT."

Yes, whoever you are, that's what you should do: get out. Leave now while you can.

A hand placed the flashlight on one of the workstations, which illuminated the room a bit more, but shadows still obscured who it was.

A small case was placed on the scarred old oak floor and opened. This revealed the contents in the dim light: several white candles and short candlesticks, chalk, a small incense holder, a silver pentacle medallion on a chain, and a black knife that I knew was called an *athame*.

I was familiar with these items, yet did not use them in my work. All of it quite standard, except for the *athame*. The intruder was obviously a practitioner, as the blade was not steel or iron, which, according to some sources, would disrupt the flow of a ritual.

Artisans carved the ritual object from a black stone, likely obsidian, a volcanic rock glass, and fashioned it into the shape of a knife. That would make sense, as it was a naturally occurring crystal and has been used to make extremely sharp knives for centuries.

This person pulled out the items, and despite the shadows, I could see the hands. They were a woman's hands — well-cared for with polished nails.

An icy dread grew in me.

She pulled out a compass and consulted the dial and put out the holders in specific locations. I knew what she was doing, placing the candles at the four cardinal directions. Once they were in place, she used the chalk and drew a circle on the floor. It took her a few minutes, and once completed, she carefully drew individual lines to form a pentagram within the circle.

She took out a small lighter and lit the candles at the four locations, and they added to the light in the room. She looked up at the mirror emblazoned with the words "GET OUT," and I saw her face.

It was Haley.

She wore the same outfit as that afternoon, and at that moment I knew I hadn't been following her. I was watching everything through her eyes.

Pulling out a fair-sized incense burner, an abalone shell with a hole drilled to fit the stick of incense, she lit the incense with the same lighter she had used on the candles.

She then picked up the black *athame* and traced the circle on top of the chalk, lightly scratching the finish on the floor with the knife's pointed blade. She repeated the process on the lines of the pentagram.

Once it was complete, she put the *athame* on the floor and observed herself in the mirror.

She removed her clothing, watching herself in the mirror while chanting quietly under her breath. Even though I was inside her head, the chants were unfamiliar to me.

She could see her reflection as she removed the small vest and threw it from the circle, then the long-sleeved work shirt. She wriggled out of her stretch denim pants, and also put her shoes and socks safely outside the circle.

She stood in her bra and panties and watched herself in the mirror again, her attention moving to her flat stomach and curving hips. Then she quickly opened her bra, which freed her full breasts. Finally, she removed her panties and tossed them aside with the other clothes.

She crossed her legs and slowly lowered herself into the center of the pentagram in the middle of the circle, gazing at her reflection the entire time. She sat in a cross-legged meditation pose, and everything went dark as she closed her eyes and drew a deep breath.

No, you have to stop, I wanted to tell her. I wanted to send the message that it was too dangerous, but although I was looking through her eyes, I couldn't touch her mind. I was a witness only, not a participant in the events.

After several minutes, she opened her eyes, and in the mirror I saw her lift her head and stand with the knife firmly in her hands. She faced one candle.

"Spirits of Air, I call on you," she stated clearly, and I could hear a rush of wind outside the house. She turned one quarter turn and spoke again. "Spirits of Fire, I call on you."

She was performing a conjuration, an ancient ceremony of ritual magic. But there at Scudder House, would it protect her or give energy to the thing that lay hidden within the house?

She turned another quarter turn. "Spirits of Water, I call on you."

I had been unsure of the McCord Psychic Institute, but they must have taught these ancient rituals to her. What else were they teaching young, impressionable minds?

She turned one last turn and said, "Spirits of Earth, I call on you." She paused for a moment, then added, "The circle is cast. Blessed be."

Once again, she turned and faced the position where she had called upon the spirits of water. With a loud voice, she ordered, "All spirits confined here must leave this house, shed your tears, and depart, lest a flood cast you out!"

Another turn to face the fire candle, and she bellowed, "Spirits of this house. Release your burning desire to remain. Go, or the flames will consume you!"

This continued as she commanded, "Spirits within this house, release this hallowed ground! Go, or you will be rent by the grinding earthquakes!"

And finally, "Spirits within this house, allow your troubles to fly off. Go, or you will be torn apart by the whirlwind!"

I knew what was coming next. A thrice repetition of the intended goal of her ritual. The Rule of Three, as practitioners know it. She didn't disappoint as she raised the knife over her head and called out, "I banish you! I banish you! I banish you! BEGONE!"

She pointed the blade at the ceiling to let the force of her will activate the incantation. At least, that was the theory behind her actions.

The floor shook as if from a minor earth tremor, and the shell that acted as an incense burner quivered, causing the small stick to wave back and forth as smoke rose and made twisting ribbons in the air.

In the mirror, I could see her pale-white face, and a small smile played on her lips as she believed she had succeeded in her goal.

That was when things went awry.

All at once, the candles went out, leaving only the flashlight on top of the worktable to light the room. A deep chuckle filled the air, and the arms which held the knife aloft slowly lowered until the *athame* fell out of them and clattered to the wooden floor.

The deep laugh continued, and I realized it was coming from Haley.

She looked at herself in the mirror, but instead of the beautiful blonde with flawless features, there was a hideous crone with white hair, a shrunken body, and fallen breasts. There was a shriek, and it was Haley's regular voice as she stepped back in terror.

No, I wanted to project to her: *Whatever you do, don't break the circle.*

She stepped back in shock, and one foot landed outside the chalk line. This broke the circle, and whatever protection it may have provided was immediately gone. She stopped and pulled herself upright in an odd, jerking way, like a marionette being yanked by the puppeteer.

I perceived her observing herself in the mirror, as her limbs trembled and jolts seemed to go through her naked body.

She must have turned toward the stairs, because I could no longer see her reflection, and a hand went to the ornate railing as she climbed.

No, no, no, I reached out to her. *You've got to stop yourself. You've got to listen.*

But she kept climbing, higher and higher, as sure-footed as if she had walked those stairs every day and knew them perfectly. She reached the top and moved into the dark hallway, and I could only see vague shadows as she continued to walk.

I could hear her labored breathing and caught quick flashes of her hands as they flailed about, not under her control.

She ascended deeper into the house's rotted core, her bare feet silent on the floorboards of a dark hallway that seemed to stretch longer than the architecture allowed. Figures appeared out of the gloom, each draped in a sickly, translucent glow.

The recognition was sharp and cold.

Elias Scudder stood stiff in his Victorian waistcoat, his eyes like hollowed knots in wood. Beside him was Lucy Scudder, forever five years old, her lace collar tattered by a century of decay.

Frances Scudder loomed tall and dour, her commanding silhouette unbent by death, while Nat Hewing cowered nearby, his spectral eyes darting in a permanent loop of terror.

They were the house's permanent collection — souls caught like echoes in the heavy air of the estate.

Haley didn't glance at them. She moved past the silent watchers with a chilling, purposeful stride, reaching the base of the circular tower. In the bruised light of a narrow lancet window, a spiraling staircase coiled upward toward the highest point of the mansion.

This was the room where the Scudder legacy had reached its dark conclusion. Elias met his end here, as Joey Thompson had only days earlier. The air grew thin and cold as the stairs wound tighter.

As she crested the last step, the tower room opened around her. Pale moonlight spilled through the dual-facing windows Elias had commissioned so he could survey his kingdom and the town below.

Haley paused, her silhouette framed by the elaborate wrought-iron lattice of the glass.

The latch was a simple, elegant thing of brass. It turned with a faint, musical creak that resonated through the silent house. The windows swung outward, and a rush of warm, jasmine-scented summer air flooded the stagnant room. It was the very breeze Elias had loved, the temperate current that had once made this hilltop a paradise.

The sight was hypnotic and terrifying. She moved into the opening; the moonlight illuminating her body as she stepped up onto the sill.

Below, the wrought-iron fence glinted like a row of silver needles in the dark.

"Stop, stop, stop," I wanted to yell, to pull her away from the edge that opened out to certain death.

She didn't look at the sky or the horizon. She kept her gaze fixed on those dark points; her knuckles white as she gripped the window frame one last time.

Then, with a terrifying, absolute silence, she let go. She didn't scream; she simply watched the sharpest of the spears rush upward to meet her, the warm night air whistling past her ears as the distance between her and the iron plummeted to nothing.

11. QUESTIONABLE APPARITION

I bolted upright; the transition from the vision to reality was so violent my heart felt like it was trying to punch through my ribs.

The room was a graveyard of shadows, the only light coming from the digital pulse of the clock on the bureau. 5:55 a.m.

The silence of the house was suffocating. Had it been real? The sensation of the wind and the glint of those iron spears still clung to my mind.

Beside me, the sheets rustled. Anna was a soft, warm weight in the dark, as she snored lightly. The memories of the night before flooded back: the heat, the touch, the brief, beautiful delusion that the world was safe.

But as I looked at her, a sharp, unbidden pang of guilt pierced through the adrenaline. It felt like I was cheating on Jyanette. A ridiculous notion for a thirty-one-year-old man months past a breakup, but the heart doesn't care about logic.

Slowly, I extracted the arm pinned beneath Anna. Pins and needles erupted along the forearm, a thousand tiny electric stabs as the blood rushed back.

I pivoted to the edge of the bed and used the bedside table to get up, joints popping like dry kindling in the quiet room. Without the folding cane, my movement was unsteady. Quickly I found my underwear on the floor in the gloom, jeans snagged from a chair and pulled on yesterday's rumpled shirt.

The folding cane was near the door, and a suit jacket lay slumped on my suitcase. Within the pockets, I found my phone and a single, stiff rectangle of cardstock:

Jorge Valentin

Barefoot, the walk to the kitchen was silent, the cold tile biting at the soles of my feet. Through the sliding glass door, the sky was indigo; the sun still hiding beneath the horizon. Stepping out into the warm morning air, I punched the numbers into the phone.

The line clicked open after three rings.

"Somebody better be dead," a gravelly, sleep-crushed voice growled.

"Detective Valentin? It's Doctor Leonard Wise."

"I hope there is a damn good reason for waking me up at five-fifty-five, Wise," he griped, the sound of a bedsheet rustling over the line.

"There's been another death at Scudder House."

The silence that followed was absolute. It stretched for several seconds, heavy with the weight of recent events.

"What?" Valentin finally whispered.

"A young woman. Last night."

"At Scudder?" The sharp click of a bedside lamp sounded over the line. "Was a body found? Is someone there now?"

"No," came the reply, voice trembling slightly. "I haven't been there yet."

A frustrated exhale distorted the speaker. "Then how do you know that someone is dead?"

"I... um... saw it."

"Saw it?"

"In a vision."

"A vision?" Valentin's voice shifted to a tone of pure irritation. "What the hell are you bothering me for?"

"The situation is serious. Someone needs to get to that property. I didn't want my team to go to the house and stumble over another tragedy. Please."

"All right," he snarled. "I'll send out a couple of uniforms to check the perimeter. But this better not be a waste of time, Doctor."

"Thank you," I started, but the line went dead before I finished.

Sliding the phone into a pocket, I stood on the deck, the sky bleeding into a pale, sickly gray. The certainty of the event felt etched into my very bones.

Why had she gone back alone? Was it the arrogance of the young, that shimmering sense of invincibility? Or had the house itself exerted some pull?

A sense of failure hung heavy. Looking out toward the mountains as the darkness faded, the weight of the coming day became undeniable.

Soon, the rest of the house was awake and moving about. I made a cup of coffee and sat outside on the porch, trying to get my head around another loss.

Eventually, Anna got up, saw me outside, and came out with her own cup of coffee.

"Lost in thought?" she asked as she slid the door closed behind her.

I gave her a sad smile.

"I thought after last night you'd be in a cheerier mood," she told me as she sat. "I mean, my spirits are certainly better."

I bent forward and kissed her, then leaned back into my chair. "Last night was fantastic."

She chuckled. "If anyone didn't know what we were doing, we certainly made enough noise to clue them in."

I looked around, embarrassed. "Sorry, I'm loud."

"Loud? Next time I'm wearing earplugs."

I took her hand. "Anna, I have something serious to talk to you about."

She immediately became solemn. "What?"

"I had a vision last night. I think someone else died at Scudder House."

"What?" she gasped. "Who?"

"Haley Wolder."

"Wow," she said, and stared at the table with a shocked look on her face. "Are you sure?"

"Pretty sure. I called Detective Valentin this morning. The police are checking right now."

She glanced up at me with doubt. "But you could be wrong?"

"I could be, but I can tell the difference between a nightmare and a vision."

The door slid open and Fritz stood smiling in the doorway. "Is this a private party, or may I join?"

"Please join us, Fritz," I suggested. Anna got up and moved around the table to sit next to me, and Fritz pulled out the chair across from us. "I hate to start your day with bad news—"

The smile on Fritz's face disappeared, and he sank into the chair. "Oh, no. Tell me."

"There's been another death at Scudder House."

"Mein Gott," he murmured.

I quickly told Fritz and Anna the details of what I saw: the circle, the candles, and finally the climb up the stairs and the leap from the window.

He listened raptly, his blue eyes focused on my face in horror as I went through each detail.

"This is terrible," he lamented when I finished. "That poor young woman. Vhy did she even try?"

"I don't know, Fritz. I think she believed she could clear the house of the entities."

Fritz shook his head sadly. "This is more bad news. Last night, the town council voted to have the house condemned and demolished. Ve have to take our equipment and go."

Anna spoke up at this point. "Maybe it's for the best. I mean, if people keep dying in that house, wouldn't tearing it down be the best thing?"

"You are right, of course," Fritz fumed. "But it is a loss from a research point of view."

"I worried that it's more than just the house," I muttered.

Both of them looked up at me, confused.

"The entity I came into contact with — it's powerful and very... I don't know... old. I think it is using the house, might even be a prisoner. If the town tears down the house, it's possible that it could get free."

Anna stared at me. "What makes you think that?"

I shook my head. "It keeps its true nature hidden. Yet when someone comes into contact with it, like Joey did with the use of the Accelerator or Haley did through ritual, they end up dead."

"What's your theory?" a voice said nearby.

All three of us turned toward the front of the house, which required Fritz to rotate his chair. Standing there was Detective Valentin, who appeared unshaven and dour.

"Detective," I greeted as I used my cane to push myself up. "Did they find her?"

"We found a body all right. A young woman who jumped out the window or someone pushed her," he added sardonically. "Officers found her stark naked. According to them, one of those sharp iron fence posts impaled her."

"Mein Gott," murmured Fritz.

Anna's hands went to her mouth, and then she blurted, "Just like Frances Scudder."

I sighed; the sadness and loss washed over me. "Dead?"

He looked at me sternly. "Quite dead. Now, you are coming downtown with me, and I want George Humphreys as well."

I looked at him with surprise. "Are we under arrest?"

"You can't!" Anna blurted. "Doctor Wise was here all night. I can vouch for him."

This got a surprised look from Fritz, but the detective only seemed annoyed. "I am detaining you and Humphreys for questioning. There are some things you have to clear up."

I turned to Fritz. "Do you have the phone number for Chuck Granger?"

Fritz stared at me for a moment. "Your sponsor? Ja, in my phone. You gave it to me in case of an emergency."

I nodded. "He's in San Francisco this week for a convention. Call him and tell him to meet me at the Brisbane Police Station."

"This isn't a social visit, Doctor. You can't invite guests," the detective growled.

I faced Valentin. "He's my lawyer, Detective. I am happy to answer questions, but I want him present."

Valentin sighed. "All right. I will not handcuff you or anything, but you'll have to ride in the back of my car, got it?"

"Of course."

Valentin pulled open the sliding door and pointed a meaty finger at George, who had risen from the sofa bed and was pulling on pants. "Humphreys!"

George leaped to his feet and stared at the detective. "Wha-?"

"You're coming downtown for questioning. Throw on some clothes."

George blinked in shock, then frantically pulled on a shirt and shoes.

Anna came to me. "If you need me as your alibi—"

"It will be fine, Anna."

The detective slid the door closed as Fritz cleared his throat. "Detective, should any of us be vorried?"

Valentin scowled and glanced at me. "I would think your 'psychic' should be."

The drive to the station was a blur of gray asphalt and rising unease; the mile-long trip was over in minutes. We veered off the major artery, passing a blue sign that welcomed us to the City of Brisbane. Its logo — a jaunty sailboat cresting yellow-starred waves against a mountain silhouette — felt jarringly cheerful compared to the leaden weight in my chest.

We skirted a modern architectural marvel, a building of sharp angles that jutted toward the street like the prow of a ship. Rows of metallic louvers shielded windows several stories up, designed to filter the sun but looking more like the closed eyelids of a giant.

Valentin swung into the rear parking lot, and we followed him toward an entrance that continued the theme: soaring glass walls and those same skeletal louvers, which I now realized doubled as part of the building's support structure.

The air inside was sterile, smelling of industrial floor wax and old coffee. We cleared a security checkpoint, the officer's eyes lingering on my cane, before Valentin led us down a long, echoing hallway. He steered us into a windowless conference room, the air stagnant and thick.

"Sit. Wait," he ordered, his voice clipped as he vanished back into the corridor.

He didn't leave us alone for long. A uniformed officer stepped inside, his hand resting near his belt as he swept the room with a look of pure suspicion. He eyed us as if he had caught us red-handed in the middle of a heist, and his gaze lingered on my rumpled clothes. Satisfied we weren't going anywhere, he turned and took up a post just outside the door, his silhouette visible through the frosted glass — a silent reminder that while we weren't in handcuffs yet, we were far from free.

George glanced around nervously, then leaned closer to me. "Should I get a lawyer?"

"You can ask for one. They are required to assign you a lawyer if you insist. But the first rule is that you are not required to answer questions at all. If you do answer questions, anything you say can be used against you."

"But I did nothing," he insisted.

"I know, but there have been two suspicious deaths, and they have to find answers."

"Two? There have been two?"

I gritted my teeth. "Yes, Haley appears to have jumped out the tower window and impaled on the fence."

"Haley?" George said and went white.

"Are you all right?" I asked.

"Haley and I have... kinda... been seeing each other. She and I hooked up last night."

I frowned. "How did you manage that?"

"I have the bed nearest the door. I can get in and out with no one seeing me."

"Did you know she was going to go to Scudder House last night?"

"No, no, I thought she just wanted... I mean... oh man."

"What's wrong?" I demanded.

"We did it in Doctor Janis's van last night."

"You what?"

"Yeah." He looked down, and I thought he might cry. "She said she was going to do a ritual, and that sex beforehand really helped her. Jesus, now she's dead!"

"You have to tell them," I advised.

"It's just… I didn't know she would go to Scudder House, really." He looked incredibly sad.

I sighed, but couldn't condemn the young man. I had been thinking with something other than my brain the previous night myself.

"Did Doctor Kohl tell you about the town meeting?" I wondered.

"I got in after they were all in bed. I heard this morning that the town wants to knock the house down."

"I only found out this morning myself."

He gave me a knowing look. "I know, you were busy with something else. I'm glad you and Anna hooked up, she has had a crush on you for the longest time. She was always saying, 'Leonard Wise said this,' and 'Doctor Wise taught me that.'" He looked at me seriously. "It's good when people can make each other happy. Haley made me happy. I mean, she was completely out of my league, but I think she liked me. I can't get my head around her being dead."

"It's tough. Trust me, I know."

Detective Valentin walked back in. "Mr. Humphreys, we'd like to talk to you in the other room, please. Doctor Wise, your lawyer is here, and you can meet with him in here."

George gave me a nervous nod and got up to walk out of the room, escorted by the detective.

A uniformed officer brought in my first AA sponsor and friend, Chuck Granger. He was six-two with a square jaw and boyish good looks. He wore a suit and tie, and a mane of dirty-blond hair. The officer left the room and shut the door.

I moved toward Chuck, who gave me a bear hug.

"Thanks for coming," I said as he released me.

"I was already in San Fran. I assume you got my email?"

"I did. That's why I had Fritz call you."

"So, sit. Tell me what this is all about."

We both sat at the table, and I went through the series of events since I'd received the phone call from Doctor Kohl and flown out to San Francisco. I told him about the strange events at Scudder House, the vision I had the previous night, and my frantic call to Valentin this morning. I edited out the part where I slept with Anna, as I didn't see how this could have anything to do with the case.

He made notes on a yellow legal pad he took out of his small leather briefcase.

"Before the detective joins us, can I ask a few other questions?"

"Anything you want, Chuck."

"Do you have anyone who can prove you were at the rented house, and didn't go anywhere?"

"I can't drive a regular car, Chuck, with my leg and all."

"Understood, but answer the question."

"Yes," I sighed. "I was with a woman from the research group."

"You slept with her?"

"Yes, and she was there when I got up."

"That's a strong alibi. And you weren't here when the other person died?"

"No, I was in New Jersey."

"Okay," he said as he made a note. Then he met my eyes. "Do you mind if I get personal?"

"Not at all, Chuck."

"Have you got a sponsor out in New Jersey?"

I looked down and exhaled heavily. "Yes, two months ago. After I had a setback."

His eyebrows went up. "Do you want to talk about it?"

I met Chuck's eyes. He had been my sponsor for over a year when I lived near Los Angeles and was aware of the strange situations my work entailed. I could've talked about the demon I had sent back to Hell as being the cause, but I knew what the truth was.

I looked down at my hands, and tears stabbed my eyes. "I had a breakup. That's not true. A woman I was very much in love with dumped me."

"And you drank?"

"I was in the hospital because of injuries, but as soon as I got out, the first place I went was a bar."

"Because you felt you needed it?"

I raised my eyes and spoke with more anger than I had intended. "Because I didn't give a damn. I just wanted to not hurt for a while."

"Did it work?"

I hung my head. "No. Fortunately, a friend tracked me down and got me home. It turns out he's an alcoholic as well and became my sponsor."

"That's good. If you want to talk, I'm here for a few more days."

"I don't know if I'll be staying. Our program is being shut down."

At that moment, there was a knock at the door, and Detective Valentin stepped into the room, holding a file. "Gentleman, may I ask my questions now?"

Chuck smiled and stood, coming over to my side of the table. "Your timing is impeccable, Detective. Doctor Wise and I were just finishing up."

Valentin grunted something incoherent and sat in the chair Chuck had just vacated. He opened the folder and began. "Doctor Wise, you called me this morning and informed me that there had been a death at Scudder House, is that correct?"

I glanced at Chuck, who nodded. "That is correct."

"And you claimed you saw this person in a vision, is that also correct?"

"Yes."

"In this vision, what did you see her do?"

"She was attempting some type of ritual magic. Your forensic team has probably already located the circle and pentagram she drew on the floor."

"Don't worry about what my people found. Tell me what you saw!" Valentin demanded in an annoyed tone.

I exchanged a glance with Chuck. "I saw her lose control of the ritual, and suddenly it was like someone else had control over her."

"Someone else? Anyone specific?"

"There is something in that house that can take control of a person—"

"You mean, like a possession?"

"Yes, but different. I saw all of the events through Haley Wolder's eyes."

"Really?" Valentin said and made a note on his pad. "If that is the case, how did she die?"

"She climbed up the stairs in the dark, as if she knew where all the steps were without seeing them. She went all the way to the highest tower, opened a window, and jumped out."

"And you 'saw' all of this?"

"Yes, I was a witness to the ritual she attempted to cleanse the house. That's why she was naked."

Valentin's head snapped up. "How do you know she was naked?"

"I saw her take her clothes off. She watched herself undress in that big mirror downstairs."

"Why?"

"I'm sorry?"

"Why did she take off her clothes? You said she was trying to cleanse the house. You think she got naked to clean?"

I exhaled heavily. "There are many schools of ritual magic, and different teachings. Being naked for a ritual is a specific technique referred to as being 'skyclad.'"

"Skyclad?" Valentin repeated, unconvinced.

"It's not sexual. Some believers claim it helps if the practitioner removes all distractions, including clothing."

"Is that what you do in your work?" Valentin asked with a raised eyebrow.

"Detective, I'm a scientist. You've seen the setup we have at Scudder House. Machines and computers and the like. What Ms. Wolder was attempting was an act of ritual magic, and she tried it in the wrong place. If she had let us know her intentions, I would have stopped her."

"Ms. Chou claimed she can attest to you being in the rented house all night. How would she know?"

I blew out my breath. "Ms. Chou and I spent the night together."

Chuck spoke up. "I don't see how that has any relevance, as they are both consenting adults."

"Just tying up any loose ends. Once you retired with Ms. Chou, did you see Mr. Humphreys during the night?"

"No. I saw him in the morning when I woke up and phoned you."

"One last thing. Do you know how to contact Haley Wolder's family? We have had little luck getting her university records so far."

I shook my head. "Honestly, I met her for the first time yesterday."

"And yet you could share this 'vision' with her?" He gazed at me.

Chuck came to my rescue. "Doctor Wise has already explained that, Detective."

Valentin closed his notebook. "Well then. Mr. Granger, can you give the doctor a ride back to where he is staying?"

Chuck frowned. "I can. Is that all, Detective?"

"For now. Please make sure your client doesn't leave town."

He rose and, with a nod to us both, walked to the door, opened it, and put out an arm to suggest we should exit.

They had left me my cane, so I used it to get up. Chuck and I headed out of the conference room toward the main doors and out into the sunlit parking lot.

"Come on, I'll buy you breakfast," Chuck offered.

I directed Chuck toward Madhouse Coffee, a weathered little haunt I'd visited with Doctor Kohl two years earlier, when the world felt a lot less haunted.

The building was a block of reddish-brown stucco, its earthy tone peeling slightly at the corners, with a quiet real estate office perched on the second floor like a watchful neighbor.

The air inside was thick with the toasted, nutty scent of dark roast and the frantic hiss of milk being steamed. I ordered a bagel with egg and melted cheese — while Chuck went for a panini that looked like a structural marvel, overflowing with a glistening assortment of breakfast meats and scrambled eggs.

We took our cardboard cups and paper-wrapped sandwiches through the rear door, stepping into a small, open-air patio. The morning air was crisp, cutting through the heavy aroma of the food. A cluster of black wrought-iron tables and chairs sat scattered across the concrete, their metal cold to the touch.

As I sat, I looked up. Fixed to a weathered wooden fence meant to shield us from the street was a large, five-pointed star carved from rough timber. It hung there, rustic and silent, a strange echo of the occult geometry that seemed to follow me everywhere lately.

"A pentagram," I exclaimed, and indicated the large wooden star made of interlocking pieces in the traditional style.

Chuck looked over at it. "Yes, they're all over the place here. You probably didn't notice now, but they light them up come December. Brisbane has earned the nickname 'City of Stars.'"

I recalled the stars I had seen on the logo at the municipal building. "Are they all like this? Five lines intersecting that way?"

"I guess, why?"

"Because it's an ancient symbol to ward off evil," I explained. "The woman who died last night used the same symbol in what she was attempting."

"So you told me. She drew a pentagram like that? Inside the circle?"

I nodded. "I've studied the use of sympathetic magic, as well as Wiccan theology and rituals in my work with Doctor Kohl." Shaking my head, I said, "That's an odd coincidence. A haunted house in a town with pentagrams everywhere."

"You have that look in your eyes," Chuck worried.

"What look?"

"The one that says you're close to something."

I hung my head. "I'm not close to anything. I have to tell you — this house — I've never been aware of anything like it. I've been to houses that overwhelmed me before, but not like this."

"Really?"

"Yes, I went to Hedden House in Maine last January," I went on. "There was an energy that really knocked me for a loop. But once I figured out the history, the truth behind the haunting, I ended it."

"Maybe that's what you need to do here, Len," Chuck said as he took another bite of his panini. He went on talking as he chewed. "I mean, I don't really understand what you do, but you've done things that have surprised me."

"Finding your wallet that one time was not a big deal," I replied modestly.

"It fell behind the counter, and I was afraid someone stole it. But you just closed your eyes, touched your hand to where it had been, and you knew where it was."

"I got lucky."

"Well, at the time, it was pretty amazing. So, tell me the truth. Are you really coping with this breakup?"

"As best as I can," I explained. "I think about her all the time."

"And this young lady, this Anna Chou? What is that about?"

"She likes me. I guess she has a crush on me. She's an amiable woman, but only twenty-four, and it's not serious. Just two lonely people making each other happy. I mean, I'm going back to New Jersey when this is over."

"Is your support system enough to keep you on the program?"

"It is now. I'm going to meetings at least twice a week and I've been working the steps."

"Good."

"Chuck, I never really thanked you for all you did. Doctor Kohl saved my life by teaching me how to use my abilities. But you also saved my life by getting me sober."

"You got yourself sober, Len," Chuck said, his voice dropping an octave as he leaned across the scarred metal table. "You surrendered to a higher power when the bottle was winning. Honestly, looking at what you've accomplished since then... I see the work of that power in every step you take."

We finished our meal in a rare, contemplative silence, the weight of his words hanging in the air alongside the steam from our coffee.

I phoned Fritz, who confirmed the team was still grounded at the rental house; the police were still crawling over Scudder House, stripping the scene for every forensic scrap they could find.

When he drove me back to the house, Chuck kept the engine idling.

"Well, back to the exhilarating world of seminars and legalese for me," he said with a wry grin. "But keep my number on speed dial. If they put the cuffs on you again, I can be back here in thirty minutes to bail you out."

I watched his taillights vanish around the bend, his words echoing in the sudden quiet of the driveway. Surrender to a higher power.

Scudder House didn't just want my logic or my equipment; it wanted to hollow me out. To find the answers buried in that stone and shadow, I knew I couldn't rely on my own meager strength anymore. I needed to find something far greater, something vast and ancient.

I hoped I could tap into one before anyone else died.

12. TRACKING THE THREAT

I walked back into the house where everyone was milling about sullenly. Fritz was sitting on the bed in the room next to the living room and speaking on his cell phone.

Anna rushed up to me, and I sensed she wanted to hug me but resisted. "What happened? Where's George?"

"They're still speaking to him. They wanted to know how I learned Haley had died."

She shrugged. "That's not unreasonable, I guess."

"No, and I don't blame them. There are still cops in New Jersey who are suspicious of me."

She escorted me back into the hall, and we both headed to my bedroom.

"Really, with all your successes there?"

"It's difficult for people to accept what I do, especially the police. Many people lie to them, and if someone shows up claiming to be a psychic, they usually just want attention."

"You would know better than I would," she said as she pulled me through the doorway, shut the door, and pressed herself against me. Her lips were warm and inviting. The memories of the previous night's delights danced in my head.

She released me with a sigh and a smile. "I've wanted to do that all morning."

"Before we get carried away, we should talk."

She sighed again. "I'd rather get carried away and then talk." She pulled back from me and sat on the bed with her hands on her knees, looking very proper. "The problem with someone over thirty is that they are harder to distract than a guy in his twenties."

"I'll remember that if I ever date a guy in his twenties," I joked. That brought a grin to Anna. "It looks like this project will soon be over—"

"Sooner than planned anyway," she observed.

"Yes, well, I'm going back to New Jersey and you'll be going back to the university."

"With a smile on my face." She gave me a quick peck.

"I just want to make sure you're okay with all of this. I don't want to take advantage of you."

She met my eyes, then stood. "Would you like to know how to take advantage of me?"

She reached down and pulled her work shirt off over her head.

She wore no bra.

I gulped. "Well, if you have specific… uh… needs."

"Yes, I do," she whispered as she unzipped her pants and lowered them. "And if you don't take care of them, I shall feel terribly taken advantage of."

Naked, she straddled my lap and pressed her mouth to mine hungrily.

We addressed each other's needs as thoroughly and as quietly as we could, with the rest of the house up and busy around us. Anna buried her face into a pillow to muffle her passion as we gasped and murmured our desires.

Sweaty and sated, we lay on the bed, naked and panting. I kissed her face.

She put her hand on my cheek. "Nice to know that last night wasn't just a fluke."

"I guess not," I wheezed. "We better get dressed. They'll be wondering where we are."

She clung to me. "Everyone knows where we are and what we are doing. And that I wanted this to happen."

"I just don't want to flaunt it to the others."

"Well, Zabella's a bit crushed. I wasn't interested in her, and Lamar and Liam are involved with each other."

"Oh, Lamar is gay?"

"Yes, that's why he wanted the bed downstairs. Then he and Liam hit it off very well."

"I'm glad for them," I said. "I noticed that Liam watches Lamar's back."

"And his ass," Anna chuckled.

We lay there looking up at the ceiling, tired from our lovemaking, yet too wide awake to doze.

Anna spoke first. "You know, I could come to New Jersey."

"Really? How would you pull that off?"

"Well, you teach Doctor Kohl's techniques at GSU, right? I could study there!"

"If I were your professor, that would preclude any of this," I cautioned. "GSU has strict policies about teacher and student fraternization."

"Well, I won't tell if you won't," she murmured and kissed my chest.

"Anna!" I replied, a bit shocked.

"Okay, okay, it was just an idea. I guess I'll have to settle for the next few days."

We both looked up at the ceiling again, and I caressed her flank.

She slipped out of bed to grab her clothes. I watched her dress, her slim body exposed to me in the curtained sunlight; her breasts, small but firm, and the roundness of her hips and the small triangle of hair that covered her sex.

She pushed her shoulder-length hair into an elastic to hold it away from her face. As she pulled her trousers over her strong thighs, layers of fabric once again hid her, and the very proper young lady prepared to get back to work.

I sat up and put on my clothes, as she went to the door and peeked out. Blowing me a kiss, she left.

I finished dressing and came out into the kitchen. It seemed there was some kind of meeting around the small standing island: Liam, Lamar, Fritz, and Zabella sat on the tall stools as Anna stood.

Doctor Kohl turned to look at me. "Ah, Leonard, it is good you are here."

"Are they going to let us back on the site?" I inquired.

"Ve do not know yet."

Zabella spoke up. "Doctor Kohl was telling us you saw Haley in a vision?"

"Yes, that's correct."

She went on. "Wasn't there anything you could do?"

"No, I could only witness what happened. I wasn't able to communicate with her."

Liam spoke. "Zabella found something interesting in the data from yesterday."

"Will it help solve any of this?" I hoped.

"No, but it might give us a place to focus our efforts," Zabella said, and held up sheets of paper in front of her. "There's a wireless printer here in the house. I printed these up. It's the data from the site."

"Which you downloaded from the cloud?" I put in.

"Yes. Remember, I mentioned the correlation between the brain waves in your meditation and the changes in the readings?"

"I recall that as I went deeper, all the machines registered higher output."

"Correct," Zabella agreed. "And you said there was something hidden. I may have found it."

"Found it?"

Liam spoke up. "The team placed sensors on the different floors of the house, which wirelessly communicate with the other machines, sending them readings from specific areas."

"You did?" I commented, surprise in my voice. "That's brilliant."

Zabella continued. "The energy readings appear to be strongest in the front room."

"Where all the equipment is located?" I offered.

"Correct," Zabella concurred with a nod. "There, and in the basement directly below it. Whatever you sensed should be there."

I leaned against the wall and remembered the basement from my first experience at Scudder House. I could recall the foreboding feeling when I had hobbled down those ancient wooden stairs.

It had been cold, the coldest part of the house. That cold wasn't just the air; it surrounded me like a living thing that chilled the blood and made me want to run — and not look back.

Though lit with electric light, the naked bulbs hadn't been strong enough or spaced close enough to cut through the gloom. Builders made the outer walls from huge blocks of cut sandstone. There were also inner walls, separating section from section and connecting support to support. Brick formed them, featuring intricate patterns and curved arches that mirrored the different sections running the length of the vast house.

The feeling of heaviness and sadness had increased in that dark place, shut away from the sunlight.

It was down there, with instructions from a poem I had recited while acting as a medium, that I located a brick wall at the far end of one room. All the outer walls were sandstone, with this one exception.

When I ran my hand along the red rectangular masonry, I had pushed on a specific brick and heard a click.

A part of the wall swung loose like a portal. Behind it was a large, rectangular metal door — an old-fashioned bank vault.

It was that vault that had contained a treasure of gold, silver, and cash hidden since the early twentieth century.

This pressed a question into my mind, and I looked over at Zabella. "Is this location, below the front room, anywhere near the spot where I found the vault?"

Zabella met my eyes, as if expecting this question. "The very place. The vault is directly below the fireplace in the living room."

I felt a chill run up my spine.

A phone rang, and Doctor Kohl pulled out his cell. "Hello?"

He listened and rose from his chair. "Vat? Yes, yes, I vill be right down." He ended the call. "Doctor Janis is conscious."

There was a chatter of congratulations through the group.

"That's good," I said. "Do they know what caused him to black out?"

"Ja. Henry says that Haley drugged him."

Fritz and I headed to the hospital in nearby San Francisco, while the rest of the team remained in the rented abode, waiting until we could return to Scudder House.

Fritz drove the six miles, and as we drew near, we followed signs to an impressive parking lot. We walked out of the lot and up the road toward the multi-building hospital complex, passing the older hospital built one hundred fifty years earlier. We headed for the front of the very new, multi-storied building, named the Zuckerberg San Francisco General Hospital and Trauma after the Facebook founder, who was married to a pediatrician.

The main building was four stories tall, which was higher than standard in earthquake-prone California.

Electronic doors slid open in front of us, and we went into a two-story lobby with a second-floor balcony and a floor made of brightly colored ceramic tiles.

We stopped at the security desk where they examined identification, took our photos, and printed paper badges for Fritz and me to wear.

Soon we were riding up in an elevator to the correct floor. They moved Doctor Janis out of the trauma center after discovering he had been drugged and identifying the substance.

We soon stood in Henry Janis' room, looking at him as he sat up in bed with a tray in front of him holding some kind of unrecognizable food.

"Henry," Fritz greeted him as we walked into the room. "Vhy are they not releasing you?"

"They want to make sure there are no ill effects from the drug, Fritz, so I'm here until tomorrow."

"Can you tell us what happened?" I coaxed.

"Ms. Wolder and I were walking through the woods on our way to the crystal cave and she offered me a small bottle of water, about eight ounces. Well, I only noticed it had an odd taste to it after I'd finished it."

"Odd taste?" I repeated.

"Yes, it was like alcohol, like vodka. As we approached the cave, I felt dizzy. And Haley helped me down to the ground and said, 'I'm sorry, it was necessary.'"

"That vas ominous," Fritz interjected.

"So, I lie on the ground, and she holds me on her lap and holds up my keys. Then she asks which is for Scudder House, and I just tell her."

"Now we know how she got into the house," I said.

"When I woke up here in the hospital and they told me I tested positive for flunitrazepam, I put it all together. I also realized that was why I told her what she wanted to know. She drugged me! That damn girl could have killed me. I am going to press charges."

Fritz and I exchanged a glance.

"That won't be necessary," I suggested.

"Of course it is! Did she steal anything else? My van? Any equipment?"

"Doctor Janis, you don't understand. Haley Wolder is dead."

He glared at me and then at Fritz, his expression hard. When he noted that we were serious, it softened. "Dead... how?"

I cleared my throat. "She attempted a Wiccan ritual at Scudder House last night."

He absorbed this. "Alone?"

"Completely," I added.

He shook his head sadly. "What on earth was she thinking?"

I wondered the same thing myself.

After we left the hospital, at my request, we drove through San Francisco and took the Bay Bridge onto the mainland to the McCord Psychic Institute in Berkeley, California.

I didn't know what I hoped to find out, but while Fritz used the GPS on his phone, I meditated and tried to calm myself so I could be open and aware once we got there.

It took twenty-six minutes, and he pulled into a parking space on the street near a mustard-yellow stucco building.

We walked in, and I tried to reach out, lowering my mental walls to lead me to someone who could give me an explanation for Haley's actions.

We came into the lobby of the gracious building with a woman at the desk. Raised silver letters were on the wall behind her: MCCORD PSYCHIC INSTITUTE.

She smiled pleasantly. "May I help you? Are you looking to get a reading today?"

Fritz and I exchanged a glance. "We're looking for anyone who might know about a student... or maybe a former student... Haley Wolder."

The smile dropped away. "You should know we are not responsible for any readings our students do once they leave the institute—"

I interrupted. "No, this is of a more personal nature. You see, she had an accident — she's dead."

No one could fake the look of shock that came over her. I felt tempted to push into her mind and rummage around to see what I could find. But she was upset and vulnerable, and it wouldn't have been right.

"D-Dead?" she repeated.

"I'm afraid so. We have no idea how to get in touch with next of kin, and we hoped you might—"

Before I could finish the sentence, she dropped into the chair as if her knees had given out. She held up a hand to stop me as she gathered her strength. Without looking up, she picked up the phone and pressed a few buttons.

She spoke into the receiver quietly and calmly. "Ms. McCord. Please come to the front desk. It's about Haley."

She hung up the phone and rose unsteadily to her feet. She gestured to a pair of padded chairs across from her, behind a low glass table. "Please sit. Ms. McCord should speak to you."

I looked at the woman who sat again, and I could see she was pale. "Will Ms. McCord know how to get in touch with Haley's family?"

She gazed up at me, and a tear slipped out of her right eye. "Yes," she croaked. "She's Haley's mother."

I walked over to the chair but remained standing, my weight on my cane. I suddenly felt older and heavier.

Not two minutes had passed when a woman in her fifties walked out. She was thin, her hair perfectly coiffed, and her nails immaculate, wearing a silk blouse with a pair of Capri pants and heels that added about an inch and a half to her height. Looking at both me and Fritz, recognition flashed in her eyes.

"Doctor Kohl and Doctor Wise! This is a surprise. What brings you gentlemen here?"

There was a stifled sob from the woman behind the desk, which made Ms. McCord raise an eyebrow.

"You know us?" I said, puzzled.

"I know of you. I make it my business to know the few visionaries who have parapsychology courses of study at major universities."

"Ve are flattered," Fritz responded.

"We need to speak to you in private, please," I spoke earnestly.

Her expression changed to one of concern. "Yes, of course, follow me."

She quickly led us down the hall and into her nearby office, where she closed the door.

The office was simple, with a desk sporting a large computer monitor, a simple four-level file cabinet, and little shelves with many knickknacks, from small crystal balls to rough pieces of quartz, and little bags which probably contained herbs. On the wall was a rather impressive astrological chart.

She got right to the point once the door was closed. "Tamara said it was about Haley. Is there a problem?"

Fritz gulped and said, "You vere avare that Haley was doing volunteer vork for Doctor Janis this summer?"

"Yes, I was." She folded her arms in defiance. "Now look here, if you complain about her doing your job better than you—"

"No," I interrupted. Then I cleared my throat and went on solemnly. "We are here to tell you that Haley is dead."

Her eyes flashed with fury. "How dare you come here and attempt this terrible—"

Fritz moved to the woman. "Dear lady, it is true. The police have verified it."

Suddenly, the implacable demeanor seemed to melt. "No, no, you're wrong. I would've known. I would've felt it."

"She tried to do some kind of ritual at Scudder House," I explained quietly. "She made a circle, lit candles, created a pentagram. Then some — thing — in that house made her see herself as a withered hag. She stepped out of the circle and broke the protection."

All at once, I could feel her mind as it reached out frantically, attempting to read me, to find the truth.

I met her eyes and reached in. "I'll show you."

Her eyes widened as our minds touched. I pulled the memory of the vision and revealed it, allowing her to see what I had seen. Usually, recalling a vision is difficult, as they are like dreams and become wispy and forgotten when the dreamer wakes. But in this case, it was clear and solid every moment. I presented the incidents like a video on fast forward, giving her the entire event in a mere thirty seconds.

I broke eye contact and turned away as tears stung her eyes. Gone was the iron resolve of this woman who had built her own school and done hundreds of readings for others over the years. She did indeed have a gift, and she had studied to improve it as best she could.

But the person before us was not a clever businesswoman or a powerful executive, but a mother who had just experienced the most devastating event a parent could face: the loss of a child.

Although we were no longer in direct eye contact, she was leaking images and memories, as grief had broken down any barriers she had put around her mind. I saw images of Haley: one right after she was born, the tiny squalling infant; another of her as a five-year-old, as she told her mother of the things she could see; then another of her as a preteen, locked in meditation as she tried to master the skills that would allow her to control her abilities.

Hundreds of images ran through my mind, as well as the crushing grief, the overwhelming sense of loss. I had to put up my own barriers, or else grief would also cripple me.

She leaned on the desk to help lower herself into the chair. "I'm going to be sick," she moaned.

Fritz grabbed a nearby wastebasket and placed it at her feet.

This caused something to click in her, and I could sense her mental shields as they rebuilt themselves. She straightened up in her chair and took a deep breath.

She looked over at me, but she had aged. She seemed almost ancient and weary of life. But with a turn of her head, she pushed down emotions and grief as the steel returned.

She looked over at Fritz and me. "I don't see why the police didn't call me."

"They've been having trouble tracking down Haley's information."

She nodded wearily. "I will contact the Brisbane police and see about my daughter."

For a moment, the resolve wavered as if the grief had won, but she tossed back her head and tamped it down again.

"There is another reason we've come," I said. "There is something in that house that is unlike anything I've ever faced. It's more than a spirit or a haunting. There is something old there and powerful."

"As I suspected," she said with a nod.

"If you could give us any insight, it would help," I implored. "Two people have died there in the last few days. The town wants to tear the building down, but I think they could set free whatever it is if they did."

She took a deep breath and exhaled it heavily. "Yes, I can see that." She moved a strand of hair out of her face. "I have researched Scudder House thoroughly. In fact, I submitted repeated requests to do research there at my cost, but Doctor Janis always denied my requests." I could see the anger in her eyes. "Since I don't have a degree like yourself and Doctor Kohl, he didn't consider my work 'scholarly' enough for consideration." Then she muttered under her breath, "Janis should have been the one that died."

"What makes the house so dangerous, do you know?" As much as I hated to press her, we needed knowledge if we were going to prevent the death of anyone else.

Her words were automatic, as if the act of speaking could hold back the waves of grief I could see etched on her face. "For centuries, the Bay Area was home to Native Americans, indigenous people known as the '*Ohlone.*' The Spanish referred to them as the *'Costanoans,'* which basically means 'people who live near the coast.'"

She stood and paced, the need to do something physical pushing her. "They lived in the Bay Area for centuries and left behind shell mounds." She pulled open the second drawer of the file cabinet and went through it.

"Shell mounds?" Fritz repeated.

"Yes, huge depositories of shells that archaeologists believed were merely garbage dumps, where the *Ohlone* threw their refuse, or burial sites where the shells were to honor the dead." She pulled a full file folder and pushed the drawer closed. "But they were wrong. The shell mounds were places of mystic power, and they intentionally put the shells in those locations to control that energy. The bodies on these sites were great shamans who had passed away. They believed their spirits could help protect the tribe."

"Not an uncommon ancient practice," I said as I thought about the pyramids and other unique mausoleums.

She nodded. "They built Scudder House on top of one of those shell mounds, but a most unique one."

"Are you sure?" I asked.

Fritz added, "Ja, do you have proof of that?"

She blinked at him for a moment, as if she had momentarily forgotten what she was doing. She shook herself and extracted a print of an old black-and-white photo. It showed a large, boxy, steam-powered machine as it cleared soil at the site of Scudder House. It was being used to dig away a small hill.

"This is one of the old photos of when Scudder House was being built. They found a mound with layers of shells in the soil.

It went further underground than any other shell mound, and after a lot of research, I believe I know the reason."

She pulled another page from the file. "There is a legend that the *Ohlone* would hold ceremonial dances underground in caves. Deep in the earth, an evil being made entirely of stone — *WiWay* — interrupted the dance. He stopped their magic and chased the participants, who fled in terror. But there was a great hero, *Kaknu*, the grandson of Coyote, who challenged the monster. *Kaknu* defeated *WiWay* with a magical spear and sealed him in the subterranean cave, which was covered over with shells to keep *WiWay* entombed there."

"I have never heard this legend," Fritz claimed, and Ms. McCord handed him the paper.

"There were also ancient stories of a great stone placed to warn the tribe and to keep the monster from returning." She pulled another photo and handed it to me. "And there was this at the location."

The photo showed the pit dug for the house with machines down in it. But there was something else: a tall, rectangular stone rising from the ground.

"Is that an obelisk?" I asked, stunned.

"That would be the closest English name for it," she said and rubbed her eyes. She was controlling her grief, but just barely. "It became the cornerstone for the entire construction."

Fritz frowned. "They built the entire house around the one stone?"

She nodded. "Elias Scudder thought it was a lucky sign and would help the house in an earthquake."

"It was already square," I murmured, and peered at the strange stone rising from the pit. "Did Haley know the legends?"

I saw another flash of pain in her eyes. The burst of energy she'd experienced faded, and she slumped into her chair.

"She believed she could defeat it," she murmured. "I told her it was too dangerous, but she's just like her father." Her eyes widened, and she shook her head. "Oh God, I have to call her father. No, no, this will devastate him." She glanced up at Fritz and me, her eyes wet again. "We're divorced, but it was friendly."

"Do you have any other children?" I asked gently.

"Another daughter, Haley's sister, Jenna. She doesn't have 'the gift.'"

I grabbed the phone receiver and handed it to her. "Call her. Ask her to pick you up. You shouldn't drive."

She took the receiver. "I have to call the police first, claim the body."

"Is it possible to get copies of any of this file?" I asked.

Her face contorted with hidden rage, and she slid the file toward me. "Take it all. I never want to hear about that damned house ever again."

"Thank you." I took the folder and then offered, "We are in town if you need to talk."

I saw the fire in her eyes. "If you find what did this to my baby, can you do something for me?"

"Of course."

"Kill it," she hissed.

13. GHOST OF A CHANCE

The drive back took us through San Francisco on major highways. As Fritz drove, I reviewed more of the file McCord had put together.

It was obvious she had worked on it for years, as it contained historical data, as well as photos of many of the major participants. There were portraits of Elias Scudder, his daughter Lucy, who died young, and Frances, who committed suicide in her fifties by jumping out the window and impaling herself on the fence, the same way Haley did.

There were also pages and pages of collected lore about the *Ohlone* people, their legends, and way of life in this part of California, before the Spanish arrival.

Still, I couldn't find anything that would help fight what I'd glimpsed at Scudder House. What if I accepted the premise that this was an ancient Native-American entity, trapped in a subterranean cave under Scudder House? How did that help me? I didn't possess any magical spears, and I didn't have a Native-American exorcist on speed dial.

Not even a good shaman.

I was searching for anything that could give me an edge, or at least deflect an attack. Whatever this entity was, it certainly did not fall into any category I had experienced before.

I went through a mental checklist:

Pyrokinetic? Yeah, I'd dealt with that.

Evil *Palero*? Check. Saved myself and others.

Insane cult leader with a drug that made him psychic? Piece of cake.

Demon from Hell? Well, that one had been rough.

I had to deal with the weird and the unusual, and not only did I stop these forces, but I also saved lives. But I had no idea what to do in this case. And there were other people who, if I failed, might end up like Joey or Haley.

Plus, there were the spirits of the dead trapped within the house. Whether they were ambient energy or actual residual personalities didn't matter. Something kept them there, something that haunted that building and wanted bad things to happen.

I was sure that whatever it was, it was tired of being stuck in that one location. It was hungry and wanted more. It sought power to escape and spread like a virus, to destroy everything in its path.

"Anything useful?" Fritz asked as we pulled off the highway and onto the side streets of Brisbane.

I shook myself out of my reverie. "A lot of information, but so far none of it helps."

"I do not think ve should go to that house tonight, Leonard. Ve cannot be safe there after dark."

"Not alone. But if we go as a team, I think we will be all right," I offered. "But I think if we let everyone on the team study this file, maybe we can find something to use."

"I also know a Medicine Practitioner who vas vith the *Ohlone* tribe. I could contact him."

I stared at my mentor in stunned disbelief, then leaned back my head to laugh out loud. He glanced over at me as if I had gone mad.

"Vhat is it?"

"Of course you would know a Native-American medicine man," I chuckled. "And one from the *Ohlone* tribe?" I shook my head. "Only you, Fritz."

He smiled as well and shrugged as he pulled the car over and parked at the curb. "I know many people and many disciplines, Leonard." Then he smiled and with a twinkle in his eye said, "But I have to admit it is a nice bit of synchronicity."

We came into the house, and the team was there at the island in the kitchen again. George sat on a stool with everyone around him.

"George!" Fritz said jovially. "They have released you."

The young man's response revealed his troubled state to me. "They think I'm a killer, Doctor Kohl."

"Vhat?" Fritz exclaimed.

Zabella spoke up, "The police said they found DNA on that girl, Haley."

"DNA?" I asked.

"From George," Liam explained.

"What kind of DNA?" I pushed.

"They didn't say," George mumbled. "But they made it sound like I raped her or something." His face grew red. "I couldn't... I mean, I would never... hurt her."

"Vat are they basing this on?" Fritz demanded.

"That detective — Valentin? He thinks I can sneak in and out because my bed is near the door."

"Look, George," I said, placing a hand on his shoulder. "This is a technique police use to get people to slip up. Just stick to your story, and everything will be fine."

"He hates me," he muttered.

"Don't worry," I said. "He hates me, too."

This broke some of the tension with nervous chuckles all around, and I looked over to see Anna give me a soft smile.

Danger...

The buzz was quick but strong, and I examined the faces of everyone there.

"Where's Lamar?" I declared, suddenly serious.

"He drove into town to get a few things," Liam said. "More coffee or something."

Scudder House...

I know that when a buzz makes the hair on the back of my neck jump up and electricity pulse through my blood, I need to take it seriously.

I turned to Anna. "You need to drive me to Scudder House."

"What?" she said, taken aback.

"Right now!"

The compact car careened up the side road at the best speed it could manage, considering it was an unused gravel path once we pulled off the main road.

"Aren't the police still there?" Anna asked, her eyes straight ahead. "Isn't it safe?"

"No, it's not safe, not safe at all," I fretted. "You need to hurry."

"Len, this is as fast as I can go on this road."

"Okay," I replied as the car bounced on a pothole. "I'm going to close my eyes, try to reach out, and get some insight into what I'm sensing."

"Got it!" she exclaimed and focused on the road.

I shut my eyes and let down my walls, trying to reach out to Lamar. I could sense his presence, but there was something wrong; he was somewhere wrong, and he was not sure how he'd arrived there.

I sought to connect with his mind. I had done it so easily with Haley, but she was skilled with her abilities, and long-range telepathy was uncommon. Lamar might not have the knack for it, and impressions from other sources could easily overwhelm his mind.

I was sure that was what was happening right now.

I felt the car bump and jostle as we came to a screeching stop in the yard of Scudder House.

The back of the white van was open, and I could hear the generator going. The electric lights were on in the house, even though it was hard to tell on this sunlit day.

I glanced at Anna as she got out. "Stay here!" I lunged forward toward the house.

"Like hell," she announced and followed me.

I turned to her and stopped. "It could be dangerous."

"What was it you said before? We should only go into the house as a team? That goes for you, too."

I couldn't argue with her, but my mind flashed with images of the women I had lost: Cathy hanging upside down, dead in our broken car; Wendy Wallace bursting into flames on her porch; Jyanette lying in the hospital, her face battered and bruised.

I pushed the memories away and shouted, "Come on!" and propelled myself forward as fast as I could.

We headed toward the house. The one major difference since the last time I was here was a brown crust on one of the tall iron fence posts. I shuddered when I realized that was the spot where Haley had impaled herself.

We reached the steps together, and, of course, she just ran up them and to the door. "No!" I barked. "We go in together. It's the only protection we have."

Fortunately, it was only a few steps, and I was up on them and at the door quickly. Yellow police tape had been covering the door, but was now torn away. I sucked in a big breath, walled up my mind, and imagined barriers to keep out anything that might be there.

We pushed through the unlocked door and into the living room. All the machines were active and clicking away. At the laptop near the Accelerator stood Lamar, his back to us.

"Lamar," I spoke quietly, but he didn't move. His dark fingers tapped away at the keyboard.

I detected an odd smell, which hit me all at once with a sense of panic: gasoline.

I glanced over to see one of the large red canisters George used to fuel the generator, as it sat near the mantle on the hearthstone of the fireplace. I tentatively drew closer to Lamar. His shirt was damp, but I knew it wasn't water or sweat.

He had doused himself with gasoline.

"Lamar!" I shouted, fighting to keep my mental barriers in place. There was something just beyond me, an energy in the air, and I needed to be protected from it, or it could affect me as well.

Lamar continued to tap away at the keyboard, and I could see he had pulled up the Accelerator's activation window and was programming it. From what numbers I could see on the screen, he was setting it to run for an hour.

If that machine were to put out vibrational energy for an hour, it would give whatever lived here the energy to do almost anything.

"Lamar, stop," I insisted and moved toward him.

He whirled around, and I saw his eyes. What was there was not Lamar. It was the cold, frightening stare of the entity that had possessed him during our previous use of the Accelerator.

He held up a lighter in his left hand. "Stay back," he croaked in an inhuman, demonic voice, "or this vessel dies."

I could see the dampness soaking Lamar's long sleeves, and the smell of gasoline was overwhelming. If he flicked that lighter, he would burst into flames right before me.

I stopped my forward momentum and held my cane aloft. "Okay, okay."

I tried to move nearer to knock the lighter from his hand using my cane, but he fixed his eyes on me and grinned. He reached with his right hand and hit the space bar on the laptop.

Numbers counted down on the screen. I had to stop it before it hit '1' or the machine would become active. I had passed out the last time, and this seemed a poor moment to do that again.

The Accelerator hummed as it warmed up and prepared to emit vibrations at the same level as all the other machines in the room were reading.

The mad look in Lamar's eyes grew brighter as he faced me. "You lose, healer!" he croaked.

And at that moment, the countdown on the screen froze, and the hum lowered in pitch as the Accelerator went dead. In fact, all the machines shut down except for the laptop.

Lamar, or whatever was using him, turned toward the screen in rage. "NO!"

My moment had come. With two quick steps, I moved close enough. The folding cane is not as solid as my cobra-headed companion. But even so, I readily smacked his hand with the head. The lighter rattled to the floor across the room.

Lamar bellowed and ran toward me. He yanked my cane from my hand and threw it, relieving me of my only weapon. He clutched my throat with both hands and squeezed, which effectively cut off my air.

The smell of gasoline made my eyes water, and I heard myself making choking noises.

I heard Anna yell, "No, stop!"

She tried to pull Lamar off me, but he just turned and slapped her with a backhand that sent her flying. Then he returned to me, his hands at my throat.

I was growing dizzy, and his grip was superhumanly strong. I couldn't break his hold. In fact, I couldn't even loosen it.

I glanced down. We were at the edge of the circle Haley had scratched into the wood with her athame.

I grabbed Lamar's wrist and pulled, jostling us to the center of the circle.

I am certainly not a practitioner of 'white magic' or any of the pagan religious practices, but I understood how sympathetic magic worked. The circle was a barrier created in the mind that shut the practitioner off from any outside influences. It worked the same way the mental barriers I used to protect my mind worked: through imagination and a force of will.

I envisioned the surrounding circle, moved my mental protections to fill the entire area in which we both stood, and focused on sealing us away from whatever had seized control of Lamar.

The grip around my neck weakened, and since I held his wrists, I forced his hands from my throat. I leaned over, gasping for air.

"What the hell happened?" Lamar questioned. "How did I get here?" He looked at his clothes. "Why am I wet?"

Anna ran toward us with a yell, clutching my cane high overhead and ready to bring it down on his head.

"Wait, wait!" Lamar and I yelled in unison with our hands up to ward off a blow.

Anna stopped dead in her tracks. "Lamar? Is it you?"

"Who else would it be?" He sniffed the air. "Do you guys smell gasoline?"

"Yes," I croaked. "It's you. You're covered in gas."

"What?" he yelped and stepped back. I grabbed his arm and pulled him to me. "Don't step out of the circle."

He looked at me with surprise, then dropped his eyes to the circle and pentagram in chalk beneath us.

"Why not?"

"Do you have any recollection of how you got here?"

He considered this. "I went shopping. Now I'm here."

"You became possessed, taken over. It must have been the presence that overwhelmed you when we activated the Accelerator the other day."

"What was it trying to make me do?"

"Burn yourself alive," I offered.

"What?" he snapped.

"And turn on the Accelerator. Fortunately, there was a glitch, and it shut down."

"That wasn't a glitch," Anna announced and handed me my cane. "I shut off the power bar that went to the machines in that corner."

"What?" I asked.

"All the power comes from the generator. Then we break it down through different extension cords, and each one has a surge protector switch. I just turned it off."

I shook my head and smiled. "I would never have thought of that."

Anna raised an eyebrow at me. "Guess it's good I didn't stay in the car."

"I'll never ask that again."

"You'd better not. I'm not some 'damsel in distress,' Len. I'm a member of this team, and I have skills that help."

"Duly chastised," I noted. "Could you bring the car around to the front and get Lamar into it?"

"I could just go with her," he said.

"I would prefer you stay in the circle as long as possible. Also, take off your clothes."

"What?"

"Just your shirt and pants. I'd prefer you not be a fire hazard." I looked over at Anna. "Can you drop him off with the team, and then come back here to get me?"

She shifted her weight nervously from one foot to the other. "I thought you shouldn't be here alone?"

"I should be okay, as long as I stay in the circle," I reassured her. "I will try to be aware of an attack or whatever."

Anna nodded and headed out the door.

"You're not very reassuring," Lamar said as he slid his pants down. He was now in an undershirt and boxer shorts, with his socks and shoes on.

"Try to go over everything in your mind — not here, but once you're back at the rented house. Anything you can remember might be helpful. And don't be alone; you're at risk."

"Liam will stay with me."

"Good. I'm glad you have backup."

Anna appeared back at the front door. "Car is running, and I'm ready."

"Okay!" I turned to Lamar. "Keep your eyes on her, move directly to the door, and let nothing distract you."

He nodded, looked down at the circle for a moment, then focused on Anna and moved across the floor to her. He got there without incident, and I sighed as Anna waved and the pair of them went out the door.

I heard the car drive away and relaxed a little, still focusing on the circular barrier around me. A chair was at the edge of the circle, and I grabbed it and placed it in the center of the pentagram to take a seat.

I tried to get a feel for the house, letting the walls down a little, and once again I sensed nothing. The overpowering presence was gone.

I thought about the *Ohlone* myth of the creature made of stone, WiWay. I wished I had brought the folder with me, so I could read more of the contents, but Anna and I had left in a hurry.

What was this entity playing at?

Even if it was this WiWay character, I couldn't see how killing people could change its situation. Unless killing gave it the energy it sought to free it from this place. But what could a disembodied Native-American monster do, even if it could break free?

And the gasoline. Lamar had poured it on himself. It was reminiscent of the way a former resident, Nat Hewing, had died — burned to death. So far, two people had died in ways similar to previous tenants. Joey hung himself in a way similar to Elias Scudder; Haley ended up impaled like Frances Scudder.

That's when the idea struck me: Haley.

I was in a circle she had created. If her consciousness was trapped here like the others I'd seen in my vision, it might mean her spirit could not move on. It might be possible to let her in and keep the big, bad WiWay out.

I closed my eyes and sought to reach out to her, keeping the image of her strong in my mind. I felt a quiet stirring all around me.

I tried to speak to her in my mind: *Haley...*

Len? Is that you...

The voice I heard was hers.

Yes. Do you know what happened...

I'm not sure...

Where are you…

Scudder House. I've been wandering around. I think I'm lost…

I paused for a moment. This was the tough point. Some hauntings I've investigated had spirits who were unaware that they were deceased.

Have you seen the others? The spirits…

Yes. They are everywhere…

Is there something keeping you here, an entity you don't know…

I sensed it, but I don't—

In the middle of the sentence, she was gone. I tried again to connect with her.

Haley…

A dark presence answered.

Healer…

I paused for a moment. The voice rumbled in my head, deep and powerful. I decided answering it was worth the risk if I could learn something.

Hello. Should I call you WiWay, or do you have another name…

Names do not interest me, healer. You need to get out of my way…

And allow you to kill people? Possess them? Use them? I can't let you do that…

You have little choice, healer…

What are you after? Perhaps there is a way to give you what you seek without hurting any living beings…

I shall choose who gets hurt and how…

There was a stabbing pain in my head, and I realized I had allowed my concentration and my barriers to relax.

I closed my eyes and envisioned the protective circle around me. I imagined the power of the candles and the incense. After a moment, my head cleared.

I was alone. Whatever had touched my mind hid in whatever place it ran to after every attempt to seek it.

It could interrupt contact with any other entities trapped in the house, which meant I would have no help from the other side. It could also hide itself from me and then overwhelm and possibly even possess me.

The choices that lay before me did not look good.

In fact, as the last few days had proved, it could be fatal.

14. CRYPTIC CONCEPTS

Anna returned to the house, and thankfully, the entity did not appear to make an encore. We exited together with no ill effects. She shut down all the laptops and every machine as I gathered Lamar's clothing. Once outside, she turned off the gasoline generator, which brought an eerie silence to the area, as the work at the nearby quarry had ended for the day. She locked the van using keys she had taken from the pocket of Lamar's pants.

She was oddly silent during this entire time. I put the clothes in the hatchback, and we got into the car and drove away before she spoke. "Were there any problems after I left?"

"It talked to me," I said. My eyes watching the road and the setting sun.

"Talked to you?" she asked.

I pointed a finger at my head. "In here."

She exhaled and focused on the road.

"Are you okay?" I attempted.

"No, I'm not okay. I thought I'd be doing research this summer. Research! You know, compile numbers, write reports, maybe the worst thing I'd get is a chill down my spine. But people are *dying*!"

"I know. Joey starting up the Accelerator made — whatever it is — active, gave it the power it needed to strike."

"And the look in Lamar's eyes," Anna recalled, as a shiver ran through her. "I don't think I have the right stuff for paranormal research."

"Anna, this situation is unusual. Most paranormal activity is not scary or violent." I gazed ahead at the road. "My experience is that usually it's the living you have to watch out for."

She pulled the car over and parked near the house.

She turned to face me. "I wanted to do field work. I guess what I wanted was to be like you." She leaned forward and kissed me. Then she pulled back and met my eyes. "Can you do it to me?"

"I'm sorry?" I said, confused by the question.

"That thing you do where you reach into people's minds?"

I turned my head. "It's not something you would enjoy."

"I just want to know what it feels like," she said, her eyes bright. "Having another person touch your mind, having no secrets."

I looked at her, but focused on the tip of her nose. "Anna, it isn't some parlor trick designed to amuse. I only use it when I have no other choice."

"I want you to."

I pushed out my breath in annoyance. "Inside. In my room. Not out here on the street. And later, after we talk to the team and make plans."

She smiled, and we both got out of the car.

I liked Anna. She was a sweet woman and an enthusiastic lover. I remembered she was younger than I was. Her years as a wallflower had made her a bit immature. One moment she felt depressed over the death of acquaintances, and the next she became excited about me reading her mind. It was a roller-coaster of emotions that seemed more like a teenager than a woman in her twenties.

A memory from last Christmas flashed through my mind. Jyanette looking at me and smiling, sitting at the big dining room table with Mrs. Higgins. The only lights were the candles, and her eyes caught the candlelight with such beauty, I could've stared into them forever.

And there it was; my heart was heavy with loss. We were so well-suited, despite my white, upper-middle-class Jewish background and her African-American, working-class Christian family. We touched in all the right places. Sure, we had arguments, even fights, but we fit together nicely. We both had our work, and we both made time to be together and wanted to build a life with each other. Events took that future away from me.

That dream, like the one Cathy and I planned; a gifted surgeon and his pediatrician wife, which was shattered on a rainy mountain so many years ago.

How many others would I love and lose? Could I ever find the stability I longed for? I believed that living with Mrs. Higgins and teaching at GSU would provide me with a nice, stable existence.

I could see that would never be my path.

We stepped into the house, and a hush came over the room.

"How's Lamar?" I asked.

Liam spoke up. "In the shower, still trying to get the smell of gasoline off himself."

George watched me fixedly. "How did you know he was at the house, that he was in danger?"

Zabella chided him. "Don't you know, George? This is the great Doctor Wise, the 'super psychic of Scudder House.'"

I could tell that the others were looking at me coldly, and I noted that Doctor Kohl was nowhere to be seen.

"Okay, what's going on?" I inquired warily.

Zabella stepped forward. "Since the others won't say it, I will. You were called here to help, but since you arrived, a woman has died, Lamar nearly had his brain fried, and George is under suspicion."

"Yes, and things have gotten completely weird," George blurted. "Now we have to worry about something getting into our heads and making us do things without our knowing?"

Liam joined in. "Weren't you here to stop it? Isn't that what you're supposed to do?"

Anna's voice silenced them all. "Stop it! Len just risked his life to save Lamar! And all you can do is blame him?"

Zabella snapped, "You're just saying that because you're sleeping with him."

Anna's face darkened as if she was going to slap Zabella into next week, so I intervened.

I kept my volume low but used the power of my voice to get the group to focus on me. "Look, this is a strange situation. I'm trying to understand it as well as all of you. But this is what this entity wants. It wants us fighting amongst ourselves."

"Oh yeah?" George challenged. "What if there isn't any 'entity?' What if you're doing all of this, getting into our heads and manipulating us?"

The front door closed as Doctor Kohl came inside. An older, short, brown man wearing glasses and a baseball cap followed him. His long-sleeve shirt bore a bold Native-American print, and he carried a small leather satchel, reminiscent of a doctor's bag from another time.

Fritz gave all of us a stern look. "I heard shouting."

The team members all milled about and looked at the floor. I was busy sensing the peaceful energy around the new arrival.

"Do not blame them, Fritz," the older man said in a firm voice. "The ancient one has touched them, and it influences their judgment."

He placed the satchel on a nearby table and opened it up as Fritz spoke. "This is Thomas Twofeathers, an associate of mine. He is a healer and herbalist and has studied the way of the *Ohlone* all his life."

He smiled at the group and bowed his head. "I am both *Ohlone* and *Cherokee*, and I have studied the ancient ways. I believe that some of the old traditions may be of help to you."

From the bag, he pulled a string of seashells and held them up. He closed his eyes and chanted a few words in a strange language with sounds I had never heard before. He then opened his eyes and moved to Zabella.

"The spirit of anger is strongest in you," he said to her and put the shells over her head. "You feel as if someone has taken things from you. But you have all you need."

George laughed sarcastically. "So now we've got an Indian guru who is going to help us beat the big baddie?"

Thomas had returned to the satchel, held up another string of small shells, and repeated his chant, ignoring George. He then approached him, and his dark eyes flashed. "The spirit of anger has long had a home within you, my son. You must let it go if you wish to walk free."

This effectively shut George up, and Thomas hung the string of shells around his neck.

He put strings of shells around Liam and Fritz as well. Lamar came out of his shower in fresh clothes but said nothing as the older man continued his work.

Finally, Thomas looked at Lamar and nodded. "You are the one he has used. Come close, my son."

Lamar looked at me with trepidation and stepped close to the man. Once again, Thomas reached into the bag but pulled out a large, handmade rattle with an eagle feather hanging from it on a strip of rawhide. He shook the rattle and chanted over Lamar's head as the young man eyed him with suspicion.

Thomas pulled a small sand dollar shell from the bag. It was a little bigger than a silver dollar, and the surface of it was a five-petal-shaped design, almost like a five-pointed star. A circle of rawhide ran over it and through a hole. He chanted under his breath as he placed the shell over Lamar's head.

"This shall protect you," he said, and Lamar, not sure what to do, gave a quick bow and backed away.

Thomas' eyes lighted on Anna. "You are the one in the most danger."

"What?" Anna said, and a deep frown appeared on her youthful face.

"Yes, you are the last link," Thomas said, and again pulled out his rattle to shake it in the air over Anna.

Anna shot a panicked look at me, but I gestured with my hand to tell her to remain calm.

Thomas pulled another flat sand dollar shell from his bag. This one was bigger, about the size of a coaster you would put under a drink. He held it up and chanted loudly, then placed the rawhide strap connected to it around Anna's neck.

He then stepped back and faced the group. "Forgive me for not explaining myself when I arrived, but I could sense the evil one reaching his claws out to you. He has captured your hearts and was fomenting discord. I needed to protect you before you could hear my words."

A mutter ran about the room, but Thomas was right. There was a much stronger sense of peace all around us.

"Many think that the old ways are dead," he told us. "There are still millions of Native Americans throughout this country, and I tell you that the old ways are being learned again. We are not a relic of the past, but a people who wish to recapture our traditions."

Liam held up the string of shells around his neck. "How did you know we would need these?"

"Fritz phoned me, and I felt the urgency of his words. I contemplated, and Coyote came to me in a vision. That is why I asked him to bring me to you, to give you charms that may protect you. You have come across an ancient evil."

"Why is it active now?" I asked.

"One of your group awoke a great spirit that wishes to be free. He paid for it with his life. I fear the disaster this ancient one might bring if it escapes confinement." He sat on the sofa, as if suddenly overcome with exhaustion, and smiled at my mentor. "Fritz, I'm getting too old for this."

Fritz moved to the sofa and sat next to his friend.

Anna stepped forward and asked, "Do you want anything — food, drink?"

"No, I am just no longer a young man." He looked at the group and announced, "You have a challenge to face. I wish I could stand by your side, but I have not the strength. I must now talk to your healer, alone."

He gestured to me.

"Come to my room," I suggested.

The older man stood, grabbed his satchel, and followed me down the short hall and into my room. He put the case on the bed, pulled out the rattle, and said a few words in that unusual language. Then he reached into the satchel and pulled out something that he kept hidden in his hand.

"I can see the light around you, though it has recently dimmed. I can see that you are in pain, and I fear more pain shall come to you."

"Great," I replied sardonically.

"I was guided to present you with a special charm."

He opened his hand to reveal one of the small sand dollars, which had several small feathers, like down, laced with thread through one hole. Unlike the others, it was not bleached white, but was brown, shiny, and appeared to be made of stone.

"What is this?" I asked, intrigued by the strange look of it.

"This is very old. It is a fossil cleaved from a rock. According to legend, a great healer and wise man wore it on his own rattle. You must tell no one you have it and show it to no one."

I met his eyes, my mind filled with doubt. "What do I do with it? When should I use it?"

He closed my hand around the small artifact. "When the time is right, you will know. Keep it on you at all times."

"I will."

He smiled slyly and said, "So the others don't think I forgot about you," then took another shell necklace from his bag, put it on me, and spoke his ancient language again. After they were around my neck, he opened his eyes, and we exited the room. We returned to the living room, and Fritz rose to his feet.

"May you all be safe and be well," Thomas told the group, and he appeared weary. "I must go now, Fritz."

"Thank you for coming out, Thomas," Fritz said. "I'll drive you home."

Twofeathers nodded, and with his satchel in his weathered hand, he waved as he left.

"That was unexpected," Lamar said, and held up his single sand dollar shell necklace. "Do you think this thing will work?"

I was still in awe, but I spoke. "I don't know, but tomorrow we're going to face whatever is in that house, so please make sure you wear these charms."

"Great, magic shells," George scoffed. "I hope they can keep my ass out of prison."

Anna drew close to me. "Would it bother you if I had some wine? It's been a freaky day."

"No, please go ahead. I'm going to look at my email. I'll be in my room," I told her as I got up and went into the bedroom and kicked off my shoes.

I had left the door open, and I saw Lamar and Liam outside.

"I'm glad you're all right," Liam said and gave Lamar a soulful kiss.

"Let's go downstairs and I'll show you I'm all right," he answered lustily. Then he looked in my door and called out, "Len, you okay?"

I had extracted my laptop and was booting it up. "Yes, I'll be fine, Lamar."

"I just wanted to, y'know, thank you for pulling my ass out of there."

I grinned. "That might not be the way I'd put it, but I appreciate it."

He held out the shell that hung around his neck. "So honestly, do you think this shell can keep that bad boy away?"

I held up my string of tiny shells. "To quote an ancient sage: 'It couldn't hurt.'"

This got a laugh, and he and Liam thundered down the stairs for some alone time. I smiled. It's good when people can find each other, even if the happiness is fleeting. That must have been what my problem was: I was trying to make more out of being with Anna. It was simply a youthful romp for her, and probably just a case of rebound for me.

I liked her, but this would never be a genuine relationship, no matter how desperate I was for one.

Yeah, that's sexy. Nothing appeals to a woman like a needy, desperate guy. What girl could resist that?

Zabella knocked at my open doorframe. "Can we talk?"

I glanced up from my computer. "Sure. Come in."

Zabella stepped in and shut the door, much to my surprise. "I wanted to apologize for how I spoke in there."

I put the laptop aside and stood up. "It's fine. We've all been under a lot of pressure."

She gazed down at the floor. "I guess a part of me was jealous. I really like Anna and I thought maybe…"

"That she might reciprocate?" I offered.

"I was getting all the signals," she explained wryly. "I guess I read them wrong. I heard the way she talked about you. I knew she had a severe case of the hots for you and was mad she didn't act on it when you lived in California."

"I'm sorry if you feel I got in the way," I said.

"Well, if she's not gay, I mean, she's not," Zabella replied. "We all have disappointments, right?"

I smiled warmly. "Yes, we do. Thank you for the apology, but it wasn't necessary."

She nodded her head, opened the door, and went across the hall to her room. Anna immediately slipped in with a half-glass of wine and closed the door again, turning the lock to prevent anyone else from coming in.

"Okay, I'm ready for you to read my mind," she said excitedly.

I sighed. "Anna, I don't want you to put too much into this."

"It'll be fun," she gushed. "Will I know you're doing it?"

"Yes. In fact, you'll experience whatever I see."

She smiled and sat on the bed opposite me. "Can we replay last night? That might be fun."

I touched my finger to her lips and spoke. "I need to concentrate."

She nodded and shut her eyes, as I did. Then, we both opened our eyes, and I reached out, my eyes focused on hers.

Memories flashed around us, snippets here and there: having breakfast, looking at herself in the mirror, kissing me, kissing Zabella.

That last one gave me pause, and I pulled back to it and saw her facing Zabella and moving in to kiss her.

When I move into someone's mind like this, they usually cannot look away and feel impelled to allow me access, but I felt a resistance. There was a feeling of both excitement and fear in that image, and I wasn't sure if it was a memory or a fantasy. I moved out and broke eye contact.

She blinked and stared at me in shock. "Wow," she murmured, but she looked troubled, and a flush traveled over her golden skin.

She got up and looked at the wine. "Sorry, sometimes I flush when I drink alcohol. They call it 'Asian Flush.' They think it's a deficient gene."

I decided to just say what was on my mind. "Is there anything you want to tell me? There's nothing wrong if Zabella attracts you."

"I don't know," she responded, and sipped her wine. "I mean, I'm around gay guys all the time, but I never considered that I might be gay."

"If you're curious to find out, I know that Zabella is interested in you."

"She's made no secret about it," she said and put her hand on her head. "It's too much to think about right now. I mean, I've wanted you for the longest time."

"I won't be hurt if you move on, Anna," I reassured her.

She looked at me long and hard, but I made a point not to slip into her mind. I just returned her gaze with a feeling of acceptance. She gulped down her wine and moved to sit next to me on the bed.

"I have some conflicting feelings, Len," she whispered, her voice barely a thread of sound. "But tonight? Right now? I just want this."

She leaned in, her mouth finding mine. It began as a tentative question but quickly deepened into an urgent, feverish demand. There was a desperation to it, a need to anchor ourselves to something solid while the world outside felt like it was dissolving into shadows.

She pulled back just enough to slip her top over her head, her movements fluid and hurried. I reached for the sand dollar shell she wore, my fingers brushing the cool, smooth calcium before pulling it off. She did the same for the string of shells around my neck, setting them aside on the bedside table.

As we moved together, the stark reality of the morning clawed at the back of my mind. Tomorrow, we were stepping into a void — facing an entity that didn't play by the rules of physics or mercy. I felt a cold spike of dread, a premonition that this might be the last quiet moment we'd ever share.

I tried to shove the thought into the dark corners of the room. *Not now. Not tonight.*

Under the heat of her touch, the dread finally began to recede, and I lay back as she rolled on top of me, my fear replaced by the sheer, grounding weight of her body against mine. She moved with a fierce, silent intensity, her breath hitching in my ear as the tension between us coiled tighter and tighter.

When the release finally came, it was like a fever breaking — a sudden, violent crashing of waves that left us both breathless and spent. We lay there in the aftermath, tangled in the sheets, still connected, our hearts hammering a frantic, synchronized rhythm.

I touched her straight, dark hair, and she fixed her hooded eyes on mine. "Do it again."

"What?" I gasped. "I might need a few minutes to recover."

"No, in my eyes. I want you to go into my mind again."

"Wasn't being inside your body enough?"

"Come on, I mean it. I want you to show me the things I'm scared to admit to myself."

"You don't need me to do that. You can do that anytime you want. Look, you've studied with Doctor Kohl, and he teaches everyone the meditation techniques. You just have to meditate on what you want to know about yourself."

"You're no fun," she chided and wiggled her hips to separate us.

She got up and grabbed a pink silken robe covered with Korean letters from a hook on the closet and headed out the door and down the hall to the bathroom.

I lay there, trying to figure out how her robe ended up in my room.

Anna felt attracted to Zabella. Well, they both were beautiful, and I could see that someone who was as shy as Anna used to be might desire the attention from either gender or even both. Or it could be deeper than that. She could have desires she feared to admit to herself, or perhaps she was bisexual. I certainly would not complain, since I was the current beneficiary.

It was not uncommon for a gay person to tamp down their desires. In the past, people had to hide the fact that they were gay, and it was only in my lifetime that such sexual practices gained acceptance as a lifestyle.

The weight of Anna's past hung over her. I knew her story: demanding parents, the crushing expectation of excellence, a childhood spent as a polished trophy rather than a girl. It had made her brilliant, yes, but socially hollow. Now, she was finally splintering away from that mold, tasting a freedom her parents would never allow.

Whatever the situation was, she would have to decide on her own. She would have to choose whom she wanted to be with and why. At least she had a choice.

I, on the other hand, was still wandering through the wreckage of my own, trying to step out from the shadow of my breakup with Jyanette, and not sure how.

Far worse, the entity we were facing didn't care about my fragile ego or my hollowed-out confidence. It had already proven it could dismantle and possess a person easily.

I was walking into a mental war zone with a clouded mind.

Tomorrow we would have to come up with a plan to stop it.

15. STRATEGIC VISION

T he gray light of a California morning was bleeding through the curtains when I drifted into a state that wasn't quite sleep and wasn't quite wakefulness.

In the hazy borderland of a dream, I felt a familiar warmth, a rhythmic weight that seemed to pull me upward from the depths. It was disorienting at first — the scent of jasmine and the cool morning air clashing with the heat of skin. I didn't open my eyes, anchored by pleasure that felt like a tide coming in, slow and relentless.

I felt Anna move above me, a shadow silhouetted against the dim room. She hadn't woken me with words; she had let my body speak for itself. The sensation was vivid, an electric current humming through the fog of my semi-conscious state.

The transition from the dream happened all at once. A sudden, sharp peak that shattered the last of my sleep, pulling a ragged cry from my throat that echoed in the corners of the room. My cries were the catalyst she needed; I felt her hitch, a sharp intake of breath as she followed me over the edge.

For a few frantic seconds, our world was nothing but the pulse of two hearts trying to find the same rhythm.

Anna let out a long, shaky exhale and rolled to the side, the mattress springs groaning under the shift. She pulled the covers up to her chin, a ghost of a smile touching her lips before her breathing slowed into the deep, rhythmic cadence of someone who had conquered the morning and gone back to sleep.

I lay there, staring at the ceiling, my skin still buzzing.

I dragged myself from the bed, pulled on my clothing from the previous day, and walked out to the kitchen to get coffee, sit on the deck, and make a brilliant plan that would defeat whatever we were up against and get us all out of Scudder House safely.

The coffee was easy. I had no luck coming up with a plan.

I tried to break it down: if the entity was trying to influence the physical world, it needed energy. Based on my past experiences, which include one with a deranged *Palero*, human sacrifice can generate powerful psychic energy. That was a safe assumption, explaining the deaths over the years, as well as the recent events.

And then there was the Accelerator. This machine used readings from the environment and created sympathetic vibrations to match and increase them. My proof that the entity needed to use the machine was the fact that it led Lamar to activate it before attempting to set himself on fire.

This knowledge still gave me little to use as a weapon. I needed to diminish its power and influence or increase my own mental abilities to be its equal.

I didn't know how to accomplish either task.

I went through the papers in the file Ms. McCord had given me. The history and research were impressive but offered little in the way of solutions.

I learned more about the tribes that had settled in the San Francisco Bay Peninsula. The dominant tribe was the *Ramaytush* who spoke their own dialect of the *Ohlone* language and had many smaller villages around the area with different names. The area that is now Brisbane had been a village known as *Siplichiquin*.

It was not surprising that people built a new town where the village once stood. This happened throughout the world, new societies rising on ancient sites and a new civilization sprouting up from the old.

Change was inevitable.

The history also went into the harsh creation of that change. The Spanish opened missions in California for the Roman Catholic Church. Initially, curiosity and offers of protection and food attracted the natives to come to them. But diseases carried by the Spanish quickly devastated the local population, and the mission became crowded with people fleeing the disease, which exacerbated the situation.

The Spanish also forced the *Ohlone* to assimilate to their ways of dress and decorum, often with harsh physical abuse for noncompliance. They also 'persuaded' the *Ohlone* to learn Spanish and Latin, and the *Ohlone* lost their own language over the years.

Most personal information included only the individual's baptism records from the old Mission of San Francisco. Between the Spanish arrival in 1777 until 1850, the Mission converted and baptized over seven thousand people. Records kept the names they received at baptism for posterity, yet omitted their former names or any heritage identifiers.

According to the Mission records, by 1842 there were a mere twelve *Ohlone* living the traditional tribal lifestyle in the San Francisco area. All the others — over ten thousand — had been converted or died.

I could understand if the entity at Scudder House held a righteous anger over the destruction of the people and culture, but I did not sense that. My feeling was that this consciousness, whatever it was or had been, was a destroyer. If indeed it had been entombed on the spot where Scudder House now stood, it had been trapped there by an *Ohlone* healer or the famed hero *Kaknu*. Therefore, it held no love for the *Ohlone* or anyone else.

Ancient entities have led to the legends of gods in mythology. They were powerful and could lay dormant for many years.

Further studies included in the file postulated that the people who became the *Ohlone* arrived by sea in the sixth century CE and displaced a people known as the *Esselen*, who had been there since prehistoric times.

McCord's research of the *Esselen* found that the most obvious remnant of their culture were painted handprints left on rocks throughout the regions where they lived. It was an *Esselen* belief that all things contained life, and if you put your hand on a large rock, you would know what had happened there.

I found this interesting. It sounded like my abilities. When I touch an object owned by someone, I often know things about them or where they are. Could the *Esselen* have been a tribe of psychics?

I shut the folder and sipped my now-cold coffee, more confused than enlightened.

Anna came out, dressed in a work shirt and jeans, and sat next to me. "Morning!"

I grunted a reply, turning the folder over in my hand.

"Why is it that I get up in a good mood and you're always grumpy?"

I lifted an eyebrow. "I get that way when I'm about to face something that wants to kill me."

"Sorry I woke you," she said with a grin.

"No, you're not."

"No, I'm not. And you should be grateful. How often does a man get a woman willing to take the initiative?" She turned from me to look out over the valley. The view was one that allowed us to look all the way to the nearby bay.

"You certainly did that."

"Two years ago, just the idea of taking charge would have frightened me. Especially sexually."

"Now, not so much?"

"Well, you were there. What do you think?" She turned to me with a smoldering look in her eyes.

I couldn't hold back my smile. "I was only involved at the end."

She sat back and smiled at me. "I can't believe you slept through most of it. That is really funny."

I lifted an eyebrow. "Yes, but the dreams I had were pretty intense."

The door slid open, and Doctor Kohl came out. "Reviewing our options?" he asked with a gesture to the folder.

"None have come to mind. This entity — consciousness — entombed spirit—"

Anna interrupted. "I thought it was called *WiWay*."

I sighed. "Sounds a lot like 'wee-wee,' but that's merely the name that appears in the *Ohlone* mythology. But they referred to the creature as 'a body made of stone,' which sounds ominous."

Fritz cleared his throat. "You mean it has *not* been ominous until now?"

"Making people throw themselves out of windows or grabbing them from a distance, like it did to Lamar yesterday?" I fretted. "We should name it 'Ominous'."

Fritz considered this. "According to ritual magic concepts, there is power in being able to call an evil force by its name."

"I had that experience with a demon," I offered.

Anna's eyes shifted to me. "A *demon*? You fought an actual demon?"

"Yes, and it wasn't an experience I recall fondly. Nor do I look forward to doing it again," I grumbled. "Plus, in that case, I had sigils and lore I could use for research and protection. The ceremonies of the *Ohlone* are long gone, and all I have is a necklace of shells."

"My shells are bigger than yours," Anna giggled, referring to the large sand dollar shell that Thomas Twofeathers had given her.

This made Fritz's eyebrows shoot up and a smile appear on his face as he looked over at me.

"I don't feel a need to compare sizes," I joked.

The rest of the house was waking up, and Lamar and Liam appeared. They were smiling at each other and talking animatedly. George got out of bed just as Zabella appeared, fully clothed and ready for the day.

Coffees in hand, we began the discussion of how best to face our foe at Scudder House.

Before we started, I insisted that we all put on our shell necklaces as protection. The group grumbled but complied.

Ideas were thrown out and rejected; new ideas were suggested. At one point, George said, "Hey, we got these shells. Isn't that enough?"

We quickly reached a point where we all felt frustrated, and Liam had shot down my latest offering.

Zabella brought up the next idea. "You say it's a matter of energy or power. This *WiWay* wants it, and you don't have enough to fight it."

"That's what he mentioned about a hundred times," Liam grumbled, still annoyed.

"What if we used the Accelerator to give *you* more power?" Zabella offered.

George interjected. "I thought we'd agreed that the Accelerator would give *Wee-wee* the edge."

"Yes, the way it's currently set up," Zabella agreed. "Right now, it's interfaced to read the machines in the room and recreate their output. But what if we changed the input?"

"Vat do you mean?" Fritz asked.

Zabella went on. "Instead of hooking it up to the measuring machines, what if we used the EEG helmet interface for the input while it's attached to Len?"

A murmur went through the group.

"Zabby, that's brilliant," Anna gushed, which made Zabella smile.

"Hold on, hold on," Liam said, considering it. "I think I could interface them together through the laptop. But what will that do to help us?"

"If our concept of how it works is correct," Zabella reasoned, "it should amplify Len's brainwaves and give him the edge he needs."

Lamar raised a hand. "But what if it does that possession thing, like it did to me? Then, *WiWay* would have Len's abilities to use on all of us."

Zabella thought for a moment. "Len, you said that circle on the floor protected you and Lamar yesterday, is that right?"

I nodded. "Yes, it's a ritual magic technique that creates a barrier of protection. That's how I got Lamar free from its influence."

"There's our answer," Zabella announced triumphantly. "We put Len in the circle and use whatever voodoo to make it a barrier while Len is attached to the Accelerator."

I looked at Fritz, who shrugged, then I spoke, "I think this might work."

"Yeah, but what if it doesn't?" Liam ventured. "Then we're all trapped in that house with that mind-possessing thing taking us over?"

"No," I stressed. "So far it has only taken possession of people who were psychic, like Haley or Lamar, or in Joey's case when the Accelerator was giving it all the juice it needed."

"Which makes me ask, why hasn't it gotten into your head?" George asked.

"I have no idea," was all I could offer.

Fritz spoke. "You vere there before and you communicated vith the trapped spirits of Elias Scudder and the others who died there."

I sighed. "Yes, but I didn't remember anything until you played the recording of what I said."

"Just like when we turned on the Accelerator," Liam mentioned. "You fell unconscious then and Lamar was possessed."

"But Lamar said we'd all die while that thing was using him," George fretted. "What if he gets taken over and tries to do it? With all due respect, Lamar, you covered yourself with gasoline and were ready to light yourself up like a Roman candle."

Lamar was annoyed at this. "So that's the other question. How did *'Wee-wee'* take me over and make me go to the house yesterday?"

"I can only assume it was because he'd already done so, from your time in the house. As far as having the power to do it, two people have died. Those sacrifices must have given it the ability to reach out."

"What can I do to not end up being his puppet?" Lamar worried.

"We keep someone near you at all times," I suggested. "Liam, can you shadow Lamar?"

"I would like to, but if we are going to make this plan work, once we get to the house, I need to focus on the machines."

George held up his hand. "I've got you covered, Lamar. In fact, it might be a good idea to have you outside with me at the generator."

Lamar looked from face to face. "I guess."

I stood and turned to the group. "So, we have a plan. The question is, when would be the best time to execute it?"

"I still vould recommend before dark," Fritz intoned, just as there was a knock at the door.

George was the closest so he went to open it.

We heard murmured voices and George backed into the room, followed by Detective Valentin with two uniformed officers: a tall brown-haired man who was skinny as a scarecrow and a short Hispanic woman who had her hands on her wide hips.

The detective cleared his throat. "We just came from the scene, and the police tape on the door was broken. Were any of you up there?"

I spoke up. "Yes, Detective, that was me. I had to retrieve some important data. Ms. Chou and Mr. Washington went with me." I gestured to Anna and Lamar.

This did not mollify Detective Valentin. "You understand we put up that tape to discourage people from entering a crime scene, right?"

"Sorry, Detective," I apologized. "I assumed since there was no active officer on duty at the location that it had been cleared."

Valentin eyed me suspiciously. "It's cleared now. You can go back. But with one less member of your group." He turned to George. "George Humphreys, you are under arrest for the murder of Haley Wolder. Please turn around."

George gave us all a panicked look but acquiesced. Valentin watched as the female officer fastened handcuffs on his wrists.

"Detective," I spoke urgently. "Mr. Humphreys told us that he was having a relationship with Ms. Wolder, which explains any DNA evidence—"

"Save it, Wise," Valentin commanded. "The medical examiner is still going over the body, but Mr. Humphreys is our prime suspect, and until we get those results, we are keeping him in police custody. We can release him if the findings prove negative." He turned to the officers. "Take him out!"

Fritz spoke loudly, "I vill contact the university lawyer, George."

"Better yet, I'll call Chuck Granger," I added. Chuck had gotten me out quickly, and since he was still in town, it was a good choice.

Valentin faced all of us and reached into his pocket to pull out a paper. "I was also asked to give this to you, Doctor Kohl." He handed Fritz the paper. "It's a court order. You are to vacate Scudder House by 6:00 p.m. tomorrow."

Fritz opened the paper and looked at it.

"The town has condemned Scudder House," Valentin said as he went out and closed the door behind him.

Fritz sighed, the paper in his hand. "It vould appear that tonight is all ve have."

16. CAST A LONG SHADOW

We all became very active at this point. Liam, Zabella, and Anna gathered in a corner with Liam in front of an open laptop. They tossed around ideas on how to make the interface with the EEG work.

Lamar and Fritz were talking about the practical side and writing a list of what we would need to bring: water, food, and clothing if the house became freezing.

I took out my phone and called Chuck.

He answered on the second ring. "Hey, Len, you're not in jail again, are you?"

"No, but one of our team members is. A kid named George Humphreys. He could use your help. I think they found his DNA on the dead girl."

"Oh my. Were they lovers?"

"He said they had an encounter right before she went to Scudder House just hours before she died."

"And he admitted that to the police?"

"Yes, he did, and he also told me they had taken a DNA swab."

"The same day that they detained you?"

"Yes."

"They did the processing pretty fast," he murmured. "Okay, well, the seminars today are terrible, so I'll take a run over. It's the Brisbane police, right?"

"Yes. Thanks, Chuck."

"Len, I'm going to have to send you a bill at some point."

I smiled. "Whatever you need, Chuck."

"I'll be in touch when I know something," he said jauntily and ended the call.

I walked over to the trio by the computer. "My lawyer friend is going to help George."

"That's good," Zabella remarked.

Liam looked up. "I think once we are on site, I should be able to make the adjustments."

"*We* will make the adjustments," Zabella corrected.

Anna spoke up. "I'm going to monitor the generator to make sure it's kept gassed and running. Lamar can help, and I can keep an eye on him."

"Great, just what I need, a babysitter," Lamar complained. "Doctor Kohl and I are getting supplies. Anything else we might need?"

The trio just shook their heads and mumbled in the negative.

"Yes," I chimed in. "Four white candles, chalk, a container of sea salt, and some kind of incense; Dragon's Blood if they have it."

"Dragon's Blood?" Anna repeated.

"It's actually a tree resin, but it's expensive. But cinnamon incense would work and should be easy to find."

Fritz nodded. "Do you really feel these things are necessary, Leonard?"

"You and I both know that these items stimulate the senses," I said. "But Haley was attempting a rite of ritual magic. It makes sense to use the items that she would use in her circle."

"Vhen Lamar and I get back, ve vill go," Fritz declared and headed out the door.

"Len, can I speak to you?" Anna asked.

"Oh, uhhh, sure," I replied, and she walked to my bedroom. I followed her, and she shut the door. "What is it?"

She pulled me close, got up on tiptoes, and kissed me, her soft mouth against mine. "I have to let you know one thing."

"That you like to kiss me?" I wondered.

"Well, I do, but that's not it. If this goes wrong, it could cause brain damage."

"What?"

"Theoretically. I mean, we're adjusting the Accelerator to your mind, your readings. In theory, it should increase your abilities, but there is the possibility it could cause a feedback loop, where your own mind is fighting you."

"I hadn't considered that."

"I've alerted Zabella and Liam, and they should be able to prevent it or shut it down if the readings suggest it is occurring."

"Good to know."

She pulled close and hugged her face against my chest. "You've gotta be careful, okay? I'd like you back with your brain intact."

"That's what I want as well."

We stepped back into the main room as Liam and Zabella talked over technical terms that I couldn't fathom. They both looked up and gave me a reassuring smile.

"Anna told me about the feedback thing," I told them.

They exchanged a glance, and Liam spoke. "It's only a possibility, and Zabella is going to observe the readings carefully."

"Okay, well, I don't have a better plan," I admitted.

"Neither do we," Zabella agreed.

"I'm open to anything, except my brain being fried." I headed back to my room and shut the door. I thought I should meditate, get myself into an altered state before going to face that thing.

I sat on the bed and focused on my breathing.

In… out. In… out.

I was not attempting to go anywhere or touch anything. In fact, it was the opposite. I wanted to do nothing but relax my mind, let go of tension, and just float.

It felt like only a few minutes later, but someone was shaking me back to consciousness. I slowly opened my eyes to see Anna's face directly in front of mine.

"We're ready," she said.

"How long was I meditating?"

"Not long. Twenty minutes. Feel better?"

"Calmer," I assured her, as I grabbed my folding cane from next to me on the bed and used it to stand up. "Are Fritz and Lamar back?"

"Yes, and ready to go to Scudder House."

I nodded and followed her out. We quickly got into several vehicles and drove off.

We arrived within minutes, the vehicles' engines dying against a backdrop of unnatural stillness. Overhead, a thick, charcoal canopy of clouds had swallowed the August sun, plunging the summer afternoon into a premature twilight.

The atmosphere felt heavy, almost liquid. In this part of California, the sky usually saved its gloom for the bone-chilling rains of January; an overcast day in late summer was a geographical glitch. I stared up at the swirling mass of gray, an icy knot tightening in my chest. This wasn't just a change in the weather. It felt deliberate, as if the house were exhaling its own darkness to shroud the hill in a metaphysical veil.

Anna and Lamar didn't hesitate and opened up the back of the white van, hooked up the big cable that sent the power to the house, and set about fueling and preparing the generator.

Liam, Zabella, Fritz, and I headed for the house, which looked even more ominous under the dark sky, the gray of the cut stones matching the heavy clouds.

We went up the steps, all of them several paces ahead of me as I took them one at a time. I had my mental barriers fully in place and clamped down in my mind. I wanted to make sure I let nothing in until we were ready.

As I came into the living room, Zabella was already holding the EEG helmet, and Liam was checking the laptop connected to the Accelerator. The wires from the cap connected to a small box, and one cable went to the laptop.

Fritz set a chair in the center of the circle. On the nearby mantel, he had placed the container of salt, a box of chalk, and the sticks of incense in a rectangular cardboard package. Haley's candleholders were lying near the hearth.

"Too soon for the chair, Fritz," I told him as I took the box of chalk, took out one piece, and bent to the floor to redraw the circle on the faded lines that were still there. It was difficult, since my frozen right leg forced me to balance myself with my left arm and left knee and draw with my right hand.

Doctor Kohl nodded and removed the chair as I continued to draw the circle, focusing on the places that the visit from the police had rubbed away the chalk.

As I drew, I spoke, "Fritz, if you can get candles in the candleholders and a stick of incense in that shell, please."

"Ve are lucky the police didn't take them away," Kohl said, and went to the mantle, grabbed the items, and began fitting each to its holder.

"The police probably didn't consider it evidence," I surmised. "By the time they got here, the candles burned out, and the candlesticks were no longer in the correct locations."

"Do you vant them at the cardinal points?" Fritz offered. "I can use the compass on my phone."

"That would help," I proposed, as I finished with the circle and drew over the five-pointed star.

While Fritz and I were busy on the circle, Zabella and Liam were doing tests on the EEG cap interface with the Accelerator and seemed pleased when they got the different computer chips to talk to one another.

The low, rhythmic thrum of the quarry machinery drifted across the hills, a mechanical heartbeat that seemed to pulse in time with the house itself. In the heavy silence of the afternoon, the sound took on a predatory edge.

It was a sudden, jarring realization: the excavators weren't just moving earth; they were jarring something loose. My mind flashed to the old *Ohlone* legends — whispers of a hollowed-out world, a vast, prehistoric cave system twisting deep beneath the foundation of this very hill.

The pieces were there, scattered across the table of my mind, but they didn't fit. A cold, prickling sensation crawled up the back of my neck. I was staring directly at the truth, but it hid in a fog I couldn't pierce. Something was down there, and the machines were screaming a warning I wasn't yet smart enough to understand.

I stood up straight as I finished the pentagram, and my mentor finished the placement of the candles at the four compass points. He handed me the chair, which I put in the center of the pentagram and the circle. I took the container of salt and slowly poured it as I walked around the circle a second time, tracing the chalk line.

"What does that do?" Zabella asked, glancing over to see what we were up to.

"According to which tradition you follow," I said, "salt can bind energy and act as a barrier. Since we are fighting an entity that likes to hide, I want something that will screw with its energy."

I pointed to the edge of the circle. "We need another chair there, where we can tape the cable from the EEG cap to the computer on its back. We don't want wires hanging down which could possibly move the salt or break the circle."

Fritz moved a second chair into position as Zabella handed me the cap. She then went to the box that had held the EEG equipment and got the bottle of saline solution.

"I'll need to place the electrodes," she insisted.

"Step carefully into the circle and be very watchful when you step out," I requested.

She nodded. With the cap in one hand and the cable held high in the other, she stepped into the circle as I sat in the chair.

Liam pulled out a roll of gray duct tape, and once Fritz had the second chair in place, he taped the wires onto the top edge.

Liam started. "Len, you don't have a lot of play in the wires, so I hope you won't start thrashing around."

"Not planning to, Liam," I soothed.

Zabella stood behind me, put the cap under one armpit, and sprinkled the saline solution into my hair and rubbed it in. "Sorry your girlfriend can't do this. I'm afraid I will have to do it."

"You're fine, Zabella," I replied. I had a desire to say that Anna wasn't my girlfriend. We had a delightful couple of days, but what was our actual involvement? Maybe 'friends with benefits?' An old crush that was finally fulfilled? A thirtyish man who had attracted a willing younger woman?

Zabella finished wetting my hair, being very careful not to let any drip to the floor where it might erase the chalk. She placed the cap on my head, even slower than Anna had, since Zabella was a novice. I faced the mirror over the mantel and watched as she progressed. She carefully placed the electrodes and soon was hooking the elastic under my chin.

"How are the readings?" she asked Liam.

"Testing the impedances," he noted, focused on the computer screen. "You'll want to adjust O2 and C4."

In the reflection, I saw her slip fingers under the cap in the back and move an electrode. Then she counted forward and jiggled one on the right side of my head back and forth into a better position.

"That's good," Liam approved. "I'm running the acquisition setup. You can step out."

She leaned close to my ear. "I know, step out carefully."

I smiled. "Thanks, Zabella."

Fritz gestured everyone away from the circle, and Zabella took a position behind a different computer station near Liam. Fritz lit the incense and then the candles, starting with the one facing north.

Once the candles were lit, he moved to join the others.

"Before we start, Zabella, can you check on Anna and Lamar?"

"Sure, Len," she said and ducked out the door.

"So, what's your plan?" Liam inquired. "When should I start the Accelerator?"

"I think the best time is when I am deep enough in my meditation," I suggested. "The other machines should show an increase in activity in the house."

"That vould be the most logical choice," Fritz agreed.

"Okay, we should start soon, Len."

Zabella stepped back into the room from outside. "They're fine, Len. Out near the van, watching the generator. Bored to tears, but fine."

"Okay," I said. "Then let's begin."

I focused on my breath and began to make it purposefully slow and deep. I released any fears or concerns I had as I focused on going deeper... deeper...

All at once, I was in the living room, though it was totally in sepia tones, dark and gloomy. I could see Liam and Zabella at their workstations and Fritz as he paced nervously. Behind them I could see the coil of the Accelerator, emitting a dull glow. It was not yet registering the vibrations of my brain waves, but it was warming up.

Where are you...?

I released the thought out like a wisp of smoke into the air.

I know you're here…

I floated around the room as effortlessly as the wind, gazing back to see my body as it breathed and my muscles twitched on their own. I had done this technique at another haunted house, and it was always interesting to see my body from the outside.

I could feel it, feel *him* hiding, waiting for a chance to strike. The presence pulsed methodically like a light in the distance. I moved to the basement door and passed through it into the cellar under the house.

In this state, there is no complete darkness, as I can perceive walls and archways, even with no light at all. I floated down the steps and into that domain, and I felt *him* even more.

He was indeed powerful, and this lightless vault was part of his domain. And yet, the basement didn't go deep enough. Someone kept this entity, whose true home was deep in the ground underneath us, confined here, preventing it from exceeding the house's limits.

I could sense him reach beyond his confines, sizing me up and preparing.

Then the Accelerator caught the frequency of my pulse, and the world dissolved. It didn't just amplify my mind; it mirrored it, catching the stray sparks of my consciousness and folding them back into a blinding, recursive loop of power.

I felt the brittle shell of 'Leonard Wise' crack and fall away.

Suddenly, the cold interior of the house was gone, replaced by a searing internal sun. My astral form didn't just glow; it detonated in a silent explosion of incandescent white. I could see myself — not as flesh and bone, but as a lattice of shimmering, woven lightning that pushed back against the encroaching rot of the room. I experienced an absolute, terrifying purity, as if my soul had distilled into a blade of light.

The entity, which had been a creeping oil-slick of shadow at the edge of my vision, recoiled. It had been tasting the air, reaching out with obsidian filaments to find the soft parts of my fear, but now it shriveled. It lashed back into the corners, shielding itself from the solar flare of my presence.

I reached out with my mind, and it wasn't just an attempt to touch another mind or a gentle opening of thoughts to me. I was a battering ram that pushed its way into the other consciousness, and it unfolded before me as if I had cracked open a walnut.

The entity — the thing we called WiWay — was no longer just a presence; it was moving, effecting change beyond the walls of its prison. My vision synced with it, and I could watch through it.

Outside, the unnatural August clouds hung like a low ceiling, pressing down on Anna. She stood near the van, a solitary figure against the gloom, her gaze fixed on the turrets of the house. She had just finished checking the generator and was standing still, trying to decipher the humming vibration radiating from the building.

I knew the exact slope of her shoulders in that moment because WiWay was watching her. It wasn't seeing her through the ether, though — it was seeing her through Lamar's eyes.

Those eyes panned toward the open back of the van. The generator roared, a mechanical beast feeding the house through the black umbilical cables. Lamar's gaze shifted downward, settling on a heavy rubber mallet resting on a toolbox. It was a common tool — a blunt, black cylinder of solid rubber — but through WiWay's lens, it looked like a prehistoric weapon.

Lamar's hand, moving with a jerky, puppet-like precision, closed around the handle. He looked back at Anna. She was still looking away, her back to him, vulnerable and unsuspecting. In one fluid, brutal motion, Lamar swung. The dull thud of rubber against bone echoed as Anna crumpled to the dirt.

Lamar didn't hesitate. He dropped the mallet, bent over her limp form, and ripped the sand dollar shell from her neck with a violent tug, tossing the protective amulet into the weeds like trash. He hoisted her over his shoulder with a terrifying, effortless strength — as if she weighed nothing — and began a steady, rhythmic march toward the shadows at the rear of the mansion.

With the power the Accelerator granted my mind, I felt as if it revealed everything to me. I could plainly see Lucy Scudder in 1894, in a pretty dress she wore for the day Scudder House opened. I could see her all those years ago as she stood on the hill and watched the fireworks as they exploded in the night sky over the San Francisco Bay.

They shot the pyrotechnics from a boat that her father had paid for. Fiery sparks whipped through the air, bursting above the crowd in the night, with brilliant slashes of light on a canvas of stars. The crowd 'oohed' and 'ahhed' as each shell exploded in amazing colors.

Lucy stood transfixed and took a step backward, and her leg caught in a small hole. But then the hole grew, and dirt fell away. It was a sinkhole, one that every land surveyor said could not possibly exist there.

As her legs sank below the surface, she reached out and pulled at the grass to free herself. She kicked her legs, which made the soil fall away farther and deeper. In mere moments, she was up to her neck, and she tried to scream, but the explosion of the display overhead muffled her cries. She fell deeper, and the loam covered up her mouth and head as she sank into the ground and suffocated.

That was the first death at Scudder House, which signaled the years of misfortune that would become a legend and the reason it lay empty for so many years.

Lamar was going to that spot to put Anna in the one place only this entity knew. He would pull her into the earth and have Lamar set himself on fire. And then the cycle would be complete.

Why? I demanded an answer from the mind I communicated with. *Why recreate the deaths of Lucy Scudder and Nat Hewing,..? What do you get from it...?*

Power...

The word didn't arrive as a sound; it was a cold, oily vibration that coated my thoughts. It was the only answer. But behind it, I tasted a frantic, jumbled subtext: the roar of quarry machines, a desperate blueprint for a physical escape, and a consciousness that was ancient and hungry, yet fractured — like a brilliant mind shattered into a thousand jagged pieces.

Then, a spike of cold reality pierced my trance. If I stayed in this form, Anna and Lamar were as good as dead.

I spun my astral form, shedding the impulse to dig deeper into the monster's origin. I needed to claw my way back to the stairs, back to the heavy anchor of my physical body, and get the team moving before events could unfold.

But as I reached the base of the cellar stairs, a wall of pure, malicious will slammed into me. It wasn't physical; it was a psychic blunt-force trauma that sent my spirit reeling, hollowing me out until I felt myself being pressed through the very molecular structure of the stone wall.

I fought back, wrenching my luminous form out of the masonry and back into the dark. There, the entity was no longer a shadow; it was manifesting as a roiling, charcoal cloud that pulsed with internal lightning. It crackled with a sick, ultraviolet light, an atmospheric storm contained within a nightmare.

It surged toward me, tendrils of static snapping at my heels.

"I don't have time for this," I snarled.

Channeling the raw, unfiltered current of the Accelerator, I thrust my incorporeal hands forward. Brighter-than-white light detonated from my palms, a solar flare that sent the storm-cloud shrieking back into the dark.

I didn't wait to see it recover. I vaulted up the stairs, passed through the cellar door, and slammed back into my body in the living room.

The transition was a physical blow. I gasped as my senses returned to the room — the hum of the laptops, the frantic typing of Zabella and Liam, and Fritz, his face pale and tight, hovering over my slumped, breathing body like a man watching a ticking bomb.

I knew what the next move for the possessed Lamar would be, and I had no time for subtlety. I moved into my body, and through the strength of conscious will, made myself take a deep breath and forced myself awake.

I sat up in the chair with a gasp, my eyes open, the darkened room lit by several work lights and the surrounding candles. My sudden movement startled Zabella and Liam. Fritz stared at me, knowing that to jump up from a deep meditation was not normal.

"Lamar!" I gasped. "You have to stop him!"

"What? Liam exclaimed, "What?" right when the power failed and the room went dark. The work lights went out, and the machines all died, except the laptop screens which remained lit, running off their own battery supply.

The only other light was the four candles that continued to burn in their holders at the cardinal points around my circle.

"Liam, it's Lamar. Stop him right now!" I bellowed and undid the elastic under my chin and carefully removed the EEG cap.

Liam sprinted for the door, followed by Fritz, as Zabella moved toward me but stopped outside the circle to reach her hands out and take the cap.

My hair was still wet from the saline solution. I pushed a hand through my hair to keep it out of my eyes. "Anna," I croaked.

She put the cap on the seat of the chair that had held the wires. "What about Anna? Is she hurt?"

"Yes," I grunted as I grabbed my cane and got to my feet. "She's in the back of the house, the spot with a view of the bay."

"How? Why?" she barked.

I stepped carefully out of the circle, and that's when I realized I hadn't taken the time to put my mental barriers in place.

The pain stabbed through my head, and I suddenly could sense the power of *WiWay* and all he could do. He was as old as time. When the Accelerator assisted me, it made me strong enough to confront him.

Now I realized I had pushed my way into only a small portion of his consciousness.

His disembodied mind struck back with all the power he possessed, fueled by the energy of death and destruction of thousands of years.

I crumpled to the floor.

"What is it!" Zabella demanded. "Where is Anna?"

"The hill," I rasped and pointed in the correct direction. "View of the bay... sinkhole..."

I knew Zabella had studied the history of the house to prepare for her work here and probably knew it better than I did.

She bolted for the door because, in that moment, she understood the danger.

I tried to focus my mind, put walls into place, but I still could not fight back. I used my cane to push myself to my feet. Then I did the only thing I could think to do and stepped back into the circle.

The effect was immediate. My mind was clear; the headache was gone. But I realized I had to go outside to help Anna and stop Lamar. Lamar had shut down the generator because *WiWay* had known it was the source of my added power. It was a good thing I noticed the entity's machinations, or I would have been fighting it in that dark basement without the additional strength.

I shut my eyes and walled up my mind with the strongest barrier I could conceive, stepped out of the circle, and headed toward the door, going as fast as my damaged leg would allow.

I stepped out into the dark afternoon and saw Lamar with a red can of gasoline in one hand and the rubber mallet in the other. He swung the mallet threateningly at Liam and Doctor Kohl, who were both out of reach of the weapon. They shouted at him, unsure how to subdue him.

I limped my way to the back of the house and saw a figure, waist-deep in the ground. As I drew closer, I saw *two* pairs of arms. One was scrabbling at the ground and actively attempting to get out, and the other pair was limp.

Zabella was sinking into the ground *with* Anna. "Len!" she shrieked as she saw me approach. "*Help!*"

I saw a sapling near the pair, and I thought for a moment I could anchor myself and reach out to them with my cane. But the cane I had brought was four tubes held together by elastic, so it wouldn't be strong enough.

Just a few feet away, partially buried in the damp leaf litter, lay a fallen oak limb—thick enough to act as a lever, yet weathered enough for me to handle.

"Hurry!" Zabella's voice was a jagged shard of panic. She was sinking, the earth swallowing her mid-thigh now, the hungry soil slipping away around her.

I didn't think. I let my cane clatter to the ground and lunged for the branch, my fingers stinging as I gripped the rough, peeling bark. I scrambled toward a spindly sapling at the edge of the collapse, the only anchor in a world no longer solid.

"Grab it! Now!" I roared. I wrapped my left arm around the sapling, the young wood groaning under my weight, and thrust the oak limb out over the void.

Zabella's hand shot out, her fingers clawing at the wood until she found a death-grip. She anchored herself to me now, but she refused to let go of Anna. She held the unconscious girl like a life raft in a storm, hauling her upward even as the ground beneath them hissed and dissolved.

The strain was tectonic. I felt the muscles in my shoulder bunch and scream, a hot, tearing sensation that threatened to pop the joint from its socket. I gritted my teeth against the white-hot flare of pain, my shoes skidding on the slick grass as the earth tried to claim all three of us.

Zabella hauled herself up the branch inch by agonizing inch, dragging Anna's limp weight with her. The soil continued to fall away in great, sickening gulps, a black maw opening wider by the second, but we were winning. I was pulling them back from the edge of the hill.

"Hold on!" I shouted. With all of my strength, I pulled myself to the sapling and wrapped myself around it, using both arms to pull the branch. The small tree bent dramatically from the weight as I gave one final yank of the large stick.

Zabella and Anna slid up onto the firmer ground, and Zabella crawled toward me, pulling the unconscious girl through the grass. I dropped the branch and dragged the stunned Anna free of the hole and slid her several feet away. Then I limped back and grabbed Zabella's hands to slide her over the grass to the safety of the sapling next to Anna.

A dark mud covered their clothing, suggesting the ground beneath them had liquefied and become slick and wet.

When all three of us were away from the opening, there was a sudden tremor. The ground under our feet shook, and the hole disappeared as it filled in with fresh dirt.

Except for the fact that the grass over the spot was missing, it looked as if there had never been a hole at all.

"That can't be natural," Zabella panted. "Sinkholes aren't frickin' quicksand."

I gasped for breath. My psychic efforts and the physical demands of the rescue exhausted me. "What happened? How did you fall in?"

"I came around the house to find Anna just lying on the ground," Zabella explained. "I got her up on her feet, and that's when the ground gave way."

"Could've lost you both," I wheezed and got my cane under me. We looked down at the unmoving Anna, who breathed steadily.

"She's not conscious," Zabella fretted.

"Try to revive her. I have to help with Lamar."

I pushed off with my cane and hobbled to the front of the house. I turned the corner to see Lamar sitting on the ground with Liam hugging him, and Fritz placing the gas can and rubber mallet back into the white van.

"Everyone okay?"

Liam looked up at me and nodded. He held a sobbing Lamar under one arm. "Yeah, when that tremor hit, Lamar just blinked and was himself again."

"Leonard," Fritz said, his face strained. "Are you all right? Where's Anna—"

"Good, I'm good," I said. "Anna is unconscious and—"

"Oh God, I killed her," Lamar wailed.

"She isn't *dead*!" I yelled, which made Liam and Lamar jump, and even Fritz turned to stare at me. "We have to get this place closed down and Anna to a hospital. We can cry about our troubles later."

Liam nodded, kissed Lamar's head, and got up, leaving Lamar to sit on the ground. "I got this," he said, and trudged up to the house.

Fritz eyed me cautiously until I nodded firmly to reassure him. "I vill roll up the cable and put it on the porch. It is going to rain."

"What should I do?" Lamar asked, wiping his face with one hand.

I spoke up. "Close up the van, give me the keys. How much do you remember of what you did?"

"I remember hitting Anna with the mallet," Lamar admitted with a stricken look.

"Well, my job right now is to keep an eye on you. Did you sabotage the generator?"

"I don't know…"

"Please look at it and make sure you just turned it off. If we want to attempt this again, we *must* have a working generator."

Lamar nodded and went to the machine, giving it a quick examination. "All the wires are the way they should be. It looks like I just turned it off."

"Good! Please lock it up."

Fritz pulled the heavy cable through the gap in the wrought-iron fence and laid it in loops on the porch under the cover of the overhang.

Thunder roared in the distance.

Lamar's gaze followed mine, tracking the way the charcoal clouds seemed to bruise the horizon, swirling in a pattern that defied every law of meteorology. The air had turned static, tasting of copper and old, disturbed earth.

"Something bad coming?" he asked, his voice barely a rasp against the unnatural wind.

I didn't look away from the sky. I could still feel the phantom hum of the Accelerator vibrating in my marrow, a warning bell that refused to go silent. The house behind us seemed to exhale a cold draft that smelled of the deep, forgotten caves below.

"Of that," I said, my voice as heavy as the storm, "I am absolutely certain."

17. PROBLEMATIC PHANTASM

Zabella, still covered in dark mud, insisted on driving Anna to the hospital. It was the same vehicle in which Anna had chauffeured me. I wanted to ride along, but I wouldn't be able to fit in the back seat.

I had seen the blow to the head she had received, and my medical training made me aware that Anna could suffer complications ranging from a simple concussion all the way to a hematoma. I doubted she experienced a skull fracture or a diffuse axonal injury, but it was best for her to be examined by professionals. They could run a Glasgow Coma Scale and determine how severe the injury had been.

It wasn't a good sign that she didn't regain consciousness. Lamar, Liam, and I had to lift her insensate body into the passenger seat of the car.

Her continued unconscious state could be the proximity of the entity. If so, I hoped that distance would remove its influence.

As Zabella drove straight to the hospital, Liam, Lamar, Fritz, and I rode back to the rented house in the minivan. On the drive, I thought about the momentary insight I had received about the quarry.

Over the years, machines had literally dug into the side of the mountain and exposed many veins of sandstone and shale. It had something to do with all this, but I couldn't imagine what.

Could the machines be approaching the place where the Shaman imprisoned WiWay a millennium ago? Perhaps the vibrations acted to awaken the ancient being from its long slumber. Could Scudder House itself, with its long history of misfortune, be calling to the creature as well?

More questions, while I had few answers.

Once we were inside the rented house, Lamar declared, "I'm packing my stuff and leaving."

This surprised the group, most of all Liam. "Why? What do you mean?"

"I'm a danger to all of you and to myself. That thing still wants me to set myself on fire, and now I've hurt someone. You can't trust me! I can't trust *myself*."

Liam stared at Doctor Kohl, who cleared his throat. "That might be for the best, Lamar."

Liam shifted his eyes from Fritz to me, and then Lamar. "It's not your fault." Liam moved to offer a hug, but Lamar sidestepped the embrace.

Lamar shook his head. "Doesn't matter. I'm compromised, and I don't have the skills to shut that thing down."

"I hate to admit it, but Lamar is right," I pointed out.

"This vill leave the team lacking," Fritz remarked sadly.

"Better that than another death," I pointed out. "When I went to help Anna and Zabella, you were fighting Liam and Doctor Kohl, but when I came back, you were yourself. Do you remember what happened?"

Lamar considered it. "Yeah, there was an earthquake or something. I mean, the ground shook, and then I was just me again."

Fritz looked at me. "Do you think it vas distracted by the tremor?"

"Or perhaps it had the power to create one," I considered. "While the Accelerator was on, I felt stronger than I can ever recall. Light filled me and I could reach out with my mind into the consciousness that is *WiWay*. I think that surprised him."

A roll of thunder cracked the air overhead, as if the sky might split apart. We all gazed up at the ceiling of the dwelling, silenced by the noise.

I considered the raw power of nature and worried about the wrath of the entity I had communed with. "I want to go to the hospital and see how Anna is," I announced.

"I can drive you," Liam offered.

"Then you can drop me off at the bus station in San Francisco," Lamar said. "Give me a few minutes to pack."

"That's like a ten or twelve-hour bus ride," Liam said miserably.

"The further I get from this place, the better off I'll be." Lamar looked at his friend. "I'll go pack."

"I'll help," Liam stated and followed Lamar down the back stairs.

"They might be a few minutes," I suggested. "They'll want to say their goodbyes."

"Ah, young people and their relationships," Fritz opined with a knowing smile. "Or should I not mention that around you?"

"I think you're trying to ask me something subtly, Fritz."

"Not subtle at all. I am concerned about you and Anna. Only a few short years ago, you vere her teacher, and now…"

He let the sentence hang for effect.

"Now, we are two lonely adults seeking some comfort with a willing partner. I wouldn't read too much into it."

"She vas not so lonely before you arrived. In fact, I might be an old fuddy-duddy—"

"Fuddy-duddy?" I repeated, surprised to hear that expression.

"But I have eyes. And Anna and Zabella vere becoming quite close. In fact, once Liam and Lamar got together, I expected her and Zabella to become the next couple."

I considered it. "Do you think I interfered?"

"I think you vere — and are — an old crush for Anna, and that she is still unsure about herself."

"She asked me to peek into her mind," I said.

He frowned. "She vanted you to do this?"

"Insisted on it. I have to say, she *has* a lot of feelings she's suppressing. Her attraction to Zabella is definitely one of them."

"And you recently had a breakup, correct?" Fritz stressed.

"Yes, but you know that."

"And you are concerned that the women you become involved with end up damaged?"

"Or dead," I said, trying to keep the concern out of my voice.

"*Ja.* Do you see vhat I am getting at?"

I frowned. "I'm afraid not."

"*WiWay* knew exactly where to strike to stop your assault on him. You had to force yourself out of your meditation to save Anna."

I considered this. "You think so?"

"It used your attraction to Anna and your fear of her getting hurt to stop you."

I stood there for a moment, trying to get my head around this. Fritz was right; I had an enormous fear of a woman I'd been involved with, slept with, getting hurt.

He went on. "Tell me what impressions you got vhen the Accelerator vas vorking."

I paced, my cane supporting me as I moved. "I think it's being held there, contained within that house, but is seeking a way to break free. That may have been why it allowed me to find the treasure there the last time."

"You think it *allowed* you to find the treasure?"

"I think it let the spirits trapped in that house use me," I said. "Perhaps it thought they would tear down the house after that."

"You believe that vould free it?"

"More and more, Fritz."

"Then how do ve finish this?"

At that moment, we heard Liam and Lamar walk up the hall, Liam helping to carry one of Lamar's two suitcases.

"We're ready to go?" I asked.

"I'm going to drop you at the hospital, Len, and then Lamar at the bus station," Liam grumbled, obviously not happy about the situation.

"It's for the best," Lamar claimed, not meeting anyone's eyes.

Liam turned away, tight-lipped, and Lamar sighed in frustration.

Fritz gazed at his young charges with sympathy. "I vill talk to Thomas Twofeathers vhile you are gone. Perhaps he can suggest something."

"Those damn shells didn't do shit," Lamar grumbled and headed for the door.

I stopped, and my eyes went to Lamar's chest. "You're not wearing yours. When did you take it off?"

Lamar frowned and his hand went to his neck, almost absently. "I... don't know. It must've been when I was checking the generator."

I moved over to Lamar and took his arm. "Lamar, please look me in the eye."

"Why?" he wondered and met my glance.

And I was in.

It was outside the white van, and Lamar recalled bending down and the rawhide strap with the shell slipped out of his shirt. The loop got caught on a small metal support that stuck out from the generator. When he stood, the knot on the cord came loose, and the sand dollar shell slipped off and fell to the ground.

Suddenly, Lamar's perspective changed; the day had an odd sepia tone. Lamar looked over at Anna, and he picked up the rubber mallet. In a few brief steps, he moved to the girl and delivered the quick blow that incapacitated her. He reached down and removed the charm from around her neck before he picked her up.

How did I not understand the importance of that before?

I broke contact, which left Lamar blinking in surprise.

"Wow!" Lamar marveled. "So that's what that feels like."

I looked up at Liam. "We need to stop at Scudder House."

"Are you sure that's a good idea?" Liam gasped.

"No, but that shell charm might help Anna," I offered.

Liam looked worriedly over at Lamar. "I'll stay in the car with you."

Lamar grunted. "That might help."

We quickly packed the luggage into the minivan and headed back toward the house.

The sky was dark with many shades of gray, like a thick woolen mantle blocking the setting sun. Colored hues on the August countryside seemed muted and dull, lifeless. I felt the air heavy with the dampness of a coming storm, and I could see no animals moving through the woods. It was as if the creatures knew it was best to seek shelter.

We pulled up the cracked roadway and stopped at the white van. As I stepped out onto the ground, I said to Liam, "Watch him, please."

Liam dutifully turned to his companion, and I hurried up the lawn, first locating Lamar's sand dollar necklace in the grass near the back of the van. I immediately retied the rawhide, adding several extra knots. Nearby, I found Anna's single round shell that Lamar had cast off her neck.

The energy around the house seemed to pulse, and I looked up at the sky where occasional lightning flashed from cloud to cloud. It was odd that it hadn't rained yet.

I got back into the minivan. "Everything all right?"

"I didn't kill him, if that's what you mean," Lamar offered sullenly. Liam turned the vehicle, and we started back down the hill.

I held out one necklace to Lamar, which he declined. "I don't need it. In an hour, I'll be far away from here."

Liam used the minivan's GPS and pulled onto 101 headed north as Lamar stared glumly out the window in the back seat. I put the charms into my pocket and found the fossilized shell still there. I again wondered what the connection was and how I could use it. It certainly had been no help in the crisis we'd faced.

Thomas Twofeathers had told me I would know when I was supposed to use it. I left the charms in my pocket, and my hand went to the necklace of shells I wore. I rubbed them for comfort.

We turned off the highway and pulled in front of the emergency room entrance for the Zuckerberg San Francisco General Hospital. I turned and shook Lamar's hand. "Thanks for helping."

"I'll try not to hurt anyone on the bus ride to Los Angeles," he murmured.

"I'll be back for you," Liam told me as I got out.

I walked into the front portico of the hospital, went to the security booth, and the guard on duty soon gave me a paper pass and instructed me on how to get to emergency services.

At the nurses' station in the Trauma Center, a friendly nurse directed me to a waiting area, and there I found Zabella.

She was sitting in a chair in a set of pink scrubs and white socks. Her mud-covered boots were on the floor next to her chair, beside a plastic bag filled with her filthy clothes.

Her hair, which she usually kept in a ponytail, now hung loosely around her face. I thought it might have been freshly washed.

"Zabella!" I said, and the girl started, looked up at me, and stood to give me a hug. She was taller than Anna, and her hug was fierce.

"Thank you," she whispered. "God, you saved my life."

"You saved Anna," I replied as I stepped back and looked at her.

"We both would've been goners if you hadn't been there."

"We got lucky," I told her, and then pointed at the pink outfit she wore. "These aren't your usual work clothes."

"A nurse took me to a shower and gave me these scrubs." Her nose wrinkled. "It's too girly for my tastes."

"You're allowed to be girly," I said.

"Well, I get dressed up occasionally. But *pink*? C'mon!"

I grew serious. "How is Anna?"

"Still unconscious, but stable. They're moving her to a different ward soon."

I noticed something that made my eyes grow wide. "Where is your necklace?"

"The shell thing?" Zabella asked. "I'm not sure. When I got undressed and showered, it wasn't there."

"Where do you think you lost it?"

"Could've been in the house. Hell, they might have done it when that *thing* nearly buried me alive. I-I don't know."

I pulled Lamar's small sand dollar necklace out of my pocket and offered it to her.

"Didn't do any good," she grumbled as she pulled it over her head.

"Can we see Anna before she's moved?" I asked as I brought out the large shell.

"We could try. Do you think the shell makes a difference?"

I examined the circular carapace in my hand. "It's hard to say. Lamar's got pulled off by accident, and it was only then that *WiWay* could use him. He took Anna's off her after he hit her."

She stared at the charm with renewed interest. "So you think it could help her now?"

All I could do was shrug. I didn't detect any special energy around it, but perhaps the protection it offered was too subtle for my enhanced senses. "I can't see any reason *WiWay* would have Lamar remove it unless it was a threat."

She nodded as if she had decided. "This way," she said.

She led me down the hall and into a large ward that was divided into many curtained enclosures.

Zabella quickly glanced around the room, and the pair of us slid behind the hanging cloth in one corner of the open space.

Anna lay on a bed with her eyes closed. An IV pole held a bag of clear liquid attached to a needle in her arm.

They removed her clothes, and she wore a hospital gown. They must also have washed her face, because I didn't see any of the mud that had covered her.

I paused, closed my eyes, and held the sand dollar shell between my hands. I moved my mind into an alpha state, then focused my energy on the charm.

After a moment, I took a deep breath and opened my eyes as Zabella watched me with suspicion. I carefully lifted Anna's head a little and hung the rawhide strip around her neck with the shell resting on her chest.

"Do you think it will help?" Zabella asked as I laid Anna's head down on the pillow.

At that moment, Anna drew a deep breath.

I turned to Zabella with a reassuring smile.

"Len!" Zabella whispered, and her eyes grew wide.

I looked back at Anna to see her blink a few times, and then her eyes opened. "What happened?" she gulped.

Zabella gave a small, strangled cry and bent down to hug Anna.

"Easy, please," Anna begged. "I've got a *terrible* headache."

Zabella pulled back, a bit embarrassed by her sudden outburst.

I spoke. "You're in the hospital. Lamar — well, *WiWay* — hit you with a rubber mallet."

Anna grimaced. "Are you sure it was rubber?"

"Yes," I assured. "But you might have sore muscles as well because the ground almost swallowed you up."

"Almost swallowed us both up," Zabella added excitedly. "Len saved our lives."

Anna squinted and looked at me. "Is this what happens to you all the time, Len?"

"Pretty much," I smiled at her, relieved that she could tease me.

"Damn," Anna muttered, heavy-eyed. "I want to sleep."

"We'll let you rest. You focus on getting well," I told her, and nodded to Zabella, who sighed and led us out and back into the hall.

"How did you do that?" Zabella asked as we headed toward the waiting room.

"Could have been the charm, could've been what I did, or it could've been time for her to regain consciousness."

"I think it was you," Zabella gushed.

We stopped walking as I turned to face her. "Can you come back to the house? We have to regroup and plan our attack."

She frowned and looked back down the hall. "Do you think Anna will be all right?"

I nodded. "I do, but I'd have to say she's out of the fight."

"So that leaves you, me, Liam, Doctor Kohl, and Lamar."

"I'm afraid not, Lamar left."

"I don't know if I blame him." She took a peek at her watch. "It's almost nightfall." She met my eyes as a realization dawned on her. "You're not thinking of going back to that house now, are you?"

"Yes. I have to, it's the only way."

We walked again and she asked, "How are you getting back to where we're staying?"

"Liam is picking me up in the minivan. He dropped Lamar off at the bus station."

"Then let me ride with you. There's a lot of mud in Anna's car. We'll need to clean it before anyone uses it again."

We stopped in the waiting room, and she put on her muddy boots and grabbed the bag with her clothes. We stopped at the nurses' station and told the on-duty nurse that Anna was awake.

We headed outside from the emergency wing to see the rented minivan idling nearby. I approached to see Liam tapping away on his smartphone. He peered up as we approached and looked a bit confused by Zabella's outfit. Then he pushed a button to unlock the doors, and we got in.

"Why aren't you driving Anna's car?" he asked Zabella.

"Full of mud," she explained simply. She then gave me a sidelong look. "Len wants us to go back to Scudder House."

"*Tonight*?" Liam blurted.

Zabella spoke up. "Len thinks we have to act immediately."

The silence that followed was broken only by the ticking of the cooling engine.

"Are you sure?" Liam worried and turned to me. "It kinda kicked our asses this afternoon."

"I know," I intoned. "But I think if we wait until tomorrow, we won't be able to stop it at all."

18. INCORPOREAL ENGAGEMENT

"**T**his is crazy!" Liam stated categorically.

We were standing around in the front room of the rented house. Zabella had changed into work clothes and pulled on a new pair of sneakers after cleaning the mud off her feet. Doctor Kohl was sipping coffee as Liam and I argued.

"Guys, we're here to discuss options," Zabella pointed out.

"Why would we try again?" Liam exploded. "We tried, it beat us and almost killed Lamar, Anna, *and* Zabella! Now there's thunder and lightning, and soon it will rain."

"Yes," I said and kept my voice calm. "I believe the storm is on purpose."

"How does a rainstorm have anything to do with this?"

"It's the lightning," Fritz spoke up, which made all of us turn to him. "It vould strike the highest point on that mountain. Liam, do you know vhere that is?"

"Sure," Liam replied, a bit cowed because it was his teacher who posed the question. "Those would be the cell towers. But what's the big deal? They're built with conductors that ground any lightning."

"*Ja*, and where does that electricity go?" Fritz asked, one eyebrow lifted.

"Into the ground," Liam grumbled as he looked at all of us. "So what? So the electricity goes into the ground. What's the big deal?"

"That vould be the ground vhere the entity is trapped, vouldn't it?" Fritz stated.

The room fell silent.

I felt a chill run up my spine. From the looks on the others' faces, they had a similar experience.

I was the first to speak. "*WiWay* is looking for energy, for power."

Fritz nodded. "Exactly. Lightning strikes into the ground vhere the Shaman trapped him. Energy he vould need if he vishes to be free."

Zabella stared at Doctor Kohl. "You think that storm's going to give him the power to break free? Tonight?"

Liam spoke up. "So *what* if he breaks free? We collect our machines and get the hell out of here. Let Brisbane deal with it."

"There vas a reason they imprisoned him," Fritz insisted.

"Doctor Kohl is right," I said. "We don't know what an entity of this strength could do."

"I'll give you a clue, Len," Liam fumed. "It could kill *us*."

We all fell silent again because, ultimately, Liam was right.

Finally, I cleared my throat and said, "So, Joey and Haley died for nothing?"

"That's not fair," Liam complained.

"Yes, it is," Zabella snapped. She turned to Fritz. "Doctor Kohl, what should we do?"

Fritz looked from person to person and then sighed. "If it vere other circumstances, I vould urge caution, take some time, learn vhat we can—"

"There you go," Liam agreed.

"However, this is a dire situation," he stated plainly. He faced me, and I saw a look of pride in his eyes. "I also know and trust Leonard. He has a remarkable gift, far beyond any other student I have ever had. His insights come from a place I cannot fathom." He took a few steps away, then turned to us. "I have taught that the paranormal is real and can affect people's lives, for good or ill. If Leonard believes ve must stop this entity tonight, then ve should help him and do vhat ve can.

I smiled at my mentor and friend. Before I met him, I thought the visions and flashes of the future were a curse, but with his help, I learned to use them to save lives. It was good to know that he believed in me.

I looked at Zabella and Liam. "I can't run the Accelerator on my own, even if I wanted to. That machine can give me the power to stop it, but it *has* to be tonight."

Liam looked at the floor and mumbled, "How can we work the generator? I mean, if it rains?"

Fritz spoke up. "I can run the generator. I vill back the van close to the fence around the house. It vill be better to keep the vires from getting vet."

I nodded. "Lamar was in control of himself, as long as he wore that shell given to us by Thomas Twofeathers. It accidentally got caught on something and fell off, and that's when *WiWay* moved into his mind."

Fritz stepped back to the island counter. "I spoke vith Thomas. After he left here, he claims he had a vision."

"Do tell," I urged him.

"He said that he saw you, Leonard, vearing a bonnet of eagle feathers. You took up a ceremonial spear to fight a foe made of stone."

"Pretty good so far," Liam offered.

"Thomas said the spear vas knocked from your hands, not once, but twice."

"Oh good," I grumbled, not happy with this prediction.

"But then, he said you transformed into coyote, the great trickster, and took the spear in your mouth to shove it into your enemy's chest."

"What happened then?" I asked hopefully.

Fritz shrugged. "Thomas said that vas vhere his vision ended."

"Not very helpful," Liam said. "Len, can you transform into animals?"

"That would be convenient," I countered. "But no, that isn't part of my skill set."

"Consider this," Zabella interjected. "The mighty war bonnet could be the EEG cap. The electrodes make it resemble a Native-American headdress… a little."

"If we can get me a ceremonial spear, that might help as well," I lamented and held up my folding cane. "I don't think this is going to cut it."

"Are we *really* going to do this?" Liam said. "It's like, eight o'clock at night already."

"Then ve should move out, now," Fritz ordered, and we gathered water, backpacks, flashlights, and anything else we could think of.

I looked over my three companions: they were all nervous, including Fritz, but I could see the determination in their eyes.

We soon piled into the minivan, and with the headlights on, Liam directed it toward the location of our confrontation. We soon turned off Quarry Road and onto the dark lane. The night rode in on a horse of pure black velvet, without either the stars or the moon to illuminate our way.

We parked near the white van, and with the minivan headlights still lighting the path, Fritz backed the white van up to the wrought iron fence that surrounded the house, just far enough away to open the rear doors.

Liam then parked close to the porch, and we exited the vehicle, clicking on flashlights to light our way. Liam and Fritz worked on getting the generator going as Zabella and I went into the house.

Despite the sultry summer night and the moist air of impending rainfall, the house was cold. It was as if all pretense had fallen away and the entity no longer felt the need to hide. It would have its power, and it would revel in it.

Beyond my mind, carefully walled away by mental barriers, I could sense the trapped former residents. And there were new voices: Haley and Joey had joined the group with the desire to break free of the prison this structure had become.

And I was about to take on the warden.

I heard the roar of the generator much closer than on previous visits. One reason they set up the generator down the hill and used the long cable was to prevent the noise and vibrations from affecting the machinery that noted any subtle changes in the environment. Now, we dropped all artifice as well.

We had only one task to do here tonight.

As the work lights came on in the room, Zabella booted up the computers. I rose to my full height as I heard another noise in the distance that seemed out of place.

"Zabella," my voice echoed dully in the room. "Come with me."

She glanced up from the screen with a puzzled look, rubbed her arms to warm herself, and then followed me out the door.

As we passed the white van, Zabella yelled to Liam. "Bring coats and gloves! It's colder than a witch's tit in there."

He gave her a 'thumbs up' sign, then yelled back. "Where are you going?"

She opened her arms. "Don't know."

I walked to the crest of the hill, being careful to avoid the spot that had gripped the ladies a few short hours ago, and peered down toward the quarry.

Zabella caught up to me. "What is it? What's wrong?"

I held up one finger. "Do you hear it? In the quarry?"

"Yeah, it sounds like machines, a bulldozer or something."

I nodded. "Do you see any headlights?"

She gazed down into the large, open pit and the many roadways carved into the earth over the decades. "I see something moving over there, heading towards the hill," she said and pointed at a dark shape far away that ambled slowly toward our mountain. "It's probably just some guy doing overtime."

"With no lights on?"

She turned to face me, her eyes wide. "Do you think it's *WiWay*?"

I nodded slowly.

"But where is he getting the power to make the machine operate?"

There was a flash of light and another roll of thunder overhead. "Any other questions?"

"But *why*? Why does an ancient monster need a bulldozer?"

"You might ask why an entombed creature would want a shovel."

"To dig itself out," she murmured. She grabbed my arm and pulled me. "Come on, we have to hook you up and get the machines going."

There was another bright flash and a streak of pure white crackled down from the menacing blanket of gray. It brightened the hot silver clouds with its blinding incandescence as the bolt connected with the cell tower at the top of the nearby peak.

The energy flashed over the outside of the tower and into the ground just as the thunder roared as if to split the air. Zabella ran on ahead as I looked in on Fritz. He had put plastic sheathing over the open back doors of the van and taped it in place with duct tape. He replaced his shoes with rubber boots and wore a clear plastic raincoat.

I stopped and smiled, and he drew near. He needed to speak loudly over the roar of the generator. "Leonard, I vish I could be there vith you."

"I do, too," I shouted back.

"I vill keep the power on. Do your best. Remember everything you've learned."

I patted his back and continued up the steps and into the house.

Liam was now inside with Zabella, both of them running diagnostics on the machines and wearing heavy coats and gloves. I could feel the cold seep into my bones. This is how I remembered Scudder House. The cold not only in the atmosphere, but a cold that reached into one's soul and froze the blood.

"George's coat is over there in the corner," Liam called out, pointing to several pieces of outerwear. I limped over and pulled on a very large winter coat. It was made for the much wider George, but the sleeves were long enough for me.

I found gloves in the pockets and decided I would put them on once everything was in place.

I relit the candles on the four cardinal points around the circle, and then I took two sticks of incense, put them in the abalone shell, and lit them as well.

I carefully stepped into the circle and verified that the lines and salt remained undisturbed, as moving them would break the protective charm.

I sat in the chair as Zabella stepped in behind me. "Ready for your shampoo and cut?" she joked as she held out the bottle of saline solution.

"Just the shampoo. I'm feeling a bit salty."

"Nice to know you haven't lost your terrible sense of humor," Zabella jibed, as she poured the cold liquid onto my head. I hissed in shock. "Sorry, we left it in the house, which is much colder than it was earlier."

"It's manifesting," I explained. "As he reaches out—"

"I know, the metaphysical effects cause a sudden decrease in ambient temperature. I studied with Doctor Kohl as well, you know."

I grinned as she rubbed the saline into my head and affixed the cap, adjusting the electrodes as she went. I could watch her easily in the mantel mirror.

"How's it going, Liam?" she asked, correctly placing each electrode and making sure they contact.

"The impedances look good. How are you, Len?"

"Chilly," I answered and pulled the gloves over my hands. "But I can be ready when you are."

Zabella leaned close to my ear. "Good luck. Kick his ass for Anna."

I nodded, and Zabella stepped carefully out of the circle and to her workstation.

"Once the acquisition setup is complete, we are good to go," Liam said. He moved over to the Accelerator and checked the connections.

I glanced at the candles on the four cardinal points, inhaled the fragrance of the nearby incense; and focused on the surrounding circle.

I closed my eyes and put my attention on my breath and began to set my mind free. I felt myself go deeper as Liam and Zabella observed the changes in the instruments.

I separated into my astral form, and soon I stood in the room, unencumbered by my cane and my bad leg. I stepped to the edge of the circle and glanced back at my insensate body in the chair with the cap on my head.

"Activating the Accelerator," Liam said, which got a quick nod from Zabella.

The coil on top of the box glowed, and light enveloped my spiritual body. I was almost surprised that the radiance did not blind Liam and Zabella, but it was invisible to them.

I floated past the circle and headed for the cellar door. I knew that whatever waited, waited down there.

There was a flash outside the windows, and a crash of thunder made my team members flinch.

I wasn't the only one charging up for this confrontation.

I passed through the door and moved down the lightless stairs. The outer walls were constructed from quarry rock, thicker than those of a medieval castle. Multiple brick archways built around the supports divided the space into separate rooms. I moved toward the vault, which stood behind a false brick wall.

I tried to remember the old photograph of the house foundation when it was dug, and the odd oblong stone that had risen from the ground. If you were going to imprison something bad, wouldn't it make sense to mark the spot with something big to warn away the unwary?

I looked around the sandstone walls, knowing that the ancient obelisk, although carved to be square, had to be rougher and larger still than the enormous stones that made up the walls.

I tried to place the old photo in conjunction with the surrounding building, but in the old picture it had only been an open pit, except for the stone that they built the house around. And where could you possibly hide a half-buried obelisk?

I looked at the false wall and the open vault I had found, with the treasures that had remained hidden down in this subterranean man-made cavern for so long.

The living room was right above me, and I recalled Zabella telling me that when the energy manifested, the sensors had shown the focal point was the front room and the basement under it.

The vault came out from the true wall, but what was behind the metal safe?

Unencumbered by the limitations of a solid form, I drifted to the vault door, then right through it, passing through the door, the shelves, and the back wall of the old vault.

Behind it, there stood the huge, ancient stone.

It had to be six feet thick and solid sandstone. In that moment, I understood why it had been easier to build the house around it than to remove it, as it rose through the ground and continued up to the floor of the room above me. In one quick revelation, I understood this stone formed the bottom of the firebox and the hearth of the vast fireplace one floor above me.

A symbol carved into the stone right below the ceiling caught my attention. This symbol seemed to possess its own power and glowed with a faint light.

I gazed at the carefully crafted design of a sand dollar. *Dendraster excentricus,* I thought, as I recalled my basic biology. But this design had more meaning, like the fact that Thomas Twofeathers gave us the actual exoskeletons of the animal with their five delicate petals so similar to the five-pointed star, the pentagram, a symbol of ancient power.

This design had an older history, one from the ancient people who once lived here, and had a hero named *Kaknu,* about whom they created many legends.

The ancient shaman had positioned the stone here and blessed it with this design to imprison *WiWay.*

That is why he wanted the house destroyed.

It made sense. It drove the people to destroy themselves as tools to bring about the destruction of the house and this special stone. That is why the monster brought such terror and was so angry at the inhabitants.

It wanted to be freed.

There was an explosion of thunder above me, and the entire house shook with it. In my incorporeal state, I rose through the floor and into the living room to see that Liam and Zabella were fine, and the Accelerator still put out its power.

"That was close," Liam worried.

Zabella glanced with concern at my insensate body. "Do you think he's having any luck?"

Liam shook his head, his face a mask of pale indecision.

Before he could speak, the front door burst open. Fritz stumbled in, his breath coming in ragged, wet gasps. His eyes were wide, the pupils blown into black saucers of pure terror.

"There is a bulldozer," he choked out, pointing a trembling hand toward the darkness outside. "Coming toward the side of the house. It's coming fast. It's going to—"

He never finished the sentence.

A sound like a tectonic plate snapping roared through the structure. The impact was cataclysmic: a violent, grinding shriek of metal meeting stone that rattled the house to its ancient marrow. The impact tossed my team like scrap wood; Zabella and Liam were hurled across the room, their bodies hitting the scarred paneling with sickening thuds. Tables upended, and delicate monitors shattered against the floor, spraying glass like shrapnel.

Then the wall itself groaned and surrendered. A massive wrought-iron fence post, jagged and rusted, punched through the brick and lath with a violent explosion of dust. It hissed through the air like a spear thrown by an invisible giant, embedding itself three feet deep into the floorboards just inches from where Fritz stood.

In the center of the chaos, my physical body sat slumped in the chair. It lurched with the shockwave; my head lolled to the side like a broken doll's. Yet my eyes remained shut, trapped in an Accelerator-induced coma.

In my astral form, I hovered over the wreckage, my heart a pulse of pure adrenaline. I looked at the machine — the Accelerator was still humming, its copper coil glowing with a defiant, thrumming violet light. Despite the carnage, the umbilical cables held. The connection was still live.

But *WiWay* wasn't just knocking; he was tearing the door down.

"Who did this?" yelled Liam, as he rose, coughing. "Who drove that thing?"

"I don't know!" Fritz coughed as plaster dust rained down upon us all from the ceiling and created a smoky mist of airborne particles.

I slipped through the vibrating atoms of the wall, my spirit-self spilling out into the night.

The scene was a chaotic tableau of twisted metal and rising dust. The bulldozer sat stalled against the defiant stone of the perimeter, its yellow paint scarred and its steel frame mangled where it had met the wrought iron. Sections of the spear-tipped fence lay scattered on the dead grass like discarded bones.

Then came the sound — a rhythmic, mechanical pulse. *Beep... beep... beep.*

The massive vehicle crawled backward, the sound of its treads grinding over the wreckage like teeth on gravel. It wasn't retreating; it was pacing itself, drawing back for a second, lethal charge.

It was a monstrous thing — a titan of the quarry, built to move mountains. Its blade was a jagged slab of reinforced steel, and its tires were massive, six-foot walls of rubber that had crushed the hillside to reach us.

In my heightened energy state, the darkness peeled away, but the driver remained a mystery. A roiling, slate-gray cloud had coalesced inside the glass-walled cab, pulsing with an internal, sickly phosphorescence. It was a cocoon of psychic static that shielded the operator from my sight.

I understood then why the cellar had been so quiet. WiWay hadn't been hiding; he had relocated. He had poured the entirety of his ancient, fractured malice into the man behind the controls.

The first strike had been a test, a brutal shearing of the iron skin that protected the house. But the path was clear now.

The bulldozer roared, the engine screaming as it shifted into gear, the massive blade lowering like a guillotine. If that steel lip hit the stone foundation at full speed, the living room would fold like parchment.

The falling masonry would crush my team, the machines, and my own vulnerable, breathing body.

I reached out to the cloud and fought to touch the consciousness that resided within.

WiWay, come forth and face me...

I held out my hands and focused. The Accelerator was giving me all the force I needed, and beams of light flashed through my outstretched arms and into the cloud that surrounded the driver's cabin.

The cloud vanished.

Behind the wheel, his eyes looking straight forward, was George Humphreys.

I floated a foot above the ground, stunned. How did George get here? I had thought he was still in jail! I wanted to call out to him, to tell him to stop, but I wasn't in a body that could do those things.

"George! George! You must stop this!" a voice yelled.

I looked over to see Fritz running toward the machine, waving his arms to get attention.

There was another flash of lightning, and thunder rolled overhead. I saw the bolt of electricity strike the cell tower and go harmlessly into the earth.

Or perhaps not so harmless.

Without warning, a gray cloud shot out of the ground as if expelled from a cannon. It blasted against my astral body and surrounded me, firing small bolts of lightning that I could feel as jolts that shocked me.

I heard a voice shout, "Len, *Len*!"

I knew it was Zabella yelling, because I was sure my real body had reacted to what my nonphysical form was experiencing and had bounced about in the chair.

Then I heard Liam shout to Zabella, "Stay out of the circle! Focus on the machines."

The bulldozer moved again, making that shrill beeping sound as it backed up to gain more momentum.

I concentrated to allow the energy that was building within me, aided by the Accelerator, to shine forth and push away the cloud. It flew back to the bulldozer and George.

I could sense the ethereal mind as he probed me, and I probed him as well. Anything to stop his influence on George.

I learned of his history, as images and knowledge sped through my mind. He was indeed old, older than I could have imagined. He had enslaved ancient peoples who worshipped him as a god. They sacrificed prisoners in his name and bowed down to him.

One day, a medicine man of great strength learned how *WiWay* controlled the people and their desire to be free. He imprisoned *WiWay* in a cave deep in this land with a great stone obelisk on top of him, binding him.

With his own hand, the healer and the tribe shaped the top of the stone to make it square and carved the symbol of the sand dollar, which was a powerful token. Then, over many years, the natives raised a shell mound to bury the entity and the ancient stone completely, and to warn others of the danger.

But *WiWay* did not depart.

He slept, barely aware of the changes and the passing of time. One day he sensed the land being cleared and desired for the builders to break the stone and allow him his freedom. He wanted to return to the world, find worshipers, and gain power through new sacrifices.

But the builders left the enormous stone in place and built the new structure around it. This angered *WiWay*, and he reached from the ground to curse the owners and have his vengeance on them.

He had limited powers, but he could open the ground. He used this ability to reach up and pull the little girl into the soil — the first human sacrifice in a millennium. Her death gave him more strength so he could reach out to torment the residents, who in the depths of despair killed themselves and gave him even more power.

In the last few days, he'd had two deaths to strengthen him and the power from the Accelerator when Joey had first used it. Now he was strong enough to call the very lightning down from the sky, as he had done in ancient times.

I projected my thoughts at him.

You can let go. You can become one with the eternal…

I was tiring. I cannot stay in astral form for long, as it burns through my personal power, even in this case, aided by the Accelerator.

Everything was unfolding in a blur of mechanical roar and psychic static. The bulldozer ground to a halt at the edge of its arc, the engine screaming as it prepared to pivot into a lethal forward trajectory.

Before the gears could engage, Fritz appeared like a ghost in the machine's shadow. He lunged at the behemoth, his fingers catching a metal step as he hauled himself up the side of the shaking cab.

He grabbed the handle of the compartment door, wrenching at it with a desperate, white-knuckled strength, but the latch held firm, sealed by more than just metal. Fritz hammered his fists against the reinforced steel, a frantic percussion against the roar of the engine.

"George!" he screamed, his voice raw. Inside the glass, George sat like a statue, his eyes fixed on the house, deaf to the world.

Desperate, Fritz swung himself around to the front, clinging to the frame and plastering himself against the windshield to block George's view.

George blinked. The haze in his eyes shifted, but it wasn't a return to clarity — it was an awakening of something ancient. He turned his head slowly, and the look he gave Fritz was one of cold, predatory malice.

With a sudden, violent shove, George kicked the door open from the inside. The heavy metal slab caught Fritz square in the chest, launching him off the machine like a rag doll. He hit the churned-up earth with a sickening thud.

Unfazed, George gripped the gearshift with both hands, slamming it into position and stomping the accelerator to the floor.

The monster lurched. The earth beneath it groaned as the massive treads found purchase, surging forward with a terrifying, inexorable weight.

My astral gaze snapped to the house. The bulldozer wasn't just aiming for a wall; it was moving towards the massive, prehistoric hearthstone that anchored the foundation.

If that stone cracked, the great fireplace would collapse inward, bringing three floors of masonry down directly onto Zabella and Liam, the Accelerator — and my body.

The truth was finally apparent from the exterior. There, etched into the ancient sandstone block, was the faded, circular geometry of a sand dollar — a sigil of binding. This side of the stone had been weathered by a century of salt air, while its twin remained pristine and hidden behind the vault.

This was the anchor. This stone was the cage that held WiWay in the dark, and it was the one thing he had to shatter to be free.

I knew that while in astral form, my physical body could sustain damage in my absence, and I might be unable to return. Which could mean *I* would be the one to join with the eternal.

With focused will, I abandoned the outdoors and slammed myself back into my flesh. It was a violent, amateurish reentry — like being shoved through a keyhole into a suit of lead. My nervous system screamed at the sudden, jarring weight of bone and blood. This was the second time today I had forced the transition, and I could feel my heart stuttering under the strain.

My eyes snapped open. I bolted upright in the chair, my face a mask of pale agony. Zabella and Liam froze, staring at me as if I had just risen from the grave.

"Get down!" I croaked, the words tearing at my throat.

I rolled out of the chair, my dead leg dragging behind me like a lead weight. Lunging across the floor, my fingers trembled as I reached for the north-facing candle — the first seal. I blew it out; the smoke curling into the air, and scrambled toward the eastern taper—

Then the world became sound and fury.

The explosion wasn't a bang; it was a rhythmic, grinding roar as the stone foundation gave way. The wall above the fireplace buckled inward at an impossible angle, the ceiling groaning as plaster and ancient lath rained down like jagged hail, burying the machines.

The massive stone mantle, a thousand pounds of dead weight, heaved upward, lurching two feet into the air as the bulldozer's blade bit deep into the house's spine.

I looked up from the floor, paralyzed, as the massive six-foot mirror slanted toward me. It hung there, suspended by a prayer, a shimmering wall of glass and silver that threatened to fall and slice me into ribbons.

Miraculously, the old mounts held.

A thick, suffocating fog of white plaster dust erupted, turning the room into a ghost-landscape. I couldn't see the others; I couldn't even see my own hands. Coughing, my lungs burning with a century of powdered lime, I clawed my way upward. Chunks of lattice and heavy stone fell from my shoulders as I tried to find my footing in the ruins.

Someone was coughing.

I used my cane to push myself up. The EEG cap was still on my head, and I undid the chin strap and pulled it off. On the floor, falling debris had broken the circle of salt. It might have helped against spiritual attacks, but was useless against a bulldozer.

The mantle leaned into the room, and I realized George hadn't smashed through the wall because he hit the thickness of the stone mantle and chimney, which gave us some extra protection.

Outside, I heard the ominous *beep... beep... beep* as George and *WiWay* reversed for another go at the ancient stone.

"Zabella?" I croaked. "Liam? Are you all right?"

"Yeah!" I heard Liam, though I couldn't see him in the choking cloud of plaster dust.

"Guys?" a female voice moaned. "I think I'm in trouble."

I stepped carefully through the room, navigating piles of fallen plaster. Another shape appeared ahead of me, which I recognized as Liam. He was caked in dust from head to foot, a minor cut bled from his forehead, and the look in his eyes bespoke the fear in his heart.

"What the hell?" he slurred.

"Where's Zabella?" I grunted.

"*Here*," came another moan.

I stumbled through the white-out, my hands sweeping the air. I found Zabella pinned beneath the wreckage of her own workstation. The heavy spectrometer, a solid block of steel and glass, had toppled during the impact, its weight anchoring her right leg to the floorboards. Above her, the ceiling continued to shed lath and plaster, clattering down like brittle bones.

"Liam, over here! Help me!" I roared, my voice thick with dust.

Liam emerged from the haze like a specter. Together, we gripped the edge of the industrial desk. We heaved, our feet skidding on the grit, until the crushing weight shifted just enough. As we cleared the machine, more of the wall crumbled away, burying the spot where her leg had been just seconds before.

We hauled her to her feet. She was unrecognizable — a statue of pulverized lime and grit. The white powder had turned her clothes, her skin, and even her dark hair into a ghostly, monochromatic mask. Only her eyes, wide and darting with shock, showed any sign of the woman beneath the debris.

"My leg," Zabella groaned, her voice tight with a pain that cut through the adrenaline.

"Is it broken?" I asked, trying to find a solid grip on her arm through the slick coating of plaster dust.

"I don't know, but I can't put my weight on it," she hissed, her face contorting as she tried to shift.

Outside, the mechanical heartbeat resumed. *Beep... beep... beep.* The monster was positioning itself for the coup de grâce.

"We have to get out of here," I said, the urgency sharp in my chest. "Now!"

"But the equipment! Our data!" Liam's eyes darted wildly around the wreckage, his hands hovering over shattered monitors as if he could stitch them back together with his bare hands.

The beeping stopped.

The sudden silence was more terrifying than the noise. We didn't wait for another word. Liam and I each hooked one of Zabella's arms over our shoulders, hoisting her up between us. We lunged toward the door, our path a treacherous gauntlet of splintered lath and rusted nails that stood up like jagged teeth from the floorboards, ready to spear through our shoes.

In the distance, the engine roared — a deep, guttural howl as the driver slammed it into gear. We struggled forward, a clumsy, three-legged animal. Zabella grunted with every jarring step, and my own crippled leg buckled under the combined weight, but terror provided its own momentum.

We reached the threshold just as the vehicle charged. I threw a glance over my shoulder and saw the Accelerator's violet coil vanish beneath a fresh cascade of falling masonry. The link was dead.

We barreled through the front door and down the porch steps. I didn't care about grace; I threw us off the landing, diving for the dirt and praying we didn't impale ourselves on the twisted remains of the wrought-iron fence.

Then it was as if the world ended.

The bulldozer slammed into Scudder House with a cacophony of screaming metal and pulverizing stone. It didn't just hit the wall; it inhaled it, the massive yellow frame disappearing entirely into the belly of the house. The ground beneath us buckled as the structure groaned in its death throes. Windows shattered outward, raining glass like diamonds into the dirt, and the house twisted on its foundations. Copper gutters ripped free, clattering down like discarded armor, before the entire side of the mansion folded inward with a sickening, heavy thud.

A pressure wave of white plaster dust erupted from the open doorway, a choking, blinding fog that swallowed us whole, turning the night into a ghost-white void.

19. CRYPTIC MENACE

We stumbled blindly through the grit, our eyes stinging and throats raw. Every breath felt like inhaling ground glass as the plaster dust coated our lungs and turned our nostrils into masks of dry, white clay.

We finally reached the van — a refuge in the gloom. All three of us slumped against its cool metal side, our bodies wracked by deep, rattling coughs that tasted of a century's worth of rot.

Out of the fog, Fritz appeared like a ghost. One side of his face was a swollen, purple bruise where the bulldozer door had caught him, and he dragged his left leg behind him, the foot trailing uselessly in the dirt.

"I tried to stop him!" he yelled, his voice cracking with a mixture of agony and failure. "The fall — I broke my leg."

The house was still settling behind us — a series of heavy thuds as the interior collapsed — but there was no time for mourning.

"Liam, kill the power! Now!" I commanded, my voice gravelly. "Fritz, can you drive?"

Fritz spat a glob of white phlegm into the dirt. "I can. My right leg is still good."

Liam shifted Zabella's dead weight onto me, my shoulder screaming at the sudden burden. He lunged for the back of the van, and the mechanical roar of the generator died instantly, leaving a silence so heavy it felt physical. He wrenched the thick umbilical cables free from the generator, threw them to the ground, and slammed the rear doors shut.

Fritz hauled himself along the side of the van, using the metal panels like a rail, and pulled himself into the driver's seat. The engine turned over with a desperate, metallic wheeze.

I hoisted Zabella into the passenger seat, helping her settle as she hissed through her teeth. "Sit," I told her. "Keep your weight off that leg."

She didn't look at her leg. Instead, she was staring at me, her eyes wide with a new alarm. She reached out, her fingers trembling as she touched the side of my head. "Len... you're bleeding."

I pulled my hand away from my ear and looked at my fingers. They were no longer white with dust; they were slick with a dark, hot crimson that was beginning to matt my hair.

"I'll be all right," I said, though the steady drip of blood against my collar suggested otherwise. "I have to get to George."

Zabella groaned as she eased her weight onto the seat, her face contorting. "George? Len, what are you talking about? What does he have to do with this?"

"He drove the excavator," I said, looking back at the gaping wound in the mansion's side. "*WiWay* didn't just find a tool; it found a host. It's inside his head, Zabella. It's controlling him."

The sky finally broke. A jagged vein of lightning split the dark, followed instantly by a crack of thunder that felt like a physical blow. Then came the rain — a sudden, violent deluge that turned the plaster dust into a grey, viscous sludge.

The droplets hammered against the van's metal roof with the rhythm of a machine gun, splashing so hard they seemed to try to scour us from the earth.

"Ve are beaten, Len," Fritz pleaded from the driver's seat, his voice trembling. "Look at the house. Ve must run!"

Liam splashed toward us, blinking through the downpour. "The van's full. You two go. I'll take the minivan and follow."

"No," I barked, my voice cutting through the storm. I reached into the storage pocket of the open door and snatched two heavy-duty flashlights. "This van is a rolling bomb with those gas cans inside. Fritz, can you make it to the hospital?"

"Vat vill you do?" Fritz asked, his eyes darting to the ruins.

I set my jaw, feeling the chilly rain mix with the warm blood on my neck. "George is still in that cab. I'm not leaving him to that thing."

"But, Leonard—"

"Go!" I cut him off. "Neither of you can help with broken legs. Get to the ER. Now."

Fritz gave a grim nod of understanding. Zabella pulled the door shut, her eyes wide with a terror that the rain couldn't wash away. The headlights cut through the shimmering sheets of water as the van began its slow, cautious descent down the muddy hill.

Liam and I stood alone in the deluge. The rain carved deep, jagged tracks through the white dust on his face, looking like silver tears under the storm's flicker. We stood in the wreckage's shadow, listening.

Deep within the hollowed-out shell of Scudder House, the bulldozer's engine was still idling — a low, rhythmic growl that sounded like a predator breathing in the dark.

Liam looked at me, dumbfounded. "Len, the entire house could collapse. There's no way we can *get* to him, let alone *rescue* him."

I handed him one of the two flashlights. "Then I'll do it myself."

I dragged my leg toward the threshold, the absence of my cane forcing me to use the handrail. Each step was a battle against the slick, treacherous debris that littered the porch. Behind us, the sky continued its violent purge, but under the sagging overhang, the roar of the rain shifted to a hollow, metallic drumming.

Liam stepped up beside me, his flashlight cutting a jittery path through the dark.

"Great," he muttered, though his voice lacked its usual bite. "Now we're soaked and you want to go back into the freezer."

"Unusual research environment, wouldn't you say?" I replied, my breath hitching from the effort of the climb.

"I was expecting to be bored, Len. Honestly, I was praying for it until you showed up."

"Glad I could liven up the syllabus for you."

"If you want to make it boring again — deadly, soul-crushing boring — I'm open to the idea."

We crossed the threshold, our boots crunching on glass and pulverized stone. The air inside didn't just feel cold; it felt charged, as if something brittle and electric had replaced the oxygen.

The bulldozer's engine was a rhythmic, mechanical snarl, the massive tires churning uselessly against the splintered floorboards with a wet, slapping sound that echoed off the hollow walls.

Our beams swept the carnage. The grand fireplace, once the room's anchor, lay uprooted and shoved like a piece of toy furniture into the center of the floor. It leaned at a sickening angle atop the yellow hood of the machine, draped in a shroud of lath, plaster, and shattered brick.

But it was the floor that told the actual story. The behemoth had punched through the foundation, its weight cleaving the ancient sandstone obelisk clean in two. The cellar's darkness now held half of the huge stone, which had sheared off. I could not even see the protective sand dollar sigils.

The bulldozer sat perched on the jagged remains of the stone, half-submerged in the floor like a sinking ship.

The "GET OUT" mirror had finally surrendered, its fragments scattered across the ruins like a million jagged diamonds that caught our flashlight beams in blinding, silver flashes.

I swung my light toward the glass-walled cab. The gray mist that had shielded the driver was gone, replaced by the grim reality of the crash.

George lay slumped over the steering wheel, motionless. A single, dark smear of crimson marked the windshield where his forehead had met the glass — a stark, human stain in the middle of a supernatural wreck.

Shining the light in front of us, we carefully stepped over and around the littered floor, testing where we trod before we dared to put down our full weight.

It was a slow process as we edged our way nervously toward the cab of the machine. At one point, I stepped on a floorboard and it gave way. I grabbed Liam's arm, and he helped steady me until I could get my footing.

The joists under our feet groaned from the weight of the vehicle and the damage done to them. I stopped about two feet from the metal step and looked at the gaping hole in the floor.

"I can't do it," I stressed to Liam. "I'd have to jump to get to the cab. With my leg, there's no way—"

"I'll do it," Liam assured me. "You just be ready to catch me if I miss."

I stared at the churning rubber of the tires, the massive treads inches away from our feet. The floorboards beneath us groaned, a long, splintering sound that suggested the entire room held together on a knife-edge. One wrong move, and the bulldozer and the two of us would disappear into the cellar.

A jagged vein of lightning strobed through the shattered walls, followed instantly by a thunderclap that shook the very air in our lungs. We both flinched, the sound echoing like a gunshot in the hollowed-out room.

"Watch the wheels," I warned, my voice tight. "If they catch your jacket, you're done."

"I've got it," Liam muttered, though his hand trembled as it braced against my shoulder. He took a measured breath, then lunged. He cleared the spinning tread in a single, desperate leap, landing hard on the metal runner of the cab.

He pulled the door handle, and it yielded with a sharp metallic snap. George's unconscious form slumped toward the opening, and Liam braced himself, catching the man by the shoulders to keep him from falling toward the still-moving treads.

In the flashlight's beam, a dark contusion was visible on George's temple, the skin broken by a thin, crimson trail.

"Come on, George," Liam urged, gently tapping the man's cheek. "We can't carry you out of here."

The floor groaned again, a deep, hollow sound of yielding timber. The string of shells felt heavy against my chest — a small bit of protection in a place that felt increasingly hostile. I pulled them over my head and held them out to Liam.

"Put these on him," I insisted.

Liam's expression tightened with concern. "Will you be alright?"

"Yeah. Just do it," I replied, glancing at the widening cracks in the floorboards. Our eyes met for a brief, heavy second amidst the dust and the shadows. "We've got to get out of here."

In one move, Liam put the shells over George's head. Some of them broke when the ceiling fell in on me, but I hoped whatever power they possessed was still strong enough to free George.

Liam again slapped George's face, and the big man roused. "Come on, George. We need you, buddy."

George's eyes blinked open, and he looked at Liam, confused. "Where are we?"

"Scudder House. Can you walk?"

"I guess." He moved his foot off the gas pedal. The wheels stopped turning, and I sighed in relief. Liam got back to the metal step and braced himself against the no-longer-moving tire, as George clumsily felt with his foot for the step and shifted his weight to it.

George's eyes darted across the devastation, reflecting the jagged beams of our flashlights. "What the hell happened?" he rasped, his voice sounding as dragged through gravel.

"A traffic accident," I said, my voice leaving no room for questions. I braced myself as best I could and held out my arms. "George, you have to jump. Now!"

I swung the flashlight beam, creating a circle of light on the most stable-looking section of the floorboards. George took a clumsy, staggering leap out of the cab. I caught his weight; the impact sending a jolt of agony through my hip, but I steered him to solid flooring.

Liam vaulted out behind him, landing lightly on his feet just as a deep, structural groan shivered through the joists beneath us.

"We have to move. Liam, take him," I ordered.

Liam gripped George's shoulder, and we made a desperate break for the threshold. The house was screaming now — a cacophony of snapping timber and shifting masonry. Above us, the rafters groaned under the redirected weight, shedding a fresh shroud of ancient dust and splinters that hissed through our light beams.

Near the door, a glint of metal caught my eye. My folding cane lay twisted in the rubble, battered and scarred, but still in one piece. I snatched it up; the familiar grip gave me the leverage I needed to propel my body forward.

"Hurry! Out!" I shouted, the urgency clawing at my throat.

The dust didn't just settle; it was violently expelled, a thick, white ghost of the house's interior spewing through the front door in a final, choking gasp. The porch beneath our feet shivered, a rhythmic trembling that felt like the hill itself was trying to shake off the parasite of Scudder House.

"Get him to the minivan!" I shouted, my voice barely cutting through the roar of the downpour.

The rain was relentless now, a vertical ocean that turned the dust on our skin into a grey, visceral slime. Liam hauled George toward the driveway, the big man stumbling through the muck like a sleepwalker.

"What about you?" Liam bellowed back, squinting against the sheets of water. "What are you doing, Len?"

"What I have to do!" I yelled.

I stood my ground, my cane anchored deep in the mud, and turned to face the ruin. The mansion was still dying. The gaping wound on the right side widened as the structural integrity failed; massive blocks of sandstone slid from the eaves, crashing into the flowerbeds with wet, heavy thuds. Another section of the upper floor groaned and gave way, the roofline dipping like a broken wing.

Through the jagged hole in the foundation, where the bulldozer had vanished, a strange, low-frequency hummed — a vibration so deep it bypassed my ears and rattled the teeth in my skull. The protective stone was broken, and the air felt charged, as if the vacuum left by the stone was being filled by something far older and much hungrier.

I pulled the fossilized shell out of my pocket and shone the light on it as the rain fell onto it and my open hand. "Well, Thomas," I murmured, "if this is going to do something, now would be the time."

I put it in my left hand and closed my eyes to focus my mind on the small fossilized shell, concentrating as the rain struck my face. I heard the rumble of more stones falling from the walls of the house.

I opened my eyes to see that my body was glowing. I apparently had been guided into an altered state once again. I looked up at the house and saw something move.

I was certain it was only my eyes that could see it: the huge glowing shape moving out from the collapsed wall. Shaped like a man, it had to be twenty feet tall and made entirely out of *rocks*.

I knew this had to be a vision, as everything had shifted into a sepia tone. Time didn't just slow; it curdled. Each raindrop hung suspended in the air like a bead of translucent amber, drifting toward the earth in a lazy, agonizing crawl.

I looked down at my hand. The sand dollar was gone, replaced by the heavy, polished wood of a shaman's rattle. The fossilized shell dangled from its neck, clicking rhythmically against the grain with a sound like a heartbeat.

In the edges of my vision, the flicker of eagle feathers brushed against my cheeks — the weight of a great chief's war bonnet resting on my brow, old and sacred.

My modern clothes had vanished, replaced by the rough, sun-warmed texture of a healer's robe. My body beneath was no longer flesh and blood, but a vessel of pure, radiant energy that pulsed with the rhythm of the hill.

Then, the last barrier fell. A second consciousness, vast and ancient, surged through my mind like a subterranean river. I didn't fight it. I opened every door, every hidden room of my psyche, and allowed the spirit of the land to possess the hollow spaces of my soul.

I raised a flint-headed spear toward the churning clouds, the stone tip honed to a lethal, glass-like edge that caught the slow-motion flicker of the lightning. The air roared with the power of a thousand ancestors.

WiWay I call you out...

The thought was not my own. I could sense the words were a language I should not be able to fathom, but I understood as it was pure thought.

The stone monster turned to face me and lifted its boulder arms.

Healer, I thought you dead and gone....

No more than you, monster...

It is my time to walk this land again...

I have watched over this land to protect it from you...

The stone man stepped menacingly toward me.

You cannot stop me this time, old fool...

I need not. You have trapped yourself...

There was a mirthless low chuckle, sounding like stones sliding into the pits of hell.

No, healer, I am free...

You are wrong. You have trapped the souls of others here. They will stop you...

The stone giant faltered, its massive, jagged head swiveling with a sudden, primitive uncertainty that sent tremors through the mud. The air, thick with the scent of ozone and ancient dust, seemed to hold its breath.

That was when the shadows in the yard ignited.

Out of the swirling grit and the slow-motion sepia rain, they emerged — not as wisps, but as pillars of incandescent light. Elias and Cassandra Scudder stepped forward first, their spectral forms radiant against the gloom. Their faces, once etched with the agony of their historical ends, were now smoothed into a terrifying, silent resolve.

Behind them followed the line of their blood: Martin and Frances, standing tall, and little Lucy, whose small hand glowed like a dying star.

Finally, stepping out from the jagged, smoking maw of the ruins, came Joey and Haley. Their spirits burned with a fierce, white heat that pushed back the darkness as they took their places at my side, an assembly of the people who had died within the house.

The monstrosity recoiled, a low, tectonic growl vibrating in its chest. For the first time, it registered a sensation it had likely never known: shock. The very souls it had harvested to fuel its ascension — the lives it had consumed to build its mountain of spite — had become the blades at its throat.

The healer's hand within mine snapped the rattle upward. The sound wasn't a mere noise; it was a rhythmic explosion, a crack of sacred thunder that shattered the silence. In response, a ghostly cheer erupted — a sound like a thousand voices caught in a windstorm — as the group of souls rose in unison. As they moved to join me, the stone monstrosity flinched, its granite limbs grinding together. Then, with a final, eerie shimmer, the air grew perfectly still. The unnatural rain simply ceased to exist, the suspended droplets vanishing into the ether.

I hoisted the phantom spear. My lungs expanded, filling with words from a powerful tongue — a war cry that tasted of wood smoke and fire. I didn't just run; I surged. The spirit-wave moved with me, a tide of brilliant light rushing headlong into the heart of the darkness.

The stone man roared, a sound like tectonic plates shattering, and lunged forward to crush me. I released the spear. It didn't just fly; it sang a high, whistling note of judgment. The flint head arced through the sepia gloom, trailing a wake of white light, and struck the beast's chest with the force of a falling star. It didn't stop at the surface. It punched through the granite hide, through the hollow, rot-filled malice of the core, and exited the other side in a violent spray of spectral sparks.

The monster buckled. It crashed onto one rocky knee.

The horde of spirits was on it instantly. They didn't need weapons; they used the raw, crushing weight of their justice. They hammered at the hard carapace with translucent fists that hit like sledgehammers and kicked at the massive stone limbs.

Composed of spirit rather than flesh, their touch acted like sledgehammers upon the creature's form. The stone began to spiderweb, white fractures racing across its chest and throat. Massive chunks of rock sheared off, disintegrating into fine, grey dust before they even hit the mud, vanishing into nothingness.

I held the rattle high, my chant rising in a beautiful, harrowing crescendo that acted as an anchor, pinning the spirits to this plane just long enough to finish the task. I watched as they pummeled the giant's face into gravel, its massive arms dissolving into grey mist under the relentless assault. It was a deconstruction of evil, brick by brick, soul by soul.

As the last remnants of the stone body disintegrated into the fog, the warriors faded.

Little Lucy Scudder vanished first with a soft, peaceful sigh that sounded like the end of a long fever. Then Elias, Cassandra, and the others drifted into the light.

Soon, the yard was silent and empty, save for the flickering, steady lights of Joey and Haley. They remained standing before me in the sudden, absolute quiet, their eyes meeting mine with a gratitude that transcended the need for words.

I met Haley's eyes, and heard her voice in my mind.

We are free... thank you...

And she was gone.

I stood swaying, my lungs burning as the world snapped back into focus. The sepia haze was gone, replaced by the reality of the cold and the dark. I wasn't a chief in a healer's robe; I was just

Leonard, drenched to the bone in my own ruined clothes, clutching the sand dollar shell so hard it bit into my palm.

The 'spear' I had thrown was nothing more than my heavy-duty flashlight. It lay in the mud, its beam casting a weak, jittery trail of light across the steaming wreckage of the house.

I shoved the shell deep into my pocket and limped toward the light, my muscles trembling with the aftershocks of a power that was never mine to keep. As the heat of the impact met the chilled air, a thick, cloying fog rose from the earth, swallowing the ruins in a white shroud.

I reached for the flashlight, but as I straightened, I froze.

Standing exactly where I had been — on the spot where the barrier between worlds had thinned to a thread — was the healer. He didn't look like a ghost; he looked more real than the rubble behind him. His buffalo robe was dark and heavy with age, and the magnificent feathers of his war bonnet stirred in a wind I couldn't feel.

He met my gaze, and the silence between us filled with a sudden, overwhelming clarity. There were no words, only the heavy, ancient weight of his thoughts pressing against mine.

"You have done well, little brother...

I made a small bow.

You honor me, healer...

I am now free to move on. WiWay will never bother this land again...

Thank you for guiding me... helping me...

A small smile played on his lips.

A man can only be guided if he allows himself to be led...

With that, he faded away.

20. RUINED REVENANT

"**D**estruction of property, malicious intent, burglary. Need I go on?" Detective Valentin said, holding his open notebook and glaring at the team.

Doctor Janis stood with Valentin. He had recently left the hospital and seemed quite upset that events had trashed his research site and damaged costly equipment.

We were all there, for better or worse. Zabella wore a support bandage on the lower part of her leg for the nasty sprain she had received. George had his arm in a sling and a bandage on his head. Fritz was using crutches, and his left leg was in a cast. Liam and I wore several bandages on various wounds, and bruises covered all of us, even Anna, who suffered the least damage in the group. She went from person to person to get us water and whatever we needed.

The previous night, when I had returned to the minivan, Liam and George stared at me in awe.

"Who *were* those people?" Liam marveled.

"And that giant thing, made of rocks?" George wondered. "Was that *WiWay?*"

I got carefully into the van, surprised. "Wait, you saw the people? You saw all of that?"

Liam turned back to me. "Yeah. You wore Native American clothing."

"And you had a spear, but it was like a ghost spear," George added.

"I'm covered with filth," I said simply. "Can we go back to the rental house and get a shower, please?"

As they drove from the house, George, now that he was in his right mind and his head was clear, realized his arm was either sprained or broken.

I also found that my ear was bleeding and practically torn off. I held it with a compress as Liam drove us to the Zuckerberg San Francisco General Hospital, where the staff isolated us in separate curtained areas in the trauma unit.

As I waited with a compress on the side of my head for the doctor to put in stitches, Anna snuck into my curtained enclosure.

"Should you be walking around?" I worried.

"Says the man who is still bleeding?" she said. "I spoke to Liam."

"Is he higher on your visitor list?"

She smiled. "No, I just located him first." She grew serious. "He said you fought a giant ghost made of stone. Is that right?"

"Probably not the way I would put it," I chuckled. "When I write up my report of the incident, I will probably suggest that the release of trapped energy ended the haunting."

"So Scudder House is safe? Free of any phenomenon?"

"What's left of it," I sighed. "The damage is pretty devastating. I don't even know if we can salvage any of the equipment. Have they released you?"

"Bumps and bruises, but I'm awake and my tests have come back with a clean bill of health; no brain damage."

"Once the doctor repairs my ear, we could go back to the house."

She paused and looked at the floor for a moment. "I want to stay here. Be here for the others."

I sensed there was something more, and I also noted that she stayed a few feet away from me and hadn't rushed up to give me a hug or a kiss.

"Sure," I smiled and cleared my throat. "You know, if there is anything you want to talk about, I am more than happy to listen."

She glanced up but didn't meet my eyes. "That's good to know, Len. I'm dealing with some issues, and I have to sort them out."

"Okay," I stated simply.

She soon moved out to keep visiting the others. A female doctor came in, gave me a local anesthetic, and sewed my ear back in place.

"How did this happen?" she asked.

"A haunted house fell on me."

She exhaled in frustration. "Okay, then don't tell me."

In a few hours, the doctors released Liam, Fritz, and me. Doctor Kohl was on crutches with his leg in a cast. Liam had come through remarkably unscathed.

We got back to the rented house; I finally got a shower. The painkillers the doctor had given me put me right out.

I slept until past ten the next morning and came out to the main room to find Liam and Anna had picked up our group from the hospital and, through their combined efforts, brought back all vehicles.

It was soon thereafter that the good detective and the angry Doctor Janis arrived. The detective asked who stole the bulldozer, and George admitted it was him, but that he had no memory of doing so, and the recriminations and threats abounded.

Fritz defended us, and I was too tired to get involved, so I sat and drank coffee as accusations flew.

Another knock at the door saved us.

Anna opened it, and who should come in but Chuck Granger, who announced, "Everyone, don't say another word."

Detective Valentin looked very annoyed by this interruption. "Counselor, we are investigating several crimes, including the damage done to Scudder House."

Chuck was unperturbed and simply proclaimed, "Scudder House? Isn't that the place condemned and ordered demolished by the town council?"

Valentin looked as if he'd just sucked a lemon. "Yes, that one."

Chuck went on brightly. "I see." He offered a card. "Please call me and we can set up appointments for interviews tomorrow. Would that be acceptable?"

"I would prefer to speak with them today," Valentin insisted.

"My clients will all come down to make statements. Look at them." He gestured around the room. "The hospital just released them. Give them a day to recover."

"But the *destruction*!" Janis fumed. "Loss of data! This will cost the university a lot of money."

Liam piped up. "We didn't lose the data, sir."

Janis frowned. "What do you mean?"

"Our automatic backups worked until the site lost power," Liam explained. "All our readings went up to the cloud. I have reviewed them and believe you will be intrigued, Doctor Janis."

Valentin angrily said, "Well, Mr. Humphreys admitted to stealing the bulldozer!"

"I'm sorry to argue," I said. "George only confessed that he got *out* of the bulldozer. And we were all here when he said he had no memory of how he got there."

"I bumped my head," George offered lamely.

Chuck turned to the detective. "So, unless you are arresting Mr. Humphreys again…" He let the sentence hang.

Valentin hissed out his breath. "Interviews. First thing tomorrow. One at a time."

"I will call you to set the appointments, Detective," Chuck said merrily as Valentin stomped out the door.

Fritz turned to Doctor Janis. "Henry, I know you've lost equipment, but we are all lucky to be alive."

Janis shook his head. "I don't know what to say, Fritz. I've always trusted your judgment in the past, but now this?"

He headed out the door, leaving only the team and Chuck.

Chuck took the initiative. "I've got to shove off as well. Seminars and all. But I will stay through tomorrow, and I'll text Fritz and Len about your appointments with the police. I'm also going to talk to the quarry company about their bulldozer, see if we can work something out."

"You're the best, Chuck," I said.

He waved as he went out the door, and we all relaxed a bit.

"How is your ear?" Fritz asked.

"What?" I joked.

"I said, how is—" Fritz stopped, as he got the wisecrack. "Not funny, Leonard."

"I'm afraid very little of this is funny." I moved to the center of the room to get everyone's attention. "I want to commend all of you for going above and beyond and for not getting killed."

This elicited a nervous chuckle throughout the room.

"I don't know about you, but I'm planning to spend the day resting. Doctor Kohl and I will discuss options, as well as plans to get everyone back to LA and me back to NJ. Liam, did Lamar get to LA all right?"

Liam held up his phone. "He did. He texted me about an hour ago to say he's headed for the university campus."

"Good. Now, I don't know about the rest of you, but I'm starved. Liam, do you mind doing a food run?"

"Sure!" he agreed. "Tell me what you want!"

As the group gathered around him, Anna approached me. "Len, can we talk?"

"Of course," I offered. "Tell Liam what you want, and I'll be in my room."

I walked down the hall and sat on the bed. The painkillers had worn off, and my ear hurt, along with my bruised arms and sore muscles.

I'm really not cut out for the hero trade.

A few minutes later, Anna came in and quietly closed the door behind her. She looked downcast and once again didn't want to meet my eyes.

I limped to her, put a finger under her chin, and lifted her face gently. "You can tell me anything. Don't worry about my feelings."

Her smile was strained. "How do you know what I want to say might hurt your feelings?"

"I'm psychic. Also, your body language is telegraphing that you have something you want to say."

"I'm afraid it might hurt me as well," she confessed.

"Tell me, and maybe between us we can figure it out."

She sat on the bed. I sat near her, but not too close.

She began. "Seeing you again has been great, and then you saved my life!"

"You don't owe me anything."

"I'm also glad that I got to act out a long-held fantasy."

I looked at my hands. "This time, I'm the one who feels there is a 'but' coming."

She exhaled and met my eyes. "It was funny. In the hospital, when I was unconscious or in a coma or whatever it was…"

"Go on."

"In my dreams, I saw myself with Zabby, and I realized I wanted to be with her, not as a friend, but as a lover."

"Did you talk to Zabella about this?"

She nodded vigorously. "Last night. We spent the entire night talking, and we laughed and joked and held hands."

"If that's what you want, Anna, then go for it."

She looked at the floor again. "I just didn't want you to think I rejected you. I mean, after your breakup and all, the last thing you need is being dumped for a girl."

This made me laugh out loud, which earned a curious look from Anna.

"Sorry," I chortled as I regained control. "I never expected it to be put that way." Turning to her, I took her hands. "I am grateful that you made love to me. You've gone through many changes since we last met, and you have more yet to realize. Do what makes you happy. Find what you want and who you love."

She nodded, her eyes wet. "Right now, it seems to be Zabella."

"Then that's who you should be with."

She reached out and hugged me.

"Easy, easy," I whined. She wasn't hugging me all that hard, but even a small amount of pressure hurt.

We came out of the bedroom, and Anna was almost glowing with happiness. I saw her go over to Zabella and whisper in her ear, and the taller woman smiled, then winked at me.

I winked back.

Food soon arrived, and we all ate and spent the morning talking over the events to make a cohesive explanation we all could relate that the police might accept.

George pointed out, "The whole, 'I was possessed by an ancient Native-American deity' story will not go over well."

"Keep it simple, and keep it honest," I stated clearly. "George, do you have any recollection of stealing that bulldozer?"

"Not at all," he explained. "I was at the police station, and Mr. Granger got them to let me go because the autopsy proved I didn't push Haley out a window or anything. The shell necklace was gone, and I didn't think about it until I got outside. Mr. Granger offered to give me a ride, and I said I wanted to walk. The next thing I knew, I was in the house, in the cab of that machine, and you and Liam were pulling me out."

We discussed different scenarios and excuses, but none of them seemed to fly. After a while, we all took a break, and Liam made another food run.

This time Zabella approached and asked to speak to me.

We went into my room, and I told her, "I should start charging for consultations."

Without warning, Zabella pulled me close and planted her lips on mine, much to my surprise. It shocked me for a moment, but I decided it was a pretty good kiss and returned it.

After what felt like two minutes and my nervous system going haywire with a combination of confusion and lust, she broke the lip-lock.

I panted. "Should I ask what that was about or should I just enjoy it and not ask questions?"

"It was an experiment," Zabella smiled. "Anna said you were a good kisser."

"I thought you were gay," I said.

"I've been with guys," she said with a grin. "They are just not my preferred choice. I just wanted to see if Anna was right."

"Okay," I said, recovering. "What's the verdict?"

"Not bad," she shrugged. "But I still prefer girls."

"Gee, so do I," I conceded. "Pardon me if I'm confused. You stole my girl and then kissed me? "

She gave my arm a gentle slap. "I didn't steal your girl!"

"I know, I'm just ribbing you."

She grew serious. "I'm grateful that you were nice to Anna about it. She was worried, and she likes you."

"I like her, too. And I want her to be happy."

"You also saved my life, so I figured I owed you a little thrill."

"That kiss was one hell of a payback," I responded. "I'll be happy to save your life anytime."

She grinned.

"Are we friends now?" I said.

"I guess. After all, you *are* a good kisser."

We rejoined the others and spent the afternoon getting our stories straight. I watched as the others drank, relaxed, and played music.

I went outside to sit at the table and drink a cup of coffee, thinking about the last few days.

I noticed I felt different, stronger. My breakup with Jyanette had thrown me, and barely surviving the demon I had faced in New Jersey months ago had made me feel I could not defeat a powerful foe except through pure luck.

But now I knew: there was help all around me.

On the supernatural side, there were forces aligned with me to fight back the dark powers on this plane of existence. Brave people, like this team, who faced a monster, and entities like the ancient healer who could help on a level I didn't even understand. They were out there, and they would come when I needed them.

On the romance side, there were women, like Anna, who still found me attractive. With time, I would find the one to heal my heart, who would join me on my journey. I wished desperately that it could be Jyanette, but if not, there would be someone. I just hadn't met her yet.

I also faced one of my biggest fears: returning to Scudder House. It had been the place of my first big success, and now I knew the site could rest in peace, along with its former residents. I felt relieved that they would demolish it, and it would cease to trouble anyone.

As I considered all this, Fritz joined me.

"So, vhen are you leaving?"

"I have to finish writing up my report, and I have to talk to the police tomorrow, but I've booked a late afternoon flight to New Jersey."

"Provided they don't arrest you," Fritz quipped.

"There is that. I hope the data you got made it worthwhile."

"I looked it over and ve vill be discussing the meaning of the machines' readings for quite a vhile," Fritz said, and then sighed. "The day after tomorrow, ve vill try to salvage what ve can from the site. By next veek, ve move on."

"I should check my email. I haven't heard from Chuck."

"Oh, I have. He persuaded the mining company not to press charges. Of course, there vill be a fee to pull the bulldozer out of the basement, but since the house vill be taken down, they can use a crane and go through the roof."

"Sounds like it will be expensive."

Fritz sighed again. "I have no doubt. But it vill keep George out of jail and ve vill be able to leave."

"Scudder House is free, as are the people who died there. I hope that counts for something." I looked at my mentor in the light of the setting sun. "Good working with you again, Fritz."

"It vas good to see you too, Leonard. You have become quite impressive with your skills."

"That's been a matter of necessity," I considered. "Stay in touch."

"You as vell."

We went back inside, and the partying continued for the kids. They danced, Zabella and Anna taking turns with Liam, George, and even Fritz, who sort of hobbled on his crutches. Then the girls danced together in a rather sexy way, showing off, as Liam and George applauded and whistled.

Everyone except Fritz kept trying to hand me a beer or a glass of wine. I politely took each one and set it down somewhere without drinking it. But the desire was there, and after fending it off as long as my will let me, I headed to bed alone.

The music was still loud in the living room, but I had reached the point where the desire to have a drink was too strong, and I either had to get out of the living room or give in. I lay in bed thinking about Jyanette and slipped into a doze.

It was about midnight when I came awake. The music had stopped, but I thought I heard voices whispering.

The room was fairly dark, but some illumination came through the slats in the Venetian blinds. I heard giggles and sat up in bed. "Hello?"

Two figures stood in the dim light, and another fit of giggles took them. Even in the darkness, I recognized both Anna and Zabella.

"What's going on?" I asked, attempting to sound casual, as if people invaded my bedroom all the time.

The girls came over and sat on either side of the bed. They both wore bathrobes, and I could smell the alcohol on their breath.

"Len," Zabella announced, focusing her attention on her pronunciation. "I have discussed the situation with Anna."

"I see," I responded, not entirely sure where this was going.

Anna spoke up from her side of the bed. "And I discussed it with Zabella!"

"Communication is important," I attempted.

Zabella took up the tale. "We have decided that a kiss is not enough for saving our lives!"

"No, it's not," Anna giggled.

"We have decided to reward you properly," Zabella finished and rose to her feet, as did Anna. I watched as both women glanced at each other and threw off their robes to expose their naked bodies to my gaze.

I gasped.

Anna whispered, "I told you he responds well."

Zabella smiled down at me. "Let's find out."

The two naked women pulled the covers aside and joined me in the bed.

It was quite a night.

EPILOGUE

The vinyl of the booth at Mindy's Diner felt sticky against my skin, a stark contrast to the sterile chill of the San Francisco fog I'd left behind.

My body was a roadmap of the last forty-eight hours—dull aches in my ribs, a sharp pull in the stitches across my ear — but I wore the bruises like medals. I'd survived a god dropping a house on me; surely, I could survive morning coffee in Mountainview.

Unlike my last night in California, the flight home was uneventful. I was tired, but I had a smile on my face and was quite pleased with myself, so I slept the entire six-hour flight.

I was at the San Francisco Airport waiting for my flight when I received an unexpected text from Jyanette, asking me to meet with her the next day. Pleased by this, I quickly texted her back with a request to get together at Mindy's.

I watched the clock above the griddle. 10:02 a.m.

Then the bell above the door chimed, and the oxygen seemed to leave the room. Jyanette. She moved through the diner like a storm front — elegant, dark, and dangerously composed in a charcoal courtroom pantsuit. She'd pulled her hair into that gravity-defying bun, a sculptural masterpiece that always made me wonder if she used pins or magic to hold it together.

When she reached the table, I stood, my heart hammering a frantic rhythm. I reached for her hand — it was cold — and leaned in for a kiss. She pivoted with the practiced grace of a matador, offering me a cheek that felt like polished marble. I considered even this small gesture progress. At least she didn't avoid the kiss altogether.

"You look incredible," I said, the words slightly breathless.

She didn't smile. Instead, she pulled her hand back, her eyes tracking the jagged line of black thread across my ear. "You look like a car wreck, Leonard. Again."

"It's nothing," I said, attempting a smile.

"What was it this time?"

"A Native-American deity dropped a house on me."

She held my gaze and raised an eyebrow. "So, the usual?"

"The other guy looks worse," I joked, though my voice cracked.

This didn't even garner a smile. "That line stopped being funny three hospital visits ago." She didn't open the menu or even unbutton her blazer. She sat on the edge of the vinyl as if she were prepared to bolt at the first sign of a tremor.

I tried to bridge the distance, my mind already rehearsing the speech about 'starting over' and 'going slow.' I wanted to tell her I could change, that the madness was behind me. "Jyanette, I was hoping we could—"

"Len, stop." She held up a hand, her palm a physical barrier between us. "You're wondering why I asked you here. It's not to talk about 'us.' There is no 'us.'"

The confidence I'd carried across the country deflated, leaving me hollow. "Then what? Is it a case? Your ex-husband?"

"No," she said, and for the first time, her composure fractured. A shadow of something — fear? Regret? — crossed her face. "It's personal. And it's going to require a lot from both of us."

"I don't understand," I whispered. The clatter of plates and the hiss of the espresso machine faded into a dull roar in my ears. The tension in the booth became a physical weight, pressing the air out of my lungs. "What is it? Can I help?"

A ghost of a smile touched her lips — bitter and tragic. "Oh, you've done quite enough."

I exhaled in frustration. "Obviously, you contacted me because you think I can do something."

Her lips tightened into a thin line. "You're going to have to do a lot of things; we both will."

I frowned. "Jyanette, you're talking in riddles."

She bit her lower lip, her gaze dropping to the scarred Formica tabletop for a heartbeat. When she looked back up, her brown eyes were shimmering, pinned to mine with absolute clarity. The diner seemed to go silent; the world narrowing down to the space between us.

"Len," she said, her voice barely a thread of sound. "I'm pregnant."

AUTHOR'S NOTE

Welcome, reader of the odd.

Specter In the Mind resolves the last major element that has haunted Len since the beginning of the series: the fact that he didn't finish the job the first time he was at Scudder House.

The book touches him in a time where he is fragile, and needs to rebuild his faith in himself and his abilities. How better than to become reacquainted with Anna Chou, a woman with an unrequited love?

I liked the elements of the tale, and I had to pour through many ancient Native American legends to get my concept of just what was causing the manifestations at Scudder House. I discovered the legends of WiWay, a being of great power and myth, and he made it all work.

Len returns from California with a renewed sense of his own worth and a big surprise that is explored further in the next book.

You'll also see that I'll reintroduce one of the best villains of the entire series in *Vengeance In The Mind.*

—Arjay Lewis

VENGEANCE IN THE MIND

DOCTOR WISE BOOK 8

ARJAY LEWIS

MIND
BENDER
PRESS

VENGEANCE IN THE MIND

The pre-dawn chill of September bit through Margaret Jamison's thin pink scrubs. She hated this drive — the transition from the quiet safety of Choctaw Lake to the sterile intensity of the hospital.

Usually, the rhythmic humming of her tires on Route 40 was a meditation, a way to mentally "put on" her nurse's persona before the 7:00 am shift began.

She checked the rearview mirror. She had sprayed her hair into its usual, rigid updo. Frank called it her "battle crown." It made her look capable. Formidable. At nearly forty, with a mortgage and two kids, "formidable" was the only thing keeping her together.

She'd skipped the hash browns at the West Jefferson McDonald's, the bitter black coffee sitting heavy in her stomach. *Ten pounds by the wedding,* she promised herself.

She could almost feel her relatives' judging eyes already. She'd starve herself for a month if it meant her cousin's wedding felt like a victory instead of a family reunion.

She looked forward to the wedding in October. The kids would stay with Frank's mom, so the pair of them could dance and stay in a hotel. Frank always got frisky at a hotel. In fact, he might be frisky several times over that weekend, and Margaret was looking forward to that as well. Careers and kids, mortgages and money concerns had interfered with the romance in their lives.

The Ohio landscape blurred past — skeletal corn stalks and trees bleeding autumn reds. People raved about New England, but Margaret found the local transition more honest. It was beautiful, sure, but it felt like a warning.

Winter was coming.

She was approaching the turnoff for the hospital complex when she looked for the landmark, a beacon that signaled she was three minutes from her shift.

It was a massive billboard, a local fixture that usually screamed into the darkness: **YOU MUST GET RIGHT WITH GOD.** The five-foot letters stood beside a life-sized cross made of weathered fiberglass.

Usually, the sign was flooded with industrial lights. Today, the sign was dark.

Margaret slowed. The rising sun caught the top of the cross, casting a long, distorted shadow across the road. There was something... extra. A shape perched atop the horizontal beam that hadn't been there yesterday.

"Disgusting," she muttered. Some overzealous deacon must have added a plastic Christ for the "shock value." It was heavy-handed, even for a believer like her. As she drew closer, she saw the dark streaks — fake blood painted to drip down the fiberglass.

Then her foot hit the brake, hard.

The figure wasn't wearing a robe. It was wearing a tracksuit.

And it had breasts.

Heart hammering against her ribs, Margaret pulled onto the shoulder and swung her compact car around. She parked directly beneath the towering sign, the engine ticking in the sudden silence. She grabbed the heavy flashlight from her trunk, her breath blooming in the cold air.

She walked a hundred feet back, her sensible nursing shoes crunching on the gravel. She needed a better angle. The sun was behind the sign now, turning the billboard into a black monolith.

"It's a mannequin," she whispered, her voice cracking. "Just a sick prank."

She clicked on the high-powered lantern. The beam cut through the shadows, climbing the wooden structure until it hit the figure.

Margaret's knees went water-thin. The flashlight slipped from her numb fingers, shattering on the concrete. Darkness rushed back in, yet the image had already seared itself onto her retinas.

She fumbled for her phone, her hands shaking so violently that she nearly dropped it.

"911, what is your emergency?"

"I... I'm on Route 40," Margaret gasped. She collapsed onto the cold sidewalk, the nurse in her fighting the civilian who wanted to scream.

I handle car wrecks, she told herself, the mantra a desperate rhythm in her head. *I handle amputations. I handle death.*

"Ma'am? I need your location."

Margaret forced her "head nurse" voice to the surface. It was cold, sharp, and detached. "I am west of OhioHealth Doctors'

Hospital, across from the Advance Auto. Send everyone. Police. Medics. Now."

"What are we looking at, ma'am?"

Margaret looked up at the silhouette against the orange sky. The girl's blonde hair caught the morning breeze, swaying gently. Heavy railroad spikes driven through her wrists pinned her to the fiberglass. The blood wasn't paint. It was dark, tacky, and very real.

"There's a woman on the billboard," Margaret said, her voice dropping to a horrified whisper. "She's been crucified."

TO BE CONTINUED IN

VENGEANCE IN THE MIND

DOCTOR WISE BOOK 8

BOOKS BY ARJAY LEWIS

Doctor Wise Series
Fire In The Mind
Seduction In The Mind
Reunion In The Mind
Haunted In The Mind
Devotion In The Mind
Asylum In The Mind
Specter In The Mind
Vengeance In The Mind
Echoes In The Mind
Infection In The Mind
Justice In The Mind
Ritual In The Mind
Vanished In The Mind

HORROR:
The Muse
Kept In The Dark
The Vanishing
Digger
Ghost Writer

ROMANCE SUSPENSE:
(with Debra Snow)
A Study In Murder

ULTIMATE URBAN FANTASY:
The Wizards Of Central Park West
The Vampires Of Greenwich Village
The Werewolves Of Washington Square

ABOUT THE AUTHOR

K nown as the "Wizard Of Odd", Arjay Lewis is an actor, magician, and multi-award-winning author.

I write tales of the strange and the horrifying.

I have spent my life as an entertainer, amusing people as a street-performer in the 1970s; a Broadway and casino artist in the 1980s; a party performer in the 1990s and 2000s; a cruise ship performer in the 2010s.

Stories have always been in my mind, and I have been writing since the 1990s. My reason to write is simple: to entertain. I write the type of books that I like to read: murder mysteries, strange tales of unnatural gifts, odd happenings and horror.

Please visit my web site and sign up for my mailing list to be "in the know" for upcoming books. Visit me on Facebook, Twitter, or my Amazon Author page.

And thank you for reading. You are the reason I write.

www.arjaylewis.com
www.facebook.com/arjaylewis
www.twitter.com/arjaylewiswrite
www.amazon.com/Arjay-Lewis